MW00422810

MADLANDS

MADLANDS

K. W. JETER

St. Martin's Press New York

Design by Glen M. Edelstein

Library of Congress Cataloging-in-Publication Data

Jeter, K. W.
    Madlands.
      p.   cm.
    ISBN 0-312-06407-1
    I. Title.
    PS3560.E85M3 1991   813′.54—dc20   91-21546

First Edition: October 1991

10 9 8 7 6 5 4 3 2 1

To Fred Duarte and Karen Meschke,
and all the other wild armadillos

MADLANDS

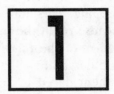

1

GELDT came riding through the city, and he smelled like blood and shit. You could smell the shit because he never washed his hands, no matter where they had been. The blood—you had to have been badly fucked over by him, to catch that whiff. Then the blood was in your nose, so it didn't mean a thing if he washed or not.

What he rode, what he drove, was a brand-new 1953 Hudson Hornet. With smooth chrome you could lick with your tongue like the ice cream of mirrors, and fenders rounded as the flanks of anthracite-hearted women. What our friends on the east side would call a *sharp short*. I was with him when he got it, but then things happened—*bad things*—and now he drove alone.

"Any you guys seen Trayne?"

Geldt was stopping along the way, every few blocks where the dark folded into an alley smelling of stale alcohol. Making inquiries with a fiver snaked around his fingers. He left the car running, door swung wide open. He knew none of these winos could get over their shakes or terminal lack of guts enough to steal it.

His shadow hung over the scrubby half-men like a club. (Half-men, quarter-men, and way in the back, an eighth of a man, weeping tears into his own open mouth.) A big shadow because of all the fivers still in his pocket. The red eyes latched onto the one in his hand, Lincoln's face the God of Another Pint.

One of them dared to speak, crouched at Geldt's polished shoes. "I seen him. Down by Traction. He was all messed up."

That's who he was looking for. He was looking for Trayne. And the news that Trayne was *all messed up* was neither new nor displeasing to him. Geldt paid off, whether the winos told him anything he could use or were just making stuff up. He got back in the Hudson and drove on, down to the avenue called Traction.

There was a sharp Countach cruising around Los Angeles that day, or what some of us liked to think of as L.A., and what other poor souls couldn't tell the difference from. Plus the usual fleet of cherry Beemers, air-conditioning locked down tight behind the sealed tinted windows. But all the hidden eyes swiveled onto Geldt's Hudson Hornet, pupils slitted in the radar of metal lust. The retro bit always racked up more points than mere expense. Only a '57 T-Bird and a gullwing Mercedes, each as new as the Hudson, competed as successfully for the hearts of men.

Out where the palm trees nodded over the sun-hissing asphalt, the rats hammocking in the dry fronds, Geldt pulled up alongside the notorious T-Bird. He got a movie-star smile in return for his split-pumpkin leer. Lock and key, the movies unreeling inside each other's skulls. The hard blonde smoked Geldt off the stop sign, and he bumbled the clutch, stalling the Hudson like the feckless asshole he was.

2

Burnt umber sat over the deco cathedral of Union Station and the Dragnet City Hall building. That had never changed, only the surrounding office buildings fading away so you could see the old city better.

Little Tokyo had lost its rough-cast concrete mini-malls and backlit plastic Hello Kitty signs, going back to dim herbalist storefronts and twenty-four-hour *pai gow* parlors. Geldt parked the Hudson and slid through the alleys, already pulling out another fiver, the flag of his own parade.

"Trayne? Seen him?"

He got a different response, this much closer to what he was looking for. A dirty mitt backhanded a smear of Mad Dog from a grey-stubbled chin. Eyes that looked like they'd been stepped on and reassembled with red thread scanned Geldt's face.

"Maybe." The squatting drunk hit the Dog bottle again. "Who wants to know?"

Geldt got loose bowels if he had to deal with a vending machine with more than three choices on it. When dealing with human beings, or even parts of them, Honest Abe was supposed to do his talking for him.

He decided to tough it out, though the smell of his sweat was already mingling with the sour-milk odors of trash dumpsters whose contents had gone archaeological.

"An old friend. That's who."

The drunk snorted at that. Friends who lasted longer than the fiver being in short supply around here. Cocking a red eye at Geldt: "Why?"

"Got business with him."

The drunk laughed grey spit into the upturned bottle, nearly drowning himself. A grinning wheeze as he pulled his ragged sleeve over his wet face.

"That's a good one, buddy." The red eye became a black hole as it gazed through the last slug in the bottle. "Business, huh?" The joke being that Trayne would have a hard

3

time now knowing the business end of anything that didn't have a screw cap on it. "Well, I'll tell you where he is, and then the two of you can do all the *business* you want together. Ar. Ar. Ar."

Geldt got decent enough directions from the drunk. The soles of his shoes were wet-sticky by the time he came feeling his way down a flight of basement steps, his hand against a sweating cinder-block wall for balance. All light left behind. The basement breathed warm and dead-still into his lungs.

Scarecrow on a mattress. Geldt's eyes adjusted enough to make out the splayed silhouette, surrounded by a beetle flock of empty bottles. Facedown into the sweat-yellowed canvas—Trayne wept and dreamt, falling through a thirsty sleep.

Geldt poked Trayne with the tip of a shoe and got a grunt in return, Trayne's eyelids clamping down tighter against the pricks and goads of that other world. Prick Geldt jabbed him harder in the ribs.

"What!" Trayne screamed, flipping over and jamming his sharpened elbows and clenched fists into the thin mattress. "For Christ's sake!" His dreaming battered its heavy moth wings against his face; he couldn't see yet. "What . . ." The scream a winded gasp now. Then a whisper as he sank back down. "What . . ."

All of this made Geldt feel so much better. The way a chicken-gutted man looks at one stuffed with sawdust, and feels the strong red blood tick over in his thighs. Now he was big and bad enough to be kind.

"Trayne . . . it's me." Squatting down beside the mattress, touching the other's trembling shoulder. "It's okay."

With a breaking sob, Trayne clutched Geldt's arm. Swarming up into Geldt's face, his own ravined for tears.

"Geldt—oh Christ, Geldt, I knew you would . . . I knew you'd come back." More trembling and gasping. A snail

4

has more teeth in its belly than Trayne had in either jaw. "I knew you wouldn't leave me . . . out there . . ."

Out there was exactly where Geldt had left him before. Hung out to dry being an even more operable phrase. Geldt had to fight down his smile. This poor bastard was still a fool, which made things easier.

"Come on, Trayne." Kindly Geldt lifted Trayne to his feet, knees wobbling. Trayne would fall boneless without this talking crutch. "Let's get you out of here. Get you something to eat. You could go for that, couldn't you? Food, Trayne—you remember."

Trayne nodded. Birdcage ribs and a bone butterfly for a pelvis—a boiled radish would round his sunken gut like a bowling ball. And . . . maybe . . . where there was food, there'd also be something more to drink. A man can always hope.

The two of them made it up the basement steps. The sun had finally died, and now the alley's shadows were outlined by the fire that caressed the night sky. Trayne clung to Geldt's arm like a drowned kitten, still weeping out his pathetic gratitude. They tripodded on to the mouth of the alley and the waiting Hudson.

Geldt cruised on out of the city's heart, out to where the dead broken freeways reared their cubist dinosaur necks, crumbling cement and twisted rebar where the heads should be. Through the Hudson's split windshield washed the flames of the burning dirigible that hung over Los Angeles night and day—Geldt's and Trayne's faces were shifting red masks in that light.

A shadow grid doubled the network of empty roads the Hudson barreled through. The grid that cast the shadows was up in the sky, tethering the dirigible to the bare ground at the city's edge. More old stuff from the archives, that same deep well out of which had come the Hudson, the T-Bird (Where was it tonight? In whose dreams?), the roads and the dead freeways and the city itself. The dirigible being the crash of the *Hindenburg* at Lakehurst, New Jersey, in 1937. The dirigible had come back, even if New Jersey hadn't—that was the fate of cities that didn't figure in anyone's dreaming, unlike L.A.

Burning and burning, and never burning away . . . Identrope was up there, a new Moses to that which burns and is never consumed. This metaphor worked, or at least could hobble along in its own crippled grace: Identrope up in the sky, at the edge of the promised land, his followers suspended in the web beneath him, in that state of grace he could never achieve . . .

The Hudson rolled on farther, to a place where the flames just tinged the asphalt.

Trayne snuffled and wiped his nose. "I won't ever forget this, Geldt."

Behind the wheel, Geldt nodded. Things were going just fine.

"And you know what?" Trayne sat up straighter. "Neither will you." And his voice was different, different enough that Geldt looked around at him, wide-eyed in surprise. Just in time to catch the blow, Trayne's fist swinging through a confined orbit, knuckles brushing the windshield glass. The blood from Geldt's mouth spattered all the way up to Trayne's wrist.

The Hudson wound up in the gravel at the side of the road. Trayne reached over and switched off the engine. Then he searched through Geldt's jacket and came up with an anonymous .357.

Geldt lay slumped against the car door, sputtering red spit. "Trayne . . . what . . ." His eyes rolled crazy and scared.

"That's right." I raised the gun and drew a line from its snout into the hinge of his breastbone. "Now you're totally fucked."

6

CLEANING a gun always puts me in a thoughtful mood.

Geldt's piece was in a shabby condition. It hurt my heart to see it. A clean gun is the sign of a healthy mind. So I got out my swab kit and broke the poor baby down.

I like the whole procedure. I like the smell of oil on metal, and the way it feels on your fingertips. As if you've become part of the machine. I worked slow and careful, taking my time.

My old partner Geldt was trussed up in the back room. There were more things I needed to find out from him, and nothing places a man in that particularly vulnerable frame of mind like having his wrists and ankles lashed together. I believe it's something to do with the sphincter being up for such potential access. Your best friend will wonder exactly what's on your mind, in that predicament. And Geldt had fallen a long way from being a friend of mine.

Sighting down the barrel, I let my mind narrow to the same tight focus. I had a lot to think about.

We were still inside the zone, right at the edge of the city's deforming field. I'd been in the Madlands for years now, longer than anybody else, except maybe Identrope. And he didn't count, as he wasn't human, or had stopped being human some time back. So I didn't sweat it anymore; I had things pretty much aced here, in terms of simple survival.

Too bad for everybody else in the field. Outside, on the sidewalks below my place, there was a lot of nervous twitching and stalking going on. All the poor bastards who'd come to this zone looking for a thrill, and now couldn't leave, what had been thrilling transformed by the calculus of need into something right up there with air to breathe. And like air, they could get all of that they wanted just by being here. Getting it wasn't what made people nervous. What set them twitching was not knowing what morning they'd wake up and they'd all be squids.

Or worse.

I ran another swab down the barrel of Geldt's piece, and studied the gleam inside.

Somebody had been watching me out there, when I'd been showing Geldt the new order. Watching at a distance, probably with binoculars. But not so far away that I hadn't been able to feel the person's presence, and recognize who it was. An old familiar knowing . . .

I came back to the smell of metal and oil. I pulled the swab out of the gun and snapped it closed. I could deal with the voyeur business later. And as for my living in a nervous neighborhood, that wasn't my problem. Identrope had a surefire cure for n-formation, anyway. A kind of cure, at any rate. Somebody with the n couldn't be too fussy, after all.

This was just wasting time. I had business to take care of with Geldt. I laid the gun down and went into the other room to talk with him.

Geldt's panic-rolling eyes greeted me. I had stuffed a rag in his mouth because I had gotten tired of his begging and pleading while I had other things on my mind.

I knew he was scared, not just from wondering what I was going to do next, but from being this long— hours—here in the Madlands. He had the horrors about catching *n*-formation. A putz like him sweated survival in this zone. I already had a lock on it.

Once, when we had still been more or less buddies, we had come across out on the street some luckless clown in the last stages of multi-cancer. A complete Wilbur Whateley-type transformation, all flopping wet dendrites and patches of dog fur and fish scales, and just enough of a human face left in the writhing center to register terminal shock. The round hole of a mouth had flopped in and out, making little noises that were a long way from the words firing in the brain remnants inside. Either the thing had crawled out onto the sidewalk when it had still had some functioning means of locomotion, or somebody had dumped it there. Geldt had staggered over to the gutter and puked. I'd found the thing's windpipe with my boot heel and stood on it until the poor bastard had finally stopped wiggling and gasping. For a long time afterward, Geldt had looked white enough to hold him up to the light and see the watermark.

Geldt was just as bloodless now. I squatted down and brought my face close to his. A strand of his sweat-slicked hair dangled between his eyes.

"Geldt—let's talk."

"Mmarf." He nodded eagerly. "*Arrm*-marf."

I fingered the end of the rag dangling out of his mouth. "First I'm going to talk. And you'll listen—okay?"

Another fast nod.

"Now, what I know is that you screwed me over." I didn't have to wait for him to agree; I could see the little

9

Oh shit flicker way at the back of his eyes. "I know you did. You're just that kind of a guy. So you got all the money—didn't you?—and I got the dirty end of the stick."

"Mrrmf!"

"Yeah, well, we'll get to that. Now here's what else I know. You've already spent all that money." I shook my head. "You just can't hang on to it, can you? So now you need more. Have I got it right so far?" I pulled the rag out rip cord fashion. The back half of it was wet and red.

Geldt panted, eyes bugged out even farther. "Trayne—I swear to *God,* Trayne—I never—"

I wadded up the rag and poked it at his mouth. His dodging made me smile.

"Come on, Geldt. I'm not interested in hearing stuff like that. What I want to know is why you come looking for me. Somebody hired you, I take it. To find me. Who?"

He shook his head. "Nobody—"

"Oh, for Christ's sake." I slammed the heel of my hand against his brow, hard enough to snap the back of his head on the floor. His eyes lost focus.

"Try it again, Geldt. Who hired you?"

He was starting to fade. "Noo . . ."

"'Knew'? Knew what?"

The words oozed around his lolling tongue. "New Moon . . ."

That was something at least. "The New Moon Corporation hired you. Okay, I got that. Now tell me why. Why'd they want me?"

Fading fast. "Don't . . . know . . ."

"The fuck you don't." Actually, I believed that part. If I were hiring a weasel like Geldt, it'd be strictly on a need-to-know basis. But just in case he did know, I motivated him again. I picked him up by the ears and dropped his head on the floor.

10

I was bouncing a basketball. He'd gone out on me, the eyes rolling up white.

It didn't look like I was going to learn anything more from Geldt, at least not for a while. I decided to leave him there and go for a little walk.

3

I was basically cruising for something to eat before I went to work.

Getting on toward midnight, the streets and sidewalks were jammed tight, the still-human bodies sliding around each other, separated by their clothes and a film of sweat. All that nervous energy prickled my skin, like taking a bath in metal filings.

I usually managed to keep track of the local faces. They came, they went. They changed and were gone. You could expect six months to a year from the time of first entry into the zone, before the n-formation started kicking in.

All of this pseudo-L.A. smelled like chili paste with garlic, and refried beans. The fallout from the Southeast Asian places and the ubiquitous—one on every corner—*pupuserias*. One of the layers of the Los Angeles that had come up from the archives had been tight with refugee culture. That had been one advantage of a collapsing empire. Years of

12

war—those little wars, not the *Big One*—in distant world parts; that was how you wound up with great cheap ethnic restaurants.

That's why I was out on the street. Mere animal hunger, the simple kind, oiling my gut and nothing more. I *knew* why I was there. But what about all these marks?—no, not marks, not suckers, because they also knew, at least a little. They weren't operating in blissful, pocket-fleecing ignorance. They knew what was ahead of them, what the zone was doing to them. Instead of food, they all had the invisible leather strap of their destiny clenched tight in their mouths. They knew what they'd come here for.

Take this one, obviously a first-timer in the zone, pushing shoulder-first through the crowd, eyes in a narrow face scanning rapid-fire, as though he were expecting death's flying tackle at any moment. Ready to bolt; not too late to go back home. But he won't.

And here's two girls, their faces sick-green under the cliché neon. (*Definitely* too much of that shit had been called back from the archives—all those sizzling ribbons of light indicated a paucity of imagination, and a pretty stiff dose of historical inaccuracy; too many grungy urban movie sets, and not the real city itself.) Forehead-to-forehead in deep calculation over a dwindling stash of money being counted out between them.

As if money mattered, to such as them. As if anything mattered at all. I walked past them, and out of the corner of my eye caught one girl's quick up-glance, of fear mingled with excitement. That giddy expectation that set her teen-age spine on fire, from pit of crotch to top of skull. Her small hand reached for my sleeve—did she recognize me, from Identrope's broadcasts?—and then darted back, a small pink animal with just enough sense to be scared. It wouldn't stay that way.

All of them—the knife-faced newcomer, the whispering

girls, everyone else on the street—they all come to the Madlands looking for thrills. And that's what they would get. If they also got Identrope and redemption as the tail end of the bargain . . . then that was a bonus. The gift-wrapped package popped out from the machinery of grace.

I found a booth in some dive where the steam rolling out of the back kitchen smelled like heavy meat action. The window next to my elbow read "Comidas Salvadorean" on the street side. Eddie the Make slid into the seat opposite me as though I had conjured him there.

"People looking for you, Trayne." Eddie's mandible-like fingers picked at the scraps on the table. "You're a popular guy."

"The whole world loves my ass." A waiter in a grease-spotted T-shirt and a ten-year-old's pencil moustache set an *horchata* in front of me. I took a sip; the rice water keeps my gut from clenching. "Anybody in particular?"

Eddie nodded, his chicken-tendoned neck jerking down to his clavicle. I kept him on a retainer, so I didn't have to feed him cash in public. He was an old-timer in the zone, and once I thought that maybe he'd scoped out the same survival ability I had—maybe it was some genetic predisposition we shared—and that he'd just go on fidgeting and alley-sneaking in these parts forever. But in the last six months, every time I saw him, I'd seen his face going progressively softer, as though the skull beneath the raddled skin were being replaced with some substance much more flexible and regrettable. He'd gotten smaller, like one of those prematurely senile children. And the bald sector of his scalp looser, depositing flakes on his negligible shoulders, less like dandruff and more like fragments of a snake's shed skin.

Eddie the Make was in the first stages of *n*-formation. The multiplying carcinoma. I'd have to start grooming some of my farm team of snitches for the big league, to replace Eddie. He'd be missed.

14

He didn't bother telling me about Geldt; he'd been the one to tell me about that, months ago. "The New Moon Corporation. They're the ones looking to get hold of you."

It wasn't his fault I'd already heard that one. Between *carnitas* bites I asked him if he knew why.

Eddie shrugged. "They're a real start-up operation. Nobody's got much of a handle on them. Could be anything."

The tortilla was disintegrating and leaking orange grease down my wrists. "What've they been up to? In general?"

"Lotta rooting around, out in the junkyard. They've got some big section out there they've fenced off." Eddie looked hungry at the last bits in my hands. "Got some major capitalization, whoever they are. Been really working, those big blue searchlights all night long and stuff."

I pushed the plate over to him. He stabbed around in the debris with his finger and sucked meat off the tip.

Pinning money under one of the plastic squeeze bottles, I slipped out of the booth. "Okay, Eddie—let me know if you hear anything more."

He looked up at me with spaniel eyes. "Trayne. I don't feel so good."

I wasn't going to lie to him. "Eddie, you do look like shit."

He sighed, growing older and smaller. You could almost see the pieces, the useless human stuff, falling off him. "Do me a favor." He was looking at the plate and talking to me. "If you see me again, and I'm . . . you know . . . *real* fucked up . . ." His sad gaze swung up to me again. "You'll do something about it, won't you? You won't let me just flop all over the place, will you?"

"Eddie. Trust me." I squeezed his minimal shoulder. "I'm enough of a pal to put a bullet through your head. Or—Christ—whatever's left of it by then."

That comforted him. He was chewing on a tortilla scrap and looking thoughtful when I left him.

15

I went to work. I work for Identrope.

Sooner or later, everybody in this Los Angeles comes to Identrope. We all have to deal with him, one way or another. I figured I got a better deal than most of these poor bastards. I still got to call most of my soul my own.

I had the keys to Geldt's Hudson in my pocket, but I didn't take it. The Hornet was such a pretty machine—all machines are pretty, but this one was especially nice—that it seemed a shame to park it anywhere near the web. There's always a rain of ash from the dirigible burning overhead. (Some low-level hustlers scrape up the ash, put it in little vials, and sell it as either holy relics or restorative pharmaceuticals.) And some other fallout, wetter and not as pleasant. I didn't want to find the Hudson's paint job all munged up when I got done with my stint and climbed back down. So I walked.

The heat from the dirigible tightened my face as I approached, though I knew there wasn't any heat, at least not any kind measured in Celsius. A cold fire, image of billowing flame. Lucky for the disciples hung in the web, or they would have been crispy-crittered a long time ago.

A superstitious dread kept clear the immediate area around the web's anchoring point. You can walk to God, but you shouldn't try to live in his neighborhood.

I walked by the empty buildings, a desolate wind tumbling the gutter trash. The grid of shadows cut the pavement into diamonds.

A hand grabbed my arm. And immediately let go, as soon as I looked around. A pudding face, mouth shocked into an O by that act of temerity.

"Mr. Trayne?" The face belonged to a soft dyke, or an even softer man. Or a highly evolved rabbit. "I—I'm sorry . . . I didn't mean to disturb you . . ."

"I woke up disturbed." The person seemed barely able to speak, so I gave him/her a prompt. "Did you want something?" I'm gentle enough with the shell-shocked.

"No . . . n-nothing." A trembling lip. "I just wanted to tell you . . . I've always been a big fan of yours."

"Well, thanks. I appreciate hearing from folks like you. I really do."

The person got up enough courage to touch my arm with pudgy fingers. "I always watch your broadcast. To see you and the dancers. I never miss a one."

"Hey, that's great." I could see my charming smile reflected in the person's irises.

"Even when they're repeats . . . I don't really mind . . ."

So fuck me already. *Mea culpa.* "I had to take a little time off. It's kind of a high-stress job." Actually, I had been schlumpfing around, waiting and baiting for Geldt. Identrope had been running tapes of my old shows for the last couple weeks.

"Oh, no . . . I understand." Nod and gulp. "I just

wanted you to know . . . it'll be nice to have you back. I mean, on the air. For real.''

I felt the person's little eyes stapled to my back as I walked on. Encounters like these make me feel like even more of a shit than I usually do. Where do they come up with such touching faith? No wonder Identrope can run such a high-voltage operation. If gullibility were spit, every one of these poor bastards could gargle an ocean.

At the anchoring point, the web's cables bit into the asphalt and concrete like mega-snakes, head down from the sky. Some of the primary cables went up to a meter in diameter. Then the smaller laterals, down to a hand's breadth. And the thin capillaries of the life-support systems, trembling with the nutrient broth and hematic fluids pumping through them. Finally the neural fibers, thin as the gossamer of spiders, electrons singing on spun metal.

I reached up and grabbed the nearest lateral, catching hand- and footholds. And started climbing. I'd done this so many times before—my regular commute—that I could do it on autopilot.

When I'd first started doing this gig, shilling on the airwaves for Identrope, there'd been so few disciples stuck in his web that you could pretty much go up any way you wanted. The bare bones, the big primaries and the laterals, were the only things in some kilometer-square areas. When I got bored, I used to go out to the web's far edges, where the tension was slackest, just to ride the flapping breeze. The Santa Anas would come hot and dry over the distant grey hills, and it was like dancing in a pizza oven. A sideways yo-yo in a mild hell. You'd have to be bored out of your skull to register that as fun.

Nowadays the web was considerably more crowded. I'd been doing good work for Identrope for a long time, and the results were all around me as I climbed. (I knew I couldn't take all the credit, or blame. Identrope had the best product to push: immortality.) I could do it without half trying, but I was still picking my way past tangles of feed tubes and brain wires. And even though I knew that none of them would feel it, I still didn't consider it polite to step right on some openmouthed face. So I'd try to be careful.

Once in a while, going up or coming back down, I'd catch sight of one of the old ones, those original spiritual pioneers, the first to catch the hook of Identrope's call. All skinned down to nothing, muscles withered to string, flesh translucent over softened, decalcified bones, bent by the mere tug of gravity. White hair fluttering, ragged pennants with an invisible emblem. The faces of martyrs who had finally seen the handle of their devotion bring up a solid row of cherries, the coin of the big payoff chiming inside their skulls. A spark of mingled envy and pity would fall behind my eyes.

This time, half or three-quarters up, I stopped for a while and let myself hang, hands above my head, feet braced on a lateral below. I could see all of L.A., or what passed for it. What would do well enough, for our purposes. Dreaming, and moving in dreams . . . It had never been any different, not even in the real city. But that had been long ago. Before my time even, and I felt real old once in a while.

Out at the edge of the city, the other direction from the web's anchoring point, the junkyard rusted in its splendor. That was a lot of territory—it had been a big war that had left all that stuff behind—and I couldn't see where this New Moon Corporation was rooting around. Whatever they were doing, they couldn't be spied on from up here.

I could see a fleet of bogged-down, trackless personnel carriers circled around a multi-cannoned tank, a land-going battleship that had been broken in two and left charred around the edges. There were people moving around the machines, a line of wash fluttering on a rope, the coils of some home-brew water condensation rig. Probably another group that had trekked out from where normal people lived—everybody has to start from somewhere like that—and were now nibbling around the edges of the Madlands while they got up the guts to take the full-throttle plunge. They were already inside the range of the field's effects, so they might as well. There was no point in catching n-formation without having the fun.

A TV antenna bobbed at the end of an aluminum pole. It pointed a chrome arrow right toward me and the web. These newcomers were all set to catch my next broadcast.

They hadn't been out there the last time I'd climbed up the web. If nobody had clued them in, they might not even be aware that I'd been on repeats. Unless they had tapes or memories of whatever they watched before they'd set out for the promised land.

"Well, here's to you, folks." I took one hand from the cable and saluted them in the distance. "This one will be going out just for you."

They didn't hear me. I wasn't on their wavelength yet. I started climbing the rest of the way up.

5

UP at the top. I walked into the studios.

"Hey, Trayne—" One of the technicians, coiling a length of coax from his hand to elbow, nodded in my direction. "Where ya been?"

Everybody wanted to know. I must be important.

"I had some business to take care of." It was getting to be automatic with me. I pointed toward the rehearsal studios. "Is Nora around?"

"Every day, pal. Waiting on you."

"Yeah, right." I'd figured as much. "Catch you later." I headed down that way.

The hallway floor's sheet metal rang like a Caribbean oil drum. The whole studio complex had been cobbled together from a fleet of mobile broadcast units—trailers, really, and a few vans, all stuffed with gear, cameras and monitors and shit—that had been left stranded out near the edge of the junkyard. Some of the equipment hadn't even had its shrink wrap peeled off. Whatever battle some ancient network crew had been sent out to cover must have scared them pissless and gone in the first five seconds. Much later, war long over, Identrope and his minions had glommed onto the gear.

The whole shitload had been dragged up the web, these days' version of the building of the pyramids. *Mucho* sweat, funky winches and hoists. You would have thought all that dead metal tonnage would have dragged the burning dirigible down, even dropped it to the concrete and asphalt below, but you would have been wrong; it stayed pinned right to the sky.

About the sturdiest of the whole construction was the flooring; they'd put a little effort into that. Through the mismatched joins of the sheet-metal walls, you could see right through to open sky. Most of the roof was as poorly done. The flames of the dirigible overhead competed with the crackling fluorescents that lit the corridors.

When I'd first started the gig with Identrope, I'd kicked up a stink about sound- and light-proofing the actual broadcast studios. The initial couple of shows had been fouled with leak-through from the complex's surrounding operations, or the cameras picking up smears and streaks from being irised down for a production number and then catching glare from some cheesy wall panel peeling open. That had given me the cue to go into a whole prima donna, offended-creative-genius routine—"*Fuck* you; I won't *work* under these conditions, you hear me," blah blah blah. I still don't know whether I was angling for the studio improvements or for getting bounced off the job entirely; I had already started getting the creeps from close proximity to Identrope. I got the walls, and was still wondering.

At any rate, the rehearsal studio didn't look like it was in imminent risk of disintegrating like a wet shoe box. I ducked into its relative dim, and pulled the door shut tight behind me.

"Ah, it's our long-lost Mr. Trayne."

Shit—my eyes were taking a few seconds to adjust, but from that smooth and oily voice alone, I knew Identrope was there. Waiting for me? I didn't know if that was a bad sign or not.

More smooth words: "I'd heard you were back from your little, ah, sabbatical. Did you have a good time? I hope you did." True, unquestionable sincerity—that was his forte, after all—made his voice ten feet wide and tall, rolling a soft truck over me. "We really appreciate your hurrying back here like this. We've got a *lot* of work to do."

My eyes had finally reached the right aperture to see him. All real stars have big heads—I mean physically big, not a matter of ego—and Identrope's achieved even more apparent mass with his brushed-back silver-fox mane. Big hands, too; big with soul, Lincolnesque, hands you could *trust*. Hanging there at the sleeve ends of his usual three-piece suit, white as though washed in the Blood of the Lamb.

He always looked immense to me, though I could look him level in the eye. And I could have pulled on his suit jacket—matter of fact, I had done that once, when I'd been cooling my heels in his living quarters and had found one of his closets unlocked—and it would fit my shoulders exactly. If he looked big to me, it was just a walking demo that perception being reality wasn't a cliché around here, it was the law.

You could get fucked by a voice and a true smile like that, and you'd enjoy it all the way down the line. Most people did. I had the goods on Identrope—I knew what he really was—and even I had to work to keep my guard up.

I nodded. "Yeah, I had a good time." I wasn't about to

23

tell him that the souvenir of my vacation was still lying trussed up on the floor of my flat's back room. "Now we can get rolling again."

"Good, good." Identrope's smile glittered, but I could see his eyes refocusing into a familiar thousand-yard gaze, his busy mind calculating elsewhere. "I'm looking forward to seeing what you're going to cook up for us, now that you've had your little rest."

Nora was standing right next to him, but his presence ate up so much of the studio's air and space—like a black hole, he seemed to bend even gravity toward himself, pumping out light instead of swallowing it—that it took a moment to detect her. Plus she had that dancer's weird fade, the bit where they disappear when they're not actually performing.

A different smile from her, one that didn't have megawatts of personality lasering through it. If a deer that was about to bolt back into the forest could smile, that would be it.

"Hi—" Smiling and looking up through her lashes at me, not even knowing the sweet effect that had. (Or did she? Had she gotten to that point while I'd been away?) "I'm glad you're back."

Standard-issue dancer gear, the stuff they wear that always looks like rats have been at it for their daily fiber quota. Sweatshirt with holes (washed-out motto: "Texas Women's College Dance Dept.") over a scooped-neck leotard that would have been revealing if she'd had more than a handful of breast; her ladder-step clavicle stood out farther. Tights with mend scars over smooth-muscled thighs . . .

I thought she looked fine. But then I thought that even when I hadn't been away for a while.

"Well, I'll let you two get down to work." Identrope's smile swept over both of us like a ground-level searchlight.

24

"Trayne, why don't you swing by after you get things nailed down here? We need to talk."

His voice made it sound like it would be pizza and beer and old movies. "Sure. Soon as I get a chance." Soon as I felt like dealing with him, actually.

The white suit with Identrope inside disappeared on the other side of the studio door. I turned back around toward Nora.

The few strands of hair that had escaped from her scraped-back *chignon* were damp with sweat. She must've been going through her own barre before Identrope showed up. She walked away from me to pick up a towel draped over the wooden rail mounted in front of the floor-to-ceiling mirrors.

"I kept the troupe working on the last number you sketched out." Her voice went muffled when she ran the towel over her damp face. "They've got it down pretty cold. We could go live tonight—if you wanted to."

My wants were tuned elsewhere at the moment. I stepped up behind her, close enough to smell the sweat filtering through the leotard. I kissed her on the salty angle between neck and shoulder, and a tremble ran through her.

We went live right then. I locked the studio door—I had to reach behind myself to do it—and laid her down on a gymnastics pad in the darkest corner.

My fingers locked into the slot of ribs beneath those small, child-like breasts. The white skin was marked with the elastic from the tights, that draped over the edge of the pad like a truncated ghost. I rubbed the marks with my thumb and felt the heat of blood come up from below.

Even as the room was falling, collapsing into that other, soft familiar room, I couldn't help thinking how much nicer it would be if she were real. As real as me.

And then I stopped thinking that.

6

IN that moment of silence, the moment afterward, that unfolds forever and is sad immortality—

We lay together on the mat, tucked in the silence of the rehearsal studio. The side of her face against my chest, one skinny arm draped possessively over me; she slept, or seemed to.

I was awake, and thinking. About a lot of things, and sometimes about her.

It had been easier with Nora when she had been even less real. Real in the sense of being human; the more human she became, the harder and more complicated everything else became.

As usual, I had no one to blame but myself. I had made Nora as real as she was. Bit by bit, as much as I regretted the process, I was making her human.

She stirred, drowsily rubbing her cheek over the spot where my heart should have been. I stroked her disordered hair and went on thinking.

How it worked—

When the Madlands had started, come into existence, there had been nothing here. Literally nothing, as in *no thing*. Space without dimension, shape without form, light without perception, darkness that started inside your skull, then stepped outside to walk around.

Different theories circulated as to how the zone came to be that way. Some believed the effect was an aftermath of the war; some weapon (tagged in this theory the "reality bomb") had punched out a hole in the universe. The hole might not be something physical in nature, but neurophysiological; the hole was in the collective sensory percept system of the species. The bomb had gone off down the length of our spinal columns. Perhaps the bomb was still going off; the hole was still there, generations after the war and all its reasons had been forgotten. The old mists of time routine, that amnesia con.

Nature may or may not abhor a vacuum, but mankind loves a monkey puzzle. Fill in the blanks. One way or another, the Madlands weren't going to stay empty forever.

Identrope was the first on the scene. Before him, the nothing. After him, there was something, all right.

He found the archives. Underground, below the reach of the Madlands' null-percept field. Or just at the downward vertical limit of the field's effects; whether the archives' contents had been scrambled from the hypothesized weapon, or had just suffered the entropic creep of the buried centuries, was impossible to know for sure. But up from the ancient data banks had come the jumbled-together readouts, the old forgotten tapes and encoded crystals—

The lost world of cheap entertainment.

Old images filtered into the blank zone, and took it over.

Out of all the range of possible reality, one narrow band locked into place. The kicker, the funny part, was that it was a reality that had probably never existed in the first

27

place, except in our ancestors' fevered little imaginations and the primitive celluloid strips on which they'd recorded all their dreaming and wishing.

A Los Angeles of the mind—that was what got imprinted onto the Madlands' blank slate. Palm trees nodding in an ocean-steamed perpetual night and desert highways paced by glitter-eyed coyotes. Pan-Pacific apartment buildings and glass-walled Neutra mansions on seismic hillsides. Matrons with refrigerated money at the Bullocks Wilshire tearoom. All the dark streets folded into one another; the tar pits hissed under the red Santa Ana winds. A starlet leaping every hour from the top of the HOLLYWOOD sign.

Historical periods all muddled together into one glistening gel. Mainly the black-and-white eras; those were the most powerful image troves from the archives. Gangsters with slouch hats and the glamorous despair of economic collapse. All that greed and fantasy had to be born out of something. The color films in the archives couldn't compete with those flat grainy archetypes.

Any powerful image would do. Like the burning dirigible—something that looked that good, the flames roiling in the ancient newsreel depths—the image came over and got incorporated.

Identrope dug it up and let it all loose, and that became this little world, the perceptual overlay of any nervous system that happened to come wandering into the Madlands. You walked in, you'd bought your ticket to the show.

And what happened to him? To Identrope? You can't mess with stuff like that and not get it on you.

He found himself in the Madlands. He *became* himself.

Another L.A. archetype/image. The media preacher. Aimee Semple McPherson warped all the ones that came later, that latched onto the true buzz of the airwaves.

Maybe he was nothing before, just like the Madlands. But he definitely became something.

Identrope was already the white suit and the silver hair, the outstretched arms and the save-your-soul smile when I came along. The broadcasts were going out—he hadn't built his studio up under the belly of the burning dirigible; that came later—but they weren't working. In the real world with real people outside the Madlands, everyone had zipty-ump channels to spin through. If viewers caught Identrope's show, they'd usually snicker and drop back down to something like Peruvian mud wrestling over a bed of live coals and greased pit bulls.

He didn't have his hook yet. The gimmick. He didn't have me.

I had come to the zone—don't ask me why—and started rooting in the archives. There was plenty more stuff down there that Identrope hadn't gotten into. Working out of a reconstructed L.A. was easier than dealing with the blank that had been there before; plenty of cheap apartments with red-tiled roofs and diners made of jacked-up streetcars. So at least you could find a place to sleep and get something to eat.

The show choreography of the mid-twentieth century—that's what I was updigging and downloading from the archives. I didn't know shit about it when I started, but I was really becoming an expert fast. Heavy on the Jack Cole—forgotten-genius time—with heavy swaths cut through the more interesting avant-garde sectors, Martha Graham and Paul Taylor, a little Merce Cunningham.

I was down in a lead-lined bunker three hundred feet underground, unreeling old movies and videotapes out of the micron-thick crystalline data structure into which they'd been encoded. For the more famous ones, famous at the time they'd been doing their work, like Graham, there was still plenty of original source material. Get into the Paul Taylor, who never really did do anything for film, or someone like Jack Cole, who was surrounded by ignorant show

29

biz bastards throughout his whole career, who wound up
having his best stuff get thrown down the crapper whenever
some dopey Broadway musical folded . . . get into those
guys, or a couple dozen others like them, and you're dealing largely with reconstructions. Fortunately for me, in the
late twentieth century, there'd been an explosion of that
kind of research, people talking to the dancers who'd
worked for Cole and Taylor and the others, when they
were still around alive to talk, and even spry enough to
show the moves. Dancers have long memories for anything
they did with their major motor systems.

I was building up my own personal trove, complete with
cross-indexing by name, probable date of first performance,
and image cluster. At the time, I'd had a vague notion of
dragging the stuff back out of the zone and peddling it to
some mainstream cable network. All those hundreds of
hours of light and motion could be boiled down to a half
hour of prestige filler, something to run late night after the
blockbuster movie, to satisfy the Feds' cultural programming requirements and give the outfit a little class on the
side.

Then I got the call from Identrope.

You answer the call, you sign on, and things aren't ever
the same. That's just life in the Madlands.

He knew what I was doing down there. He asked me to
do a little something else for him. The hook, the gimmick.

I became the choreographic director for Identrope's
broadcasts. As long as I didn't have to move on camera,
I'd be all right. At least I knew what the stuff was supposed
to look like.

I needed dancers—he created a troupe for me. Out of
the same formless void that he'd pulled this pseudo-L.A.
from. An even dozen: eight leggy girls, four smiling an-
drogynous boys. You could have popped open any one of
their skulls and dropped a quarter in, and you would've

30

had to wait a long time to hear the tiny distant splash at the bottom. But they could move, and take direction, and move, and look good on camera.

Nora I promoted to rehearsal mistress and de facto leader of the troupe, just because there was more of a flicker behind her wide-open eyes than in any of the others'. She could run them through their paces while I was down rooting around in the archives for more material.

At first I'd figured the gig would only run a couple of weeks, a month at most, until Identrope realized that this wasn't drawing in the marks, either.

Three years later, I was still working for him.

Cursed by success. The dancing caught the viewers—I initially thought the broadcast audience must all be on some huge retro kick, then bit by bit it dawned on me that they actually liked the stuff, and there wasn't anything else like it, on the cable or elsewhere. And more importantly, for Identrope at least, it wasn't just a matter of the ratings going up; the marks stayed tuned in for his sermons. Come unto me, ye lambs of God. Come to the Madlands and let me put the tiny glittering pieces of your otherwise insignificant souls into the great mosaic of the web. Tie into the real immortality, folks . . .

They started drifting into the zone, and Identrope was waiting for them.

I got into deep grave-robbing, down in the archives. I didn't have shit for choreographic sense; my big creative strokes would be to mirror-double a nightclub duet for the whole troupe, or insert an *Angst*-ridden Graham pose into the middle of a Cole tango. If my stuff was going over, it just went to show how hungry the broadcast audience was for it. I even achieved my own fifteen minutes of fame, getting introduced from the wings in my severe tux.

Nora was the side effect. She went from nothing to something; the blank started to get filled in.

The dancing did it. I'm sure of that. She was the one who showed the others what to do; her mind had to start working with the big concepts, like time, and emotion, even if only the simulation of it. Whatever was inside her pretty skull had to evolve, become more complex, in order to wrap around those notions.

· She started becoming human. She wasn't there yet, but I could see down the line, to what she would eventually be, and I didn't know if it was a good idea or not. She was falling from that state of innocent grace, and I was the one who'd handed the apple to her.

Everything became more complicated. Before, at the beginning, I'd been able to sleep with her, and not a word had to be spoken. And if that was sad in some basic way, it was at least easy. For a few moments, I could drift back back down to her preconscious level.

Now there were words, and questions. There was a lot she wanted to know, to find out. That's how it all starts. Lying on the mat with her, I stroked her hair and hoped it all wouldn't be too hard on her.

Somebody out in the corridor rattled the knob of the locked door. That woke Nora; she reached across me to drag her discarded sweatshirt toward her.

Questions, like now. Sitting upright, lifting her loosened hair over the sweat's raggedy collar . . .

She turned and focussed her big eyes on me.

"Who are all those people trying to kill you?"

7

"AW, Christ—"

I reached over and pulled my own clothes toward me.
This wasn't the first time I'd heard this. I seemed to attract
every loose cannon in L.A. This time around, I had a deep
suspicion that it had something to do with Geldt's whole
jazz.

As I buttoned my shirt, I watched Nora smoothing her
hair back with the flat of her palms and reassembling her
chignon. "So who wants to kill me?"

She looked my way and shrugged. "I don't know. That's
why I asked you."

I tried a different tack. "How did you know that's what
they wanted?"

Another shrug. "They just looked that way. There was
two of them. They came around while you were gone. One
of them was that guy you used to hang out with all the
time. You know, the one that always looks like he's just

been oiled. And he smells bad." She wrinkled her nose.

That was Geldt, all right. "Anything else? Besides the way they supposedly looked?"

"He walked funny. The bad-smelling one." Where she sat cross-legged, Nora tilted herself a few degrees. "Like he was hauling around a great big weight in his coat pocket. I could see the lump."

That idiot—Geldt always liked to carry around that piece that just about weighed more than he did.

I tied my shoes and stood up.

My own jacket was tugged down by a weight slightly less than Geldt's piece. I hauled out a sack of videocassettes and handed them to Nora.

"We'll go live tomorrow night." I trusted her that the other dancers were ready; they'd had plenty of time, after all, while I'd been gone. "Take a look at these—" The cassettes were dubbed-off copies of another couple old movies I'd dug up. "Saturday, we can start working up the new routines."

She set the tapes on top of the playback unit mounted on the studio's wall. "Trayne . . ." Her voice sounded as though the words were being bolted together on some slow assembly line inside. "I've been thinking . . ."

"That's good." It wasn't good. Thinking was how she had changed already, and where further sadness lay. As the man says, I've been down that road before. "What about?" I was edging toward the door.

"Oh . . . things . . ."

The bad things. "Like what?"

"Like us . . ."

The *old* bad things."

"Us . . . and Identrope . . ."

That was new. "What about him?"

Her face went troubled, gaze reflecting inward. "I don't know, Trayne. I just wonder sometimes. Whether the

34

things we do for him . . . the work and everything . . . whether that's—I don't know—*okay*." She shook her head. "I don't know what I mean."

I did. She had entered the steep acceleration part of the becoming-human slope. First comes consciousness, then, not too much later, guilt. It's the human condition. Only assholes who are going the other way, becoming less human, like Geldt, slide out of it.

Her face stayed troubled, turning away from mine to hide, as I held her for a moment. There was nothing I could tell her, except the usual stupid things like *Don't worry about it,* or—

"We'll talk about it some more. Some other time." Guys who say that are optimists, hoping the world will end in fiery cataclysm before that other time ever comes. "Look, I gotta get going now. I've got some other business to take care of."

She nodded, that small motion enough to dislodge a single tear, that soaked into a spot on the leotard's neckline.

I was out the door and down the corridor, feeling like a colossal shit. I was the one who'd gotten her into this whole sorry soul-robbing business with Identrope—she wouldn't have even been summoned out of happy nonexistence if it hadn't been for me—and I was nowhere near being the one who would get her out. I couldn't even get myself out.

Thinking about the sad state of humanity in general had reminded me of Geldt in specific. I had almost forgotten about him, probably because I would've liked to. Having somebody tied up and gagged in your apartment is more trouble than a house cat—a cat can at least feed and water itself. If I wanted more info from Geldt, I'd have to get back home and make sure that he didn't die on me.

Before I took care of Geldt, though, there was some other corporeal maintenance I had to see to. As long as I was up here in the web, I figured I should look in on myself. Or at least that part of me made of flesh and blood. The raw meat I'd started out with.

I climbed down the web until I was out of sight of the studio complex. Then, instead of continuing on down to the ground, I tacked leftward into another sector of cables and wires.

The ranks of Identrope's followers were thick through this section. They rocked in their cradles of feed tubing and neural net, the metal strands glistening as they caught the angle of the sun. I worked my way between them, shifting my handholds from one cable to the next. The blind eyes stared past me, the gazes behind the cloud cataracts locked on the great communion singing inside their skulls.

This bunch of acolytes was starting to grow skinny, having been too long on the short rations pumped into their veins. I could see their knife-edge ribs and, on some of the more advanced hunger cases, the print of their teeth through the hollowed cheeks.

I'd have to move my own body pretty soon, to another zone of relative newcomers to the web. My body would stand out too much from these starvation types. When I'd first smuggled it in, I'd hooked it up to a double set of feed tubes, with the second one threaded down the middle of a support cable, and the tap into the body's veins at its lower back, safely hidden from snooping eyes. That kept my body more or less at its starting weight. I'd always been a skinny bastard, anyway, and hadn't a lot to lose. I'd even had to put a limiter choke into one of the feeding tubes, to keep the body from actually putting on weight—that would really have made it stick out, some gross porker swelling up out in the middle of the web. Just as long as it didn't waste away—I had grown up in that body, I had great sentimental attachment to it. It was the only thing my mind and soul had lived in before I'd found my way to the Madlands, and things had changed for me.

36

Coming up close to where my body hung suspended in the cables, I looked over my shoulder to make sure no one had been following me. I was clear—Identrope's busy little crews usually didn't come out into the web until the morning after the big Saturday night altar call, when they had plenty of new disciples to wire up and plug in.

Finally I stood over my original body, one hand above my head, holding on to a lateral cable. I looked down into my face, my first one.

That mirror-familiar face—not too different from the one I was currently wearing. Perhaps just from habits too engrained to break, I always went for narrow-browed, dark-haired, and slightly sinister-looking types when I picked up a new body. If nothing else, it kept the early morning shock when I washed and shaved from being too severe. If somebody were to line up all the bodies I had gone through in my Madlands years, they'd probably look like a rogues' gallery of feral carnival-ride operators. One of these days, I'd have to try something a little more upscale.

Sleeping face. Dreaming . . . The few times I'd slipped myself back into that body, I'd felt the blood-temperature wind of those dreams wrapping around me, ghosts of desire, the small children of memory, all pressing their own dark faces close, as though for a kiss or to whisper their wordless secrets.

Hair all in disarray, a few grey streaks starting around the temples, grown long to tangle in the wind around the cables. Bearded now—I hated to see that. As though the body were unloved, forgotten, with no one to mourn its absence from human affairs. I supposed I could have brought up scissors and a razor, to tidy it up, but that would have been a dead giveaway in the middle of this crowd.

At least my face's eyes weren't zoned out like those of the true disciples surrounding us. A subtle difference, but

37

I could see it. Dreams, that private paradise (or hell) being preferable to Identrope's programmed communal nirvana trickling over the metal filaments. I'd had to pull a sneaky on that front, too: the wires going into my body's skull were fakes, an inch of nonconducting fiber spliced in to insulate my former head from the signals sent out from Identrope Central. To avoid this being detected by the web's built-in monitoring feedback loop, I'd rigged a battery-driven microtransmitter on-line, sending back the happy *bleepity-bleep* of a human cerebrum getting Identrope's holy word.

I'd gone to a lot of trouble with all this, and I still wasn't sure why. Crouching down beside the body, I peeled back the artificial skin near the spine that hid the battery pack. I popped in a couple of fresh ones that I'd brought up with me; line fluctuations on the feedback loop were fairly common, so the dip while I changed batteries wasn't anything that would set off an alarm.

A lot of trouble . . . I'd shifted the body, my body, a couple of times already this year, on the sly. Just to keep anyone from finding out that it wasn't tied in to Identrope's neural network. Of course, the problem was in a sense self-generated: the only reason the body was up here at all was to take advantage of the soup line percolating into all the bodies' veins. Laziness on my part, I supposed; I could have rigged some homeostatic maintenance setup down on the ground, fed and taken care of my vacated body myself. But that would have been a major hassle—worse than a cat or a trussed bundle with big scared eyes—and subject to discovery by all these people who seemed to have an inordinate interest in the comings and goings.

No, the big question—at least for the moment—was why I didn't just let Identrope's wire snake into my old body's head and shimmy its salvific dance in there. I wasn't using it; I doubted if I ever would get inside it again. I had left it behind, an empty shell on this aerial beach.

Sentiment; I couldn't figure out any other reason. A soft heart for the old homestead. The same sort of pang you get when you drive by some place you used to live, some place where you had been happy, before you knew better; maybe the place where you had lain with your arms around the woman who had been your wife, in that other world . . . you drive by that place now and see the windows cracked or covered with greasy cardboard, and the strip of grass gone brown and specked with broken glass and a dried-out condom; a devolved infant squalls behind the door you used to walk through, in those other days . . .

"Shit—" I said the word aloud. I had plowed myself into a deep melancholy. Around me, the dead eyes watched nothing, their stoppered ears heard only another voice's whispering. Only my own eyes mirrored the ones I saw through. *It's all right,* my own lips murmured in silence. *I understand.* I bent lower to hear. *Go in peace . . .*

I put everything back in order, sealing the skin flap down and otherwise erasing any sign that I had been there. I stood up from my crouch and turned away. I had some other business to take care of.

8

GELDT'S lips were parched. The desert winds that came up around the outskirts of the pseudo-L.A. had started to dehydrate him. If I'd left him any longer, he would have shriveled up like a pink raisin.

I squatted down beside him and trickled a glass of water down his throat. He sputtered and came to.

"Good morning, sunshine." It was already late afternoon, but he didn't need to know that. "Feel like talking?"

It took him a moment to realize the gag wasn't stuffed in his mouth. He jerked a bit until it was obvious that he was still tied up. His wide eyes focussed on me.

"Trayne—" His tongue had swollen, and looked like something from a deli counter. "Y-you got to believe me—"

"I don't *have* to do anything." I used the tip of one finger against his brow to push his head back down to the floor. "Believe you, least of all."

"Trayne, I *swear*—I didn't—"

"Didn't what?" I picked up the gag and balled it in my fist, in front of his eyes. "Come on, Geldt. Tell me."

Something in my voice must have scared him. His eyes darted apprehensively, trying to read a message from mine. His mouth flopped open for a second, then clamped shut.

"All right. I'll talk." I used the gag to mop his sweating brow. "I'll tell *you* something. You came looking for me; upstairs, in the web. And you were dragging around that boat anchor you call a gun then. Somebody else was going around with you. Are you starting to remember all this now? Nod for yes."

A couple of seconds passed before Geldt's head waggled above his taut-tendoned neck.

"Fine. We're making progress. Now, a friend of mine saw you and your buddy trooping around up at Identrope's—and I put a lot of credence into her feelings about things. And she got the notion that you, and your buddy, and your gun, you were all looking to do me bodily harm. Kill me, even." I lowered my smile toward Geldt's face. "Would you care to comment on that?"

"She—she's nuts, Trayne—I wouldn't—"

I put the ball of my thumb on one of his eyes and rang for an elevator. Just a little push. "Don't call my friend a liar. Think about it some more."

Geldt twitched his face out from beneath my hand. A red thumbprint marked one eyelid. "It was a mistake. I didn't know—they didn't tell me what they wanted—"

"You know, I'd like to think it's always a mistake, when somebody's looking to kill me." My thumb drew a circle around one of his staring eyes. "Now, who's this *they* you're talking about? It wouldn't be something called the New Moon Corporation, would it?"

I loved being a step ahead of him. It was as good as a poke in his eye. His head rocked back against the floor.

41

"You—you know . . ."

I could have peeled his face off and used it for a dish towel—he had gone that pale.

"Damn straight, I know. You got a lot of nerve, Geldt, trying to sneak around and pull shit in my own backyard."

He looked like he was about to pass out on me again. I gave him another sip of water.

"Lucky for you, there's still a few things I'm not one hundred percent clear on." I set the empty glass on the floor beside Geldt's head. "Exactly who are these New Moon people, anyway?"

"I . . . I don't know . . ."

"You don't know. You're working for them, and you don't even know who they are. For Christ's sake, Geldt, you hung around with me enough, I would've thought a little smarts would rub off on you." I shook my head in disgust. "That's how you get in trouble in this world. Doing shit, and you don't know why."

Geldt licked his cracked lips. "They paid me . . ."

"Come on. That's not good enough. Look where it got you." I shifted position, my crouched legs getting tired. "Let's start at the top. This New Moon Corporation—they hired you, right? Did you go to them, or the other way around?"

"They came to me . . . Honest, Trayne . . ."

"And they wanted you to kill me?"

A hasty shake of the head. "No—honest to God. That was a mistake." Geldt's words tumbled out rapid-fire. "I fucked it up at the beginning. They told me they wanted to get you, and I . . . I thought that was what they meant. You know—*get* you."

It figured a weasel like him would assume the worst possible meaning. I wasn't flattered that it had seemed natural that total strangers would want me offed.

"So you went cruising around Identrope's headquarters

with that goddamn cannon in your pocket. And what if you had found me there—you were going to blow me away right in front of Identrope's goons? And then what? Jump off the web? You were packing a parachute, too?"

"I didn't think . . . about that . . ."

"Yeah, right." I rolled my gaze up to the ceiling for a moment, then back to his sweating face. "Who was the other guy with you? Somebody from New Moon?"

Geldt nodded, the back of his head rubbing against the floor. "His name's Harrison—"

That didn't ring any bells with me. "He's your contact with these people, I take it?"

Another nod. "He was the one who first called me."

"And paid you?"

"Yeah."

"And somewhere along the line, he found out you had this little, um, *misinterpretation* about what they were asking for? And he straightened you out."

"That's right. Honest, Trayne—I didn't want to kill you."

"But as long as that's what you thought you were being paid for, you were willing to rise above these petty personal concerns. I'm flattered." I stood up, rubbing the kink that had settled into the back of one leg. "So this Harrison guy worked it out with you, that you were just supposed to find me and bring me in to them. So they could talk to me, or something."

Geldt's wide eyes looked up at me. "That's what I was doing . . . when I found you."

"Did they say anything about why they wanted to talk to me?"

"No—" A flicker of wheels turning in one of those dark spaces behind Geldt's damp face. "They just said—they said it was something good. Something you'd be real interested in. Something profitable."

I looked down at Geldt. The last word he'd spoken was the magic key to everything inside his own head, so naturally he assumed it was in mine, too.

The stuff before that, there was a good chance he was lying.

"So—" I smiled down at him. "I guess we've had our own little misunderstanding. Really; you can't blame me for being a little paranoid, can you? We've had our ups and downs. But honestly, I didn't know you were trying to do me a favor. I guess I should just untie you, and we can be friends again."

A smile wobbled onto Geldt's face. "You got it . . . I swear to God, Trayne . . . I wouldn't have fucked with you—"

"Bullshit." I kicked him in the side of the head, not hard, more for punctuation than damage. "You think I'm going to start trusting you now? Forget it."

His eyes had gone all unfocussed. I walked over to the other side of the room, squatted down, and rooted through the little pile of stuff I'd taken off him.

In his wallet I found a card for a Clay Harrison. Board of Directors, New Moon Corporation. They had a subtle little logo, a foil-printed crescent that sparked in the light.

I pocketed the card and stood up. "I got some phone calls to make—" Geldt's blank gaze floated past me to the wall. "Don't go anywhere, okay?"

9

HARRISON had a smooth voice.

"Mr. Trayne—I was hoping to hear from you."

I tapped the edge of his card on the table in my apartment's kitchen. The guy hired assholes to do his work for him, but other than that I had nothing against him.

The telephones in my section of town had come up out of the archives as squat black monsters, a seriously ancient kind with those rough-woven cords, and no buttons. That was fine by me; I liked taking my finger around the dial, and the *clickety-click* in my ear as each number went through. I rubbed the edge of the dial with my thumb as I talked to this Harrison.

"Your messenger service leaves a lot to be desired. Next time, drop me a postcard."

He chuckled, the way people do when nothing's funny, but they're trying to show that they're nice guys. "Yes, well, a lot of people here thought that Mr. Geldt was some-

45

thing of an odd duck. I take it he found you all right?"

"Could say."

"I hope you'll accept our apologies, Mr. Trayne, for these rather unorthodox communication methods. It's not our usual way of doing business. But—we were at something of a loss about how to get in touch with you. You seem to have a certain knack for disappearing."

I put my finger in the zero hole on the dial. "I work at it."

"It's a talent that might serve you well. That is, if you decide to pick up on a certain business proposition we'd like to present to you." He put a little *Luftpause* before the word "business." Enough to let a mysterious hint leak through, without actually saying anything at all.

Took my finger out. "I suppose this is something you'd like me to come on in and talk to you folks about."

Harrison's voice was so smooth it puddled. "We would appreciate it. Of course, we'd be happy to recompense you for your time. Whether you join our little team or not."

"I don't know . . . I'm not big on traveling." Truth was, I'd been so long in the Madlands, I wasn't comfortable outside it anymore. I like the flux around me. Things staying the same all the time gets me nervous.

"You wouldn't have to go very far. We have a field office quite close to you. I could meet you there."

I could guess. From what Eddie the Make had told me. "Over in the junkyard?"

"Is that what it's called? Yes, I suppose we're talking about the same place."

The field office wouldn't be hard to find. Any of the 'yard rats slinking around the wreckage could direct me to it.

"Harrison—I got a question for you. Before I come out and talk. I've had to deal with a lot of crossed wires recently. What I want to know is, do you people want to kill

46

me?" I didn't see any point in dicking around on this topic.

"What?" Harrison sounded genuinely surprised. "Mr. Trayne . . . I assure you . . . what we're interested in talking to you about is just about 180 degrees different from that."

Odd phrasing, but it at least seemed to translate into their not wanting me dead. I believed the guy, but I asked, anyway. "Why should I believe you?"

"Mr. Trayne. Please." Patient corporate voice. "It stands to reason. If that were all we wanted, we could have figured out a much easier way of accomplishing it."

These are the comforts I live with. I told him I'd meet him in the junkyard, and hung up.

The rats came out to greet me.

I was hardly into the 'yard—I'd driven Geldt's Hudson out from the city's edge—when I heard them scuttling about, and felt the needle-push pressure of their eyes upon my back. I got out of the Hudson; the junkyard was too crowded with rubble and war debris to penetrate with a car. Made sure all the doors were locked—I didn't want to come back and find some retro technophile drooling on the dashboard gauges.

One came dancing out. He'd made himself a hula skirt of multicolored transistors strung on black PVC. A Shockley T-shirt ripped to expose body paint lifted from old circuit boards, gold traces on sick green; a clattering boogaloo as he twitched in front of me, desiring my attention.

"Not bad, huh?" He paused and panted for breath, hands on knees, looking up at me from his half-crouch.

He was standing right in my way, but I didn't want to touch him, shove him aside; the paint looked wet.

The rat gave another shake. His blond dreadlocks were braided with ribbons from a shredded Hefty bag. "Really—pretty good, don't you think?"

47

It dawned on me. He was *auditioning*. Even in the junk-yard, people knew who I was. And my connection to Identrope. The big money (or so they'd like to think). Fame and immortality (that latter part was at least true). They figured since I was listed on the end credits as choreographer, the road to a dance gig on Identrope's broadcasts ran in front of my judgmental eyes.

I could just see a kick line of these hard-core technophiles, a little old-style Rockettes action, a time step garbed in fragments of old machines. The tin can chorus.

"Hey, pal—it's just not working for me." I hated always being the one to have to break it to these types. That their lives were futile and their hopes a gut-hollowing delusion. The only contact this poor bastard was going to have with Identrope would be to sign up for the web. "I don't think it's the kind of thing our audience would go for." Unless they all went blind or something, but I didn't say that.

This all came as news to the rat. He stared at me in bewilderment. "You're kidding."

That was the problem with these 'yard types. They were all so in love with the bright sparkly bits, the ancient once-powerful scraps of metal and silicon, that they couldn't imagine anyone else not being wired to the same thrill.

"Seriously." I moved to step around him and continue on my way. "Keep working at it, though." I didn't have the heart to tell him to give up and die.

He fell back, crushed like a dead leaf. If steel trees dropped aluminum leaves, that is. Without looking behind me, I knew the 'yard rat was drifting into shadows, blown by a wind of no consequence.

Somebody had been working amongst the junk. The farther I got into this zone, the more I saw evidence. More open space—I could have driven the Hudson in, if I'd known how much things had been rearranged. Big lanes had been created by shoving piles of the metal debris to either side. The soft dirt was marked with the tracks of some major operating machinery, cranes and loaders and stuff like that. I could even see the gantry of one such piece, fresh and unrusted, tapering over a pile in the distance.

Whoever these New Moon people were, they had definitely made an impact in this little corner of the world. Different outfits had gone rummaging in the junkyard before, looking for various scraps of military and even prewar technology that could be turned to profitable use. Not much ever came of these expeditions; if someone dug up a flesh-boiling laser that could be made to work, there was little commercial application other than as the ultimate toaster or something like that.

Nobody had ever hit the 'yard this heavy before. This was way beyond mere pot-hunting, as the archaeologists would say. There was some effort—read bucks—being expended here. New Moon was either getting results or expecting them soon.

Where the scraped lanes converged, I spotted the New Moon field office. The company logo rippled on a flag over a potted xeriscape of scrubby desert plants.

The office's air-conditioning chilled the sweat on my face. I told the receptionist—it looked like a skate job for her, with zip people coming by this lonely outpost—that I was there to see Harrison.

I got taken down a bolted-together prefab corridor, and shown in. The receptionist closed the door behind me.

Harrison sat behind the desk, leaning back in a high brown leather chair, and playing with a gun. The twin of Geldt's.

I didn't even get to sit down. Harrison stretched his arm out, pointing the gun right at my chest.

He smiled over the barrel. "Nice piece, huh?"

10

"IT'S lovely."

My heart went on ticking at its normal speed, but my gut had done a small clench. Intestines are always cowards, probably because it would hurt more there.

The little black hole moved away from me, as Harrison used the gun to point. "Have a seat."

I did an irritated slump in the chair. It annoyed me having to deal with all these amateurs. The way they flopped these cannons around with no respect, as if nobody could get hurt by accident. It showed they were civilians who didn't handle these things on a regular basis, and hadn't gotten over their movie-stroked fascination with them.

Harrison laid the gun down on the desk. He looked like a nice enough guy, like his voice over the telephone. Like a third-generation photocopy of a real person. I had been prepared to find him okay, until I had come in on him dicking around with the firepower. Don't people in air-conditioned offices ever have any real work to do?

Now he'd have to work to get back into my good graces. I folded my hands over my stomach and waited for him to talk about money.

"Mr. Trayne." He smiled at me. "Trayne . . . is that what people call you?"

"My friends do." I wasn't giving anything away.

"Your friends . . ." Harrison's face went all thoughtful. He obviously thought it unlikely that I would have any such commodity.

He tossed a manila folder beside the gun. "You're an interesting character . . . Mr. Trayne."

Characters are what you see on the tube. I was getting more pissed off by the minute. I leaned forward and hooked the folder—Harrison made a grab for it, but settled back in his own chair when I glanced up at him.

I always enjoy seeing what people think they know about me. My name was on the folder's tab, but there wasn't much more beyond that of any value. Some telephoto shots taken on the sly of me going in and out of my apartment . . . nothing too recent. I had grown my sideburns long a while back, a side effect from unearthing a trove of Patsy Cline recordings from the archives. The photos were all from before I'd whacked the 'burns back off.

Harrison had recovered his face. "You've been hanging out in the Madlands for quite a while, haven't you?"

No big secret there. Anyone could have figured that out from the list of my broadcast dates tucked in with the photos. I nodded. "A while."

"Most people don't last that long. As long as you have."

"Guess I'm just lucky."

He was giving me the bug-under-a-microscope look. Leaning back, making a cage out of his fingertips. Expression of mild distaste. "You know, I've seen some medical reports. On people who . . . stayed too long. Out here.

51

What's the term—" His gaze drifted away, searching for vocabulary on the ceiling.

"Multi-cancer. Or *n*-formation. Take your pick."

"That's right." Again, the smooth smile. "They're not quite the same thing, though, are they?"

I had to give him credit for knowing that much. "No. One's a precursor of the other."

"I imagine you might be quite an expert on the subject." A shrug. "There's not much to know. Only a couple things you have to remember. The disease is peculiar to the Madlands. The cause is uncertain. The symptoms are kind of unpleasant."

Harrison shook his head, the corner of his mouth curdling in distaste. "You know, it's a real mystery to me . . . to a lot of folks I work with . . . about just why these people come out to the Madlands, and hang out until they come down with something like that. I mean . . . what could possibly be the attraction?"

What he really wanted to know was what could be the attraction, compared to staying all your life in normal territory and working for whatever megacorporation was venture-capitalizing this New Moon outfit. Watching cable in your little apartment and paying off the car through the credit union. Who in their right mind would turn their backs on all that?

You'd have to be out of your mind. Harrison, and the crowd he ran with, obviously weren't on that wavelength. He was insulated. Probably taking all the approved precautions, limiting his exposure to the Madlands' field, and so forth—and none of that was even necessary in his case. He was so far off the zone's wavelength that he would never pick up the buzz; if he didn't feel the attraction, he'd never feel the ill effects, either.

What could be the attraction . . . He wanted to know, so I told him.

"It's all got to do with loss of pattern discrimination." I had given this canned lecture before—I knew it by heart. "People come into the Madlands mainly because of that. You've got this zone here, it has certain properties the actual neurophysics of which I don't even want to get into. These said properties are the ones that produce the *n*-formation disease, which is basically a loss of pattern discrimination on the cellular level; that's what causes the stuff you saw in those medical reports. You following me so far?"

Harrison nodded.

"Now, the properties of the Madlands zone—" Christ, I could reel this stuff off. "—the properties apparently also extend to all other modes of pattern discrimination, and not just to that which determines a life-form's physical existence. The concept that you have to get into your head is that the whole cellular replicating process encoded in the DNA is merely a small subset of all possible information. Like radio signals are a subset of all possible electromagnetic radiation—you got that? Now, the reality that is normally perceived—you know, this stuff we see when we look out the window?—well, that's a subset extracted out of the larger set of all possible realities. The normal percept system is a filter that excludes all other realities and lets pass through only the commonly perceived reality. Now—"

"Excuse me." Harrison coughed. He looked apologetic for interrupting me. "But, um . . . this is all just a theory."

"Yeah?" I looked at him as if he were a bug. "So?"

"Um. Nothing." A nervous little smile. "I just wanted to make that point."

"Yeah, well, you made it." Now shut the fuck up. People buy the ticket, they should take the whole ride. I didn't say any of this to Harrison, because there was still the smell of money in the air. I might still be doing business with him. "As I said, only the commonly perceived reality passes through the filter. You don't get unicorns and people who can set fire to their own methane production and fly through the air—at least not out in the ordinary world. In the Madlands it's different. The zone's properties, the loss of pattern discrimination, set in, in a major way. The percept system's filters begin to break down. This allows progressively wider and wider ranges of other realities to be perceived. Now, you may not think this is a great idea, but for the people who come to the Madlands voluntarily, this is exactly the attraction. The reality filters breaking down, and all the new sensations and perceptions that come flooding into the neural system under discussion—that's considered to be a neat thing. Very pleasurable and exciting. Worth making the trek to the zone for. Worth even winding up as a cross between a rubber glove and a squid, with two big blue eyes staring up, when your cells go all mega-squamous. Historically speaking—tell me if I'm losing you here; I only know this stuff because I spend a lot of time rooting around in the archives—this might be called 'consciousness expansion,' a phenomenon touted for certain neuro-specific drugs a long, long time ago. Not that those actually did anything, apparently. However, as with those chemicals, hanging around in the Madlands to get that buzz also has its inevitable drawbacks. You play, you pay. It's easy to get addicted to the sensation, all those new worlds opening up to your nervous system. You come into the zone for a little taste, you wind up staying for the whole banquet, right down to the dessert, which is yourself. There's the risk—actually more of a sure thing—of contracting the n-formation disease due to prolonged exposure to the zone's field. There's also the eventual loss of the ability to distinguish the commonly shared reality of the human species from all the others that are now perceived. Sort of a mental equivalent to the mere biological condition of multi-cancer that results from the n-formation disease. You could call it *multi-schizophrenia,* maybe. Not just a

54

split from the rest of the world, but many, an infinite number of chasms between the mind and everybody else's reality. A real maze to get lost in."

"Jesus." Harrison actually looked sick, a little green blush moving up from his gagging throat.

I couldn't resist; I wanted to see if I could push him all the way to the vomit point. I'm always entertained by how squeamish people get when you talk about dicking inside one's head. "Now, another way to look at it—another whole system of metaphors—is to think of it in terms of acoustic science. There you've got a distinction made between what is called 'white noise'—which is more or less the result of all possible frequencies being played simultaneously—and what is called 'pink noise,' which is the result of all possible frequencies *within the range of human hearing* being played simultaneously. So you could posit a 'pink reality,' which would be all possible sensation comprehensible to the human nervous system, and even, I suppose, a 'red reality,' which would be that little narrow band of sensation that is the commonly perceived reality. You got me on that? So—theoretically, of course—in the Madlands it would be possible to go all the way to 'white reality'—all possible perception, regardless of comprehensibility to the human nervous system. In theory, this progress could be made, and maybe that's what some of these poor bastards hanging out in the zone are after. The big one, everything at once. In practice, however, it doesn't go down that way. If somebody hangs out in the Madlands long enough to approach that point, the n-formation gets him. It's that loss of pattern discrimination ability, what keeps you you, and not a porcupine or a jellyfish. That's what n-formation is. An individual who comes down with it eventually dies of multi-cancer, a biologic anarchy where *all* cells become increasingly disordered, taking on all the characteristics of all

55

other possible life-forms at random. It's not a pretty way to go."

"Excuse me." Harrison got up from behind his desk and headed for the door, at a quick trot.

I leaned back in my chair and smiled. This made us even, for the bit with him greeting me with that stupid gun.

The usual problem with these prefab buildings. The walls are thin. I could hear him from down the hallway, redecorating the porcelain in the executive toilet.

HARRISON came back, mopping his lips with a stained handkerchief.

I was sunk low in my chair, legs sprawled out, playing with a fountain pen I'd taken from a block of travertine marble on his desk. It'd taken a bit of work, but I felt in control of the scene now.

A blue flower glistened on my fingertip; Harrison glanced with irritation at the use I made of his toys. He swept the papers off the desktop and into a drawer.

"It's kind of stuffy in here," announced Harrison. I only inhaled the cool, dehumidified sting of the air-conditioning, but his nose was loaded differently now. "Why don't we go out and get some air?"

I followed him down the corridor and past the receptionist. A white flash bleached her face as she leaned over a photocopier. The smell of money, the kind made without work or pain, billowed up from each step on the carpeting.

We walked in the shadows of the junkyard. I could feel the 'yard rats watching us, from their Indian perches on top of the larger piles, but Harrison seemed oblivious. He bent the line of his grey three-piece by slouching around with his hands shoved in the pockets.

"You're probably wondering—" People say that whether you give a shit or not, but they have this burning desire to tell you something. "—just what it is we're up to out here." Harrison was in a deep musing mode, rubbing his chin as he walked. He looked over at me. "You can tell this is a big operation, can't you?"

I shrugged. Maybe it was, maybe it wasn't. This New Moon bunch had certainly done a lot of moving stuff around, treating the whole junkyard like some kind of rusting chessboard. That didn't necessarily mean they were accomplishing anything.

Harrison took my silence for being all impressed. He nodded slowly. "A big operation . . . A lot of changes are going to be made. Lot of changes . . ." Muse, muse, stroke chin. "This is going to affect everybody." The look came my way again, something gleaned from a dark lab seminar at a sinister Dale Carnegie course. "Everybody, Mr. Trayne. You catch me?"

It would've been hard not to. I was trying to crawl out from under this fogbank he'd laid on me. "Yeah, I got it. Big changes. Everybody. Just like that."

More slow nodding and rubbing of chin, gaze gone off to that distant inner horizon. Goddamn corporate ideologues always expect you to get on their wavelength, operate by telepathy or something. He'd have to come up with something solid pretty soon, or I was going home.

He must've caught that one. Pulled himself upright. "I'm sorry, Mr. Trayne. I hope you'll forgive my woolgathering." The nice-guy smile dazzled in my direction. "We've all been working pretty hard, gearing up for this. And it's something we all really believe in."

"Great. God hates a half-devil."

Harrison actually laughed. I could see the silver in his molars. "That's good. I like that. There are no half-devils out here, are there?"

I shook my head. "There aren't even any half-saints. It's not that kind of a place."

"It's good to know where you stand. Eliminate all the grey shades, and then you can start to do business."

That's just what I was hoping for. "So, uh, just what is it? That you're doing out here. That you wanted to talk to me about."

He looked smug, pleased with himself and his bomb-dropping capacity. "We're going after Canal Ultime."

It took a moment for that to register. The old wheeze about fish not knowing what water is. I didn't do a lot of thinking about Canal Ultime on a day-to-day basis, simply because it was more or less the world I swam in. Me and Identrope; CU made our operations possible. The air we breathed.

"'Going after'?" I had fallen a step behind, and caught up with Harrison. "What, you're talking about putting them out of business?" That was hard to believe. Canal Ultime were pretty locked down. They owned that world.

"Good Christ, no." Harrison smiled and shook his head. "Really—you people outside the corporate loop . . . you tend to get overdramatic about business maneuvers. One company goes up against another, nobody's going to wind up being put out of business. In this regard, we do have to tolerate grey areas. It's not like boxing or something, where you can think about knocking the other guy out of the ring. No, we're talking about relative market share here. Much less dramatic."

"Yeah, but isn't CU's market share one hundred percent

right now?" Where did that put these New Moon people?

Shake of the head. "Not quite. There are still some fringe cable operations. Very specialized markets—stock quotes, deviant music enthusiasts, things like that."

"Still, you're talking about the high nineties for CU's market share."

Harrison shrugged. To show he wasn't impressed, intimidated. "High ninety-nines, actually. Point something or other. Really, Trayne, we wouldn't be targeting them if they didn't have the meat in their jaws."

"Yeah, right. That's good thinking." Maybe. For me, when I thought about things with jaws, I usually also considered the big long teeth they carried around in them. "But this New Moon thing—you people are a start-up operation, right? So your market share now is at zero. Am I correct on that?"

"Oh, sure." No big deal—for him. "But you have to remember, Mr. Trayne. Zero is a starting point."

In the worlds I ran in, zero was the end point.

We had walked on farther into the junkyard. Even more signs of activity. Fences with razor wire strung along on top had been thrown up, to keep the pesky rats out. Harrison got us through a card-locked gate. On the other side, the empty spaces were scraped even wider, the shiny new earth-moving equipment arrayed on either side.

Harrison led the way into this mini-zone's heart. His pace had picked up from the previous meditative stroll. He looked back over his shoulder at me, his eyes holding a genuine excited spark.

"Near one hundred market share—you're absolutely right about that, Mr. Trayne. But it's not going to be that way for long."

He'd have to work hard to convince me on that point. You didn't have to be big into history to know that when some entity has a monopoly situation, it can go way beyond

60

rational limits in defending it. Especially a high-profit corporate entity such as Canal Ultime, where a particularly
vicious defense could be paid for out of the petty-cash accounts.

Canal Ultime had started out—I knew this from my ar-
chive rummaging—as a fairly low-level special-effects outfit, contracting services out to what had been the majors
back then. An influx of Euro-capital had enabled them to
get into feature production, and finally, picking up a piece-
meal distribution network. Somewhere along the line, the
dog-French name change—*The Last Channel*—had come
about, along with some distinctly Napoleonic empire-build-
ing ambitions.

All of which they'd made good on.

One hundred market share; forget those splinter cable
deals, ticks on a rhino's back, so big it wouldn't even know
they were there. On the battlefield of broadcast communications, Canal Ultime was the big winner. Omnivorously
so; they hadn't just beaten their competition, they'd eaten
them. If it was being broadcast, and somebody was watching it, then it was CU's game. One hundred percent.

New Moon thought it was going to cut into that kind of
locked action? They were crazy. Harrison's smile was a
loon's smile.

That loony smile widened as Harrison watched the
thoughts bouncing around behind my forehead. You didn't
need telepathy to know what I was thinking.

"'O ye of little faith—'"

"Little faith, hell." I was trying to remember if he'd left
the gun on his desk, or whether he'd slipped it into his
pocket on the way out of his office. I didn't care for people
with everything packed in tight waving those things around
in close proximity to my flesh; I *really* didn't like that kind
of hardware in the hands of people with this much exposed
wiring. "If that's what you're up to, I can only wish you

61

and your friends the best of luck." I scanned around for whatever would be the quickest way out of this 'yard sector.

Harrison laughed. "I can appreciate your skepticism, Mr. Trayne. When I signed on with New Moon—and believe me, I was recruited fairly late in the process—when they told me what they were planning, I thought the venture capital they'd rounded up would be better invested in lottery tickets. At least there's a measurable chance on those. But all that was before I saw . . . certain things, let's say." He gestured with a curl of his index finger. "Step over here."

We'd come to a hangar-like building of riveted sheet metal. It bounced the sun into my eyes, all fire and tears. I heard, rather than saw, Harrison draw back a big rattling door. Another welcome blast of air-conditioning bathed my face. Generator hum massaged the darkness.

"Well? What do you think?"

I blinked and looked around. Harrison had left my side and now stood in the middle of the high-ceilinged space. A proprietary hand rested on the flank of a white cylinder, its curve higher than his head.

I could see fins and the dark snouts of a propulsion system at one end, tapered nose at the other. A missile lying on its side. This was it? Their big deal? Their idea of competing in the marketplace was to go military? That wasn't even all that original—you watch enough of those *noir* films dug up from the archives, you could pretty easily get the notion that organized crime was just ordinary corporate activity with better firepower.

"This something you found here in the 'yard?" I looked the missile over. It was a blank, no identifying insignia.

Harrison shook his head. "Most of the old ballistic stuff left around here—even if you could get it to work—it's all short-range hardware. Basically, we needed something that

62

could get us out of atmosphere, up to an orbital level." He rubbed his hand on the slick white. "This is pretty much your standard commercial piece, right off the shelf from our supplier in Jakarta. The import license was a bit tricky. We finally had to smuggle the pieces in, flatbed trucks down from a hydraulics plant in Ottawa. Everything was labeled as sewage treatment components, right down to the control electronics."

It had been the big criminal enterprise of his life; he radiated a happy smugness about it.

"So this is just a freight jobbie?" I rapped my knuckles on the metal and got a hollow *bwonng* in return. "No exploding payloads?"

A little smile as Harrison shook his head. "I'm afraid not."

"Oh." I was actually a little disappointed. Some part of me had been hoping for something a little more fun, crazier. I could see where this one was going, and it wasn't anywhere special.

"You see—"

"No; let me guess." Arms folded, I leaned a shoulder against the missle. "You're going to put up some kind of home-brew communications satellite. And that's your big blow against the empire. That's how you're going to go up against Canal Ultime." It was sad, really. They'd get creamed into something you could spread on toast. What were they going to do for programming, for one thing?

"It's not as simple as that, Mr. Trayne. Come over here."

He led me around to the other side. The missile's cargo bay hung open; wires dangled out to a squat ovoid riding on an equipment cart.

"It's true we brought the missile system in ourselves. But we brought it in, to this spot, for a reason. What we're going to be putting up with it isn't something we've built

63

ourselves. To put it bluntly, we've found something out here that is of, let's say, considerable interest. A really fine piece of technology. And it is of military origin."

Harrison was obviously referring to the big egg on the cart. It radiated that dull grey nonsheen of the old stuff, mysterious and sinister. Personally, I wouldn't have trusted it, no matter where they'd dug it up.

"Yeah?" I laid a finger on it and got a small static shock, a blue spark in the dry air. "What's it do?"

"Well, it is a communications satellite. You were right about that—"

I'm always right about these things. To my great disappointment.

"—but it is a little different from the ordinary run of those things. As I said, it's a military device—"

Big deal. They could've been using it to beam down armed forces video to the troops in the field. Tit shows and reruns of old sitcoms.

"—and it has some rather unusual capabilities. That's why New Moon is investing the money to get it up and running. Under our control, of course." The smile blossomed on Harrison's face again. "Basically, it's the device's anti-jamming abilities that attracted us to it. That we could see the commercial possibilities in. Some of our technicians refer to it as *sneak-wave propagation*. Up till now, Canal Ultime has been able to shove any possible competition off the band, blank them right out of the sky. This baby—" He gave the egg an affectionate pat. "It can use Canal Ultime's own signals as a carrier medium, without affecting the original signal's content; CU won't even be able to drag us before their pet FCC on any bullshit jamming charges their lawyers might be able to come up with. And the beauty of it is that they won't be able to use their own jammers on us. Our signal becomes a parasite on theirs, that can't be destroyed without killing the original. It's a

64

bulletproof arrangement. We can be on the air with this thing, and Canal Ultime will never know what hit them."

The guy was in love with this device; it showed. They probably all were, the techs and the money bosses alike.

"Well, that's real fine." I folded my arms across my chest. "Let's assume that your people have got this thing working, and it can do all that neat stuff. You've still forgotten a few things. Canal Ultime still has all the programming and the advertisers. Technically, you might have this wired, but your economics are screwed. Nobody's going to switch over from a CU broadcast to watch your test pattern."

"That's a good point." Harrison nodded. "I like talking to someone who can anticipate these things. It makes it so much easier. You're right; Canal Ultime has a lock on the software and the revenue accounts. That's where you come in." He reached into his jacket pocket.

Christ, he did have the piece with him. I should have spotted the gun's weight tugging his jacket askew. He hauled it out and displayed it to me, the muzzle pointing up in the air for a welcome change. His smile metamorphosed to a wacked grin.

"We'd like you to accept a little commission on our behalf, Mr. Trayne."

"Yeah?" I was ready to duck around the other side of the missile, just in case he lost all control. "Like what?"

"It's Identrope." Smile and nod. "We'd like you to kill him." Harrison held the gun butt-first out toward me.

That was it? I had to laugh.

My laughing echoed up in the high ceiling. Harrison kept watching me and smiling.

The smile grew nervous when the laughing didn't stop. "What's so funny?"

I couldn't tell him. It was too good a joke.

The laughing went on until I couldn't see Harrison any

longer, tears squeezing under my eyelids. I threw my head back and tasted one drop at the corner of my mouth. Like drowning in a small salt ocean, sinking beneath furious self-damning waves. Identrope's corpse floated by, his throat blossoming in a red cloud where a shark with one of my faces had razored him.

That was the joke. To pay the shark that had been circling in my heart for so long, pay for murder that had already been sealed in my long-night dreaming a thousand times . . .

Who wouldn't laugh?

12

MEMORY, not dream; my laughing had triggered it.

Someone else laughing, and I was in my original body, the one that was sleeping up in the web now. This must have been before I'd gone disguised and wound up working for Identrope. Because he'd been the one laughing, standing at the entrance of his headquarters, with a bunch of his studio hacks standing around him. Laughing at what, I didn't know; I'd been standing yards away, scoping things out. Long ago. But I remembered the sound of Identrope's laughter, and it had been easy to remember.

Shuffling bodies, you find out that sensory inputs differ from one person to another. Shifts and gradations, filters and processing variations. Nearsighted or slightly deaf, and subtler than that: a slide up the spectrum in this one's optic tract, an accent on the treble in another's cochlea. Things always looked a little different, sounded a little different—like getting into a car and adjusting to the tilt of the steering wheel.

But one thing I'd noticed. Whenever, over the years, I'd heard Identrope's laughter, it had always sounded the same. As though it skipped over the crude sense receptors, and wired straight into my skull. Even my own laughing, echoed in bone and sinus cavity, had never stayed just the same from body to body. Just Identrope's. That had been spooky and I'd come to hate it.

But it wasn't why I'd be happy to kill him . . .

Harrison and I went walking back to the field office.

My hilarity had died down, an ocean receding on the rocks of Harrison's dud personality. All that smiling, and if he'd ever found anything funny in his life, I was the Pope of Iguanas.

We finally got back down to business. My dark heart faded behind the numbers, but didn't entirely disappear.

"You figure offing Identrope is going to do it for you, huh?"

Harrison nodded. "That's our projection."

"As corporate warfare goes, that's pretty much hardball."

He shrugged. "We don't really see any alternative. New Moon is well capitalized, but there's a limit. Our investors want to see black ink on the bottom line pretty quickly. Even with our satellite's ability to elude Canal Ultime's jamming efforts, we don't want to spend years nibbling away at their market share. We want results. Also, we don't want to take a heavy hit, spending time and money on programming development and kissing advertiser ass. We want those people to switch *en masse,* over to us. We think we can take CU's market share from one hundred down to fifty, easily, if we play our cards right."

Maybe, maybe not; I couldn't see it myself. "What's Identrope got to do with all that?"

Harrison tried out a thoughtful expression. "I don't think you realize, Mr. Trayne, exactly what a pivotal figure your employer is; his exact importance to Canal Ultime's operations."

"Identrope pays them a lot of money to carry his broadcasts." I knew; I'd seen the account books.

"That's true. The receipts from Identrope constitute a nice piece of Canal Ultime's revenues. Hardly enough, though, on its own, to put them into profit mode, given their overhead. No, that's not where the real value of Identrope to CU lies. It's something just a little deeper than that. Consider, Mr. Trayne: do Identrope's people—his accountants and such—they get ratings from CU, don't they? A readout on how well the broadcasts are doing, number of households watching, that sort of thing?"

"Of course." That was how the payment to Canal Ultime was figured, an incentive ratchet: the more people tuned in to Identrope's broadcasts, the more we paid CU.

Harrison raised an eyebrow. "And do you trust those figures?"

I hadn't thought about it before. "What, you think CU's padding them?"

"On the contrary—and this isn't a matter of what I think, this is what New Moon *knows*—Canal Ultime is sitting on those ratings, keeping them low."

That didn't make any sense to me. "Why would they do that? That would just be cutting into their own revenues."

"They'd have to have very good reasons, wouldn't they? Now, we have certain key people—employees of Canal Ultime, some of them quite high on the ladder—whose, shall we say, allegiances have switched over to New Moon. While they're still at CU. And these people have told us some very interesting things about CU's accounting and viewer-tracking practices. Suffice it to say that CU has been deliberately underreporting the Identrope's ratings—"

"Yeah? By how much?"

"A lot, Mr. Trayne. A whole lot. The figures before

CU's people screw around with them show that Identrope's broadcasts—your broadcasts also, Trayne—are the most popular thing on all of the Canal Ultime's distribution networks. More popular than all the rest of the programming combined."

If that were true—and just looking at Harrison, I started to get the feeling it was—then that wasn't just a matter of fudging a little around the edges. There was some mega-money involved.

"I still don't get it. Why would Canal Ultime do something like that?"

Harrison put on his corporate wisdom look. "There's a couple of good reasons. One is that if they stuck to the original payment schedule, they'd bleed Identrope dry. There's no way he could come up with the kind of money that the original contract calls for. In that sense, Identrope would be a victim of his own success."

We had gotten back into the old rubble section. Late enough in the day that the rusting cliffs had us deep in shade.

I was trying to read whatever lay behind Harrison's smooth face. "So what's the problem with that? Canal Ultime could just renegotiate the contract with Identrope. That kind of thing's done all the time."

"They had a better idea. At that point in CU's thinking, the actual cash revenue coming in from Identrope was a negligible factor. The spin-off effects from Identrope's broadcasts were much more important. Their research showed a tremendous pull-through factor; your audience tends to spill over into watching all the rest of CU's programming. If they segment the Identrope broadcasts throughout the day, they can jack up their networks' total viewing audience by four to five hundred percent. Believe it; they went through a period of experimenting with time slots, and I've seen the reports that came out of that. It's

70

solid numbers. So the decision was made to clam up about the spin-off effect. Better to underreport Identrope's ratings, and forgo the additional revenues that would technically be owing to them, than to give somebody outside the company—namely Identrope himself—that knowledge about how dependent they were on him."

Now it was all coming clear. Feed in enough points, and you can predict where the line is going.

I nodded, right on Harrison's wavelength. "So if one person's that important—the way Identrope supposedly is—and you can eliminate that person . . ."

"Exactly, Mr. Trayne. We've put quite a bit of deliberation into this. At one point we were debating the advisability of having you killed. That might be where our friend Geldt got the wrong idea. A certain faction on the New Moon Board of Directors felt that your participation on Identrope's broadcasts—the choreography, the maintenance of the dance troupe—that that was the critical element drawing in the high audience numbers. And certainly your death would have had an effect, at least on a short-term basis. But the consensus finally was that you weren't absolutely essential to Identrope's operations. Your style and methods were well enough established by this point that you could be replaced, probably by one of the dancers in the troupe. Some research of our own had established that you've already turned over quite a bit of responsibility to one individual. So even though there were some points in favor of that particular action—for one, you would've been much easier to get to than Identrope—the vote finally went against having you killed."

"Thanks."

"It wasn't anything personal. We try to keep things on a strict business level."

Strict business, all right . . . "So you took another vote and decided to ice Identrope."

71

Harrison nodded. "I'm sure you can see the logic of it. With Identrope gone, the broadcasts end. With the broadcasts eliminated, the spin-off effect from them is over. Major audience drop-off for Canal Ultime. That's our window of opportunity. We've got our unjammable satellite already up, so there's no quick and dirty way CU can get back at us. CU's advertisers and other programming sources see what's happening, viewers disappearing from CU's networks, and we snap them up. Maybe even more than fifty percent. That big one hundred market share could be ours in a couple of months."

"You're forgetting something. Fifty, one hundred, whatever—it'll be a much smaller market. If Identrope's broadcasts are what draws them in, you get rid of those and the audiences are going to shrink back down."

A shrug from Harrison. "We'll deal with that afterward. Corporate planning can only go so far. It might be something that you and I will want to talk about after the event. Maybe there'll be a place for you in a new programming venue. At any rate, our feeling is that all of a small pie is better than none of a big one."

"Yeah, well—" I looked around at the reddening metal. "You're also forgetting that you're talking about me being definitely out of one job; there's no maybe about it. If I do this little thing for you. How much do you think you're going to be able to pay me, to make that worth it?"

"We're prepared to make you a very lucrative offer, Mr. Trayne. I'm not talking about a mere lump sum payment for services rendered. An ongoing slice of the action—that's what we're prepared to cut you in on."

Slice and *cut*—the man liked to talk bloodthirsty. "What kind of slice are we looking at?"

"Half of one percent of all net revenues generated by the New Moon satellite."

From blood talk to air talk; it didn't mean shit to me. I

decided to see how far I could push him. "That's not good enough, Harrison. I'll need a full one percent."

He didn't blink an eye. "It'll take board approval, but I think we can swing that."

I had spent so much time rooting up Hollywood stuff from the archives, I knew what else to bite. "On the gross, not the net."

Little soft gems of sweat welled up on his forehead. "Whoa. That's asking a lot."

"Gross, or I walk. You can get yourself some other boy."

He caved. "All right—"

"And I want all this on a stock ownership basis, not just some contract for royalties."

"Sure. Whatever you want."

None of it meant diddly; I'd been around the block enough times to know that they could still screw me blind. We hadn't even gotten into defining *profit participation,* or any of that tight creative accounting stuff.

The dying sun stained the ground appropriately red as Harrison walked with me toward the Hudson. One 'yard rat was tongue-kissing the hood ornament as we approached, but scurried away when he spotted us.

"One more question, Harrison." I leaned against the Hudson's fender and fished the keys from my pocket. "Why me?"

"Why you what?"

"Why me to kill Identrope? There are people whose main line of work is this sort of thing."

Harrison's face stayed smooth and blank. "It's a simple question of access. You're tight with Identrope. You've been working for him for a long time. It's no problem for you to get to him. In private."

"Really?" I rubbed the ignition key between my thumb

and forefinger. "If I'm so tight with him—how'd you know I'd be willing to do it?"

He looked puzzled. "But that's why we made you such a good offer. So you would do it."

Little concepts like *loyalty* or *friendship* were words on tissue paper inside his skull.

There's always something insulting about it, when people just automatically assume that you're the same sort of creature they are.

I unlocked the Hudson and got in behind the wheel. Harrison tried to hand me that gun of his through the rolled-down window, but I pushed it away. "Christ, I don't want that thing. I've got my own tool kit."

I drove away, generating a dust cloud large enough to block the sight of Harrison in the rearview mirror.

My laughing had stopped a while back. Killing Identrope—being *asked* to kill him—was still a funny notion to me, but not that hilarious.

All Harrison's money talk had done was push, with one fingertip, a boulder off the edge of a cliff where it had been teetering for a long time. As was so often the case, somebody else's word would be father to my deed.

As I one-handed the steering wheel, the low L.A. skyline up ahead, I mulled over the exact spiritual ramifications of murdering this world's—my world's—true and bogus Savior.

13

I drove out of the junkyard, with the hot eyes of the rats locked on the Hudson's exhaust pipe. Their lust for smooth metal tailed me onto the road, until the dust cloud boiling behind blotted it out.

Heading back to what passed for L.A., the skyline inching up in the windshield, I mulled over Harrison's business offer. For the mere cost of my immortal soul and a laundry list of strange psychological ramifications—I could screw over myself *and* people who trusted me!—it seemed as though I might have cut myself in on a nice piece of change.

Change in all the senses of the word, not just the jingling stuff in my pocket, but the winds of that other air, the breezes and tornadoes whistling holes through our meager lives. Constant mutation had been the theme song of the real L.A., ages ago, and the pseudo one had taken the melody down to the molecular level and beyond, every particle humming the grand dissolve and recombinant chorus. Nothing lasted forever, and in these parts the shelf life was traditionally measured in some range from hours to milliseconds.

My gig with Identrope had lasted years already; I could probably have picked up the Madlands trophy for conceptual longevity, if there'd been one. I had already bucked the odds for a run way beyond the average. I couldn't reasonably expect the deal to go on forever, though a certain mental hysteresis always led me to believe that it would be there tomorrow, and even the week and month after that. Thinking about Change was like thinking about Death, and I'd already penciled that in too on my dance card. You know the icy fist is knocking on a door somewhere, but it's not on your street, and if it is, it's not on your block, not yet. And other horseshit lies.

It made cold sense at this point, when the long run was due for termination, to cash in my trusted relationship with Identrope for a big payday. A whole gravy train of paydays, a slice of New Moon's gross for the rest of my life. With that kind of money, I could walk away from my principles, keep walking right on out of the Madlands. I could put my checkbook where my soul used to be, write *Death to Memory* on the Payable To line. You could do a lot with serious grease like that. This was, of course, all assuming that everything that Harrison had talked about—all New Moon's business plans—came to pass. But I already had the certainty, the rock in my gut, that it would, given the precedent factor of my arranging Identrope's demise. I was the hinge of history, and which way I swung spelled fate for a whole lot of people.

I kept on driving, musing on these deep dark things, as I aimed the Hudson's hood ornament for the heart of the pseudo-L.A.

Climbing up the Ivar cul-de-sac to the Alto-Nido Apartments—I left Geldt's Hudson down on the corner, where the streetlights were brighter—I dug my apartment key from my pocket. I already had it in the lock when I heard the sounds coming from inside. They didn't scare me, but they had me worried.

I reached in and switched on the light. The sounds, no longer muffled by the door, were decipherable as human if inarticulate. They had a certain edge of panic to them.

In the back room I found Geldt right where I'd left him. Eyes bugged, the gasping sound coming from him—he'd made a heroic effort, given the limited scope of action available to him, and had chewed partway through the gag I'd stuffed in his mouth, his tongue shoving the spit-damp cloth far enough aside to allow his bleat of fright to emerge.

Geldt didn't even look at me as I came into the room. With his hands tied behind his back and his ankles cuffed, he'd managed to scoot himself back against the farthest wall. I tracked his sight line to the other side.

"Christ—" I smelled it at the same time I saw it. The odor of spilled urine and worse. This mess had obviously had both a bladder and a lower intestine. But not anymore.

It was still alive. I walked over and stood looking down at it, my sight and other senses recoiling. The mess oozed and shimmered, a puddle with a tremor. Two rudimentary eyes focussed on me; the wet flesh around them was translucent enough that I could see the workings of striated orbital muscles. The whole thing had a diameter of about a meter at its widest point.

Empty clothing under one side; I pulled them out with the point of my shoe. A shiny snot-like substance clung to the different fabrics. Pants, coat, shirt with the buttons still done up; a deflated scarecrow. And something I recognized, a faded brocade vest from a Mexican wedding suit, a thrift-store item that had been bought for forty-nine cents and worn as a joke, the joke being that it couldn't really be from a Mexican wedding since there weren't any holes from the traditional knife fight out in the parking lot. Eddie

77

the Make's joke, the ethnocentric little bastard; Eddie's vest. He'd been wearing it yesterday when I'd been talking to him while chowing down.

Now I felt sad. The hole went right through my heart, and it wasn't from any knife fight. The mess on the floor was Eddie. The n-formation had hit him, just the way he'd been afraid it would.

I fished through the empty trousers pockets and came up with the apartment key I'd given him some time back. A rare token of my esteem; I didn't hand out keys to my place to just anybody. And the only reason I'd given Eddie a key was so he'd have a floor to sleep on whenever he didn't have the two bucks for his regular flop at the Hotel Stanford down on Eighth and Alvarado. That had probably been the case tonight—he hadn't looked too prosperous yesterday.

He must've let himself in, thoughtfully locked the door behind himself, and left the chain off so I could get in. Likely heard Geldt whimpering and sniffling back here, came in to look . . . and that was when the n had got him.

At least it had gotten him all at once, from the looks of it. That happened sometimes, but not very often. He'd lucked out. He would've hated going through a protracted multi-cancer siege, feeling his cells slipping out from underneath him one by one, waking up every morning a little less human than when he'd gone to sleep the night before. And the process had gone all the way to complete cellular anarchy, too, with no stop-off somewhere along the line, no intermediate stage like a PVC lobster or a dog with a lady's hands.

The whimpering behind me went up in pitch, and I looked over my shoulder. Geldt had come to enough of his senses to realize that I was there in the room. His bugged-out eyes signaled to me.

I went over and knelt by my guest-in-bondage. I tugged the gag down to his chin.

"Oh Jesus, Trayne—" He moaned my name and the

78

Other Guy's. "Thank God . . . thank God you came back
. . . it was fucking horrible—"

I looked at him with blank innocence. "What was?"
When people make it this easy, I can't resist.

Geldt's eyes looked as if they were going to come flying
at me like ground-stroke tennis balls. "For Christ's sake!
Right over there . . . you were just looking at it!"

"Oh, that." I shrugged. "You know, sometimes these
things just happen."

He started to gibber. Nerve sweat drenched his face.
"The guy . . . he just walked in here . . . it was that guy,
that Artie or something . . . he walked in here, and he
looked all funny, he looked right at me . . ." Geldt's eyes
unfocussed, rolling over the bumpy ground of his short-
term memory. "And then . . . and then . . . he just . . .
just *changed*. Went all like that . . . over there." The pro-
truding gaze fastened on me again. "Get me out of here,
Trayne." He pleaded, lips trembling. "Get me away from
. . . *that*. I'll do anything for you, Trayne. Anything."

Geldt disgusted me more than the Eddie-mess. The big
wimp. It just showed what an essential novice to the Madlands he was. If he'd spent much time here at all, he'd have
gotten used to stuff like this.

"Anything, Trayne . . . you name it."

I was already planning on taking him up on that offer.
He was, in fact, going to do a lot for me whether he offered
to or not.

My bad knee creaked as I stood up. Looking down on
him from way above, I shook my head. "Afraid I can't
oblige you just yet. I need you here—"

That got a shriek. "For the love of God, Trayne!"

I liked the Poe reference. "Tell you what, though. I'll
take *him*"—Eddie still got my respect, even if he'd slid out
of the definition of human; I wasn't going to say *it*—"out
of here. Then you'll feel better, I promise you."

Geldt tried to give me some argument on that point, but I stuck the gag back in his mouth. I went to the other bedroom, the one I used for sleeping, dumped out some books, and came back with an empty cardboard box.

I squatted down beside what Eddie had become. Poking around with one forefinger, I found rudimentary kidneys, the coil of a simple digestive system, other bits and pieces. In the thickest part of the rippling gelatin, two fists of pink stuff bumped up against each other, with a segmented tail extending about half a meter; that was his brain and neurosystem. The eyes stayed focussed on me, following my prodding investigations. I felt sure that Eddie was still in there, alive and conscious.

There was more than just consciousness in the eyes. That little soft spark, from his brain to mine. He was pleading with me to remember my promise. He had no way to speak, except in my remembrance of what I'd told him I would do, when it came to this time.

That was why I'd brought out the empty box. I tried to slide him into it, but that didn't work; the floppy tissue snagged against the rough edge of the cardboard. I set the box back upright, and tried a different tack, less pleasant. I got my hands under the Eddie-mess—like snails and slugs, it looked slimier than it actually was to the touch—and folded him up like an omelette that someone had forgotten to cook. With the thinner parts brought over the middle, Eddie made a small enough package that I could pick him up on the flats of my hands and lay him down inside the box. Tenderly as possible; that was mandatory under the circumstances.

I carried the box with the Eddie-mess in it out to the little weed-choked yard behind the apartment building. The other thing I carried out, tucked into my trousers pocket, was Geldt's overweight cannon. For some reason, I didn't want to use my own personal piece to do this; maybe to

80

avoid getting bad memories tied onto something I might want to use again someday.

Looking down the hillside, I could see the L.A. lights doing their murky dance. I'd set the cardboard box down at my feet. From inside it, I could hear the stuff that had been Eddie moving around, something like tapioca slow-sloshing in a quart mayonnaise jar. And even something like a little sigh, as though he'd realized that I hadn't forgotten my promise to him.

I turned back the box's top flaps. Inside it, Eddie's eyes caught enough of moon- and starlight for me to see them gazing up at me.

"Okay, pal." I wasn't sure if he still had anything like ears left. Snakes don't, and they can pick up vibrations. It didn't matter; I was talking more to myself than anything else. I pulled out Geldt's piece and cocked it. The metal-on-metal click bounced loud down the hill. "It was nice knowing you. I mean that."

The cerebral matter was right behind the eyes. I aimed between them, my arm laid straight down. The shot rang like a safe dropped on an iron sidewalk. Goddamn these over-amped loads.

The optic remainders had gone dull, no longer reflecting on either side of the newly drilled hole. The bottom of the box was already soggy. Eddie's cells, not too organized already, were into the liquefaction stage, and leaking into the stubbled ground. That was okay; it saved me the trouble of digging a hole to slide him in.

I straightened up, the gun heat rolling into my wrist. Eddie's eyes weren't looking at me any longer, but somebody else's were. I had a good idea who.

I held Geldt's piece up by my ear, and talked to the night. "All right—" I cocked it. "Come on out."

I looked over my shoulder as Eastern showed herself, stepping out from behind the corner of the apartment building.

"Hello, Trayne." She smiled at me. "Isn't your arm getting tired, holding that thing up there?"

Geldt's piece lowered itself; all I had to do was relax and uncock. I was actually glad to see Eastern. It had been a long day, stocked with unpleasant faces.

"Not a good idea." I tucked the gun back into my pocket. "Sneaking around people in fire mode."

"But you're so slow. You always have to think." She walked over to me. "What're you doing, blowing away kittens?" She looked down into the cardboard box. "Eeyuck." Her nose wrinkled.

"Just my friends." I nudged the box away with my foot, where its contents weren't so visible. "Paying off old debts."

"Anybody I know?" She was hip to the score, that it was

an *n*-formation basket case I'd been out here dispatching.

"Eddie the Make."

"Eddie? That was Eddie? Awww. Shit." She shook her head. "He was on my payroll. I was just about ready to go round and see him, pay him a little something on account."

"Well, you don't have to now." Eddie had been a walking info shop for a lot of people besides me. Even for a line cop like Eastern.

She looked genuinely sad about a snitch's demise. That was what I liked about Eastern. She didn't give off cop radiation. Actually, she smelled rather nice—she was that close to me, her cropped hair at about the level of my shoulder. Not perfume, but just the way some women can smell with mere soap.

"Poor little sonuvabitch."

"Tell you what." I pulled Geldt's piece out of my pocket, holding the butt with my thumb and forefinger. "Let me go stow this someplace where it won't hurt people. And then maybe we can go and have a drink. I'm kind of depressed about this."

"Yeah, sure." Eastern hunched her shoulders up inside her denim jacket. "I'll meet you down by that ugly car you've been driving."

She had been watching me for a while. I had known that it was her I'd felt, the gaze on my back. That was something we needed to talk about, the why of it.

In the apartment, Geldt had passed out. Still breathing, but basically asleep. I cracked the windows to air out the sour smell of Eddie's terminal metamorphosis. Geldt's piece I tucked up on top of the bookcases. I locked the door behind me and headed down the sidewalk to the Hudson and Eastern leaning against its fender.

Eastern and I went a long ways back. We had both drifted into the Madlands at about the same time, but from different directions. And different motivations: if she'd been looking to get away from something, the way I'd been at the time, I never found out what it was. She'd inevitably blanked me on that angle of inquiry. Of course, it was always possible that she'd come into these parts just out of curiosity, which was a much more dangerous reason for doing things. That was how you got into trouble. I should talk. Here she was with an official-type gig, working for the Feds, and I was the one out on the margin, helping operate Identrope's long-running scams and now signed up in my head to off my employer.

"You're looking good." I said that because she was, in this latest body she was walking around in. We had that in common, the shuffling in and out of other people's flesh and bones. Where she'd stashed her original body, the one she'd been born in, I didn't know. That was a good secret for people like us to keep locked up, even—or especially—from each other. Regardless, I always recognized her—something in the eyes, if you looked way in the back where the soul hung on its bone cross. Plus she always went for dark *gamine* types, small-breasted and fast, the sports cars of the female form.

"Thanks." She always recognized me, too. We had these tags on each other. "You look like hell."

We were sitting in a red booth in the dim Formosa, the Leatherette under our butts mended with duct tape. Over in the corner beneath the signed photos of Elvis and Marilyn. Moisture had leaked under the picture frames' glass, causing a brown leprosy-like fungus that had eaten most of the stars' faces. They all looked like tryouts for poster boy and girl in some campaign against rampaging entropy.

Eastern was halfway through a tall Scotch, the same thing I had in front of me. She was the type who always ordered what you did, not to flatter, but because it was all the same to her what she drank.

"I've been busy." I rattled the ice in my glass. "I don't

have some cushy government job, so I got to spend more time making a living. That cuts into my personal maintenance time."

"Your ass." She smiled, teeth sparked blue from the sputtering neon in the window. "'Cushy'—I wish. I'm on perpetual overtime just keeping up with you."

"Why?"

"Christ, Trayne, it's my job. That's why."

I shook my head. "You know what I mean. How come all of a sudden I rate this much tail activity? I always thought you people had better things to do."

God's truth on that one; it was why I wasn't one hundred percent happy to see her again. About the time I'd signed on with Identrope, Eastern had joined the enforcement wing of the FCC. The federal telecommunications agency was naturally locked into a hip-tight embrace with Canal Ultime, their biggest player. Most of the time, Eastern and the other line cops were busy enough drawing down on scapegraces doing illegal feeds off CU's entertainment network. Protecting corporate profits was their business, and rightly so.

Eastern tapped a finger on the rim of her glass. "You crack me up. You really do. Sitting there and acting like you haven't been doing shit. Come on—you know you've been a busy lad. With all that dropping out of sight, and stuff."

"Yeah, well. That was personal business. Between that asshole Geldt and me."

"Your *personal* business hooks up with my professional business." Eastern wasn't smiling at me now. "Geldt was dealing with some off-the-wall people."

I shrugged. "He's an off-the-wall kind of guy. That's why I stopped having anything to do with him."

"So why was he going around looking for you?"

She had her ear out on the street, that was for sure. I

85

gave her another shrug. "Beats me. If I see him again, I'll ask him."

Eastern sent back a look that I could read out as meaning she knew I'd had lots of contact with Geldt recently. Maybe she knew that I even had him wrapped up back at my apartment. "You sure know how to piss me off, Trayne."

"So change the subject."

"All right. New Moon."

I played dumb. "Is it? I thought we were having a full moon tonight, the way everybody's been acting so weird."

Eastern drained her glass down to the ice, while I watched one of the waitresses squeeze between the tables on the other side of the room. If somebody ever got around to inventing high-heeled air-pillow shoes, these old bats would think they'd died and gone to heaven.

"You know, Trayne, I used to think you were a halfway intelligent guy."

I brought my gaze back to her side of the booth. "I don't get paid just for being charming."

"You could get paid for being the world's ugliest paperweight, and I wouldn't care." It must've been something I'd said—I hadn't seen her in this bitchy a mood before. "Beats me why Identrope keeps you around." She just kept rolling. "Those cornball dance numbers you put on the air—Christ, I expect you to come on some night in a Day-Glo tuxedo, jump up, and shout, *Live! From the Copacabana!*" She shook her head in disgust.

"Hey. Fuck you." I was genuinely wounded. "Look, Ms. PMS, I never went around saying what I do for Identrope is great art or anything. People like it, so sue me. And besides, if it were really my stuff, you could say anything you want about it, and I wouldn't give a shit. But I've stolen all those moves from a lot of dead people whose memories I've really come to respect. Slag me off all you

86

want, but not Jack Cole. Okay?" I knocked back the dregs of my own drink.

Our voices had risen, and a couple of barflies turned around on their stool perches and looked at us.

Eastern didn't care. She was already zipping up her jacket. "I can't believe I'm having a conversation like this with you. As if I give a fuck about you and your stupid tap-dancing show. Your goddamn rumba extravaganzas."

"That's it?" I watched her sliding out of the booth. "I thought maybe you had something important to tell me."

"Important? You want important. Fine. I'll tell you something important." She put her palms down on the booth's table and lowered her glare to my level. "Watch your ass with these new friends of yours. This New Moon bunch. They're a hinky operation. Strictly nonkosher."

I shouted after her as she headed for the door. "Thanks for the advice. If I did what cops would like me to do, I'd be selling magazine subscriptions for a living—" She didn't hear the last bit; she was already gone.

The waitress plodded over and gave me the tab. I was hugely pissed off by now, mostly at myself. The shouting matches weren't the sector of my past with Eastern that I'd been hoping to revive.

I'd been really glad to see her again. I'd been looking to get laid. It looked pretty certain that was off the agenda for this time around.

I left money on the table and walked out.

15

I lay on my bed, thinking. I had a cigar fired up, a hand-rolled anonymous jobbie from a resurrected Cuban refugee on Fairfax. Not because I liked smoking it—I took a couple of hits to keep it going, and that was enough to vulcanize my tongue—but because I liked to smell it burning. As long as I had the place opened up, so the night Santa Ana wind could blow the smoke out over the city's distant lights. In the room's dark, I could hear Geldt on the other side of the wall, snoring around the gag in his mouth.

More to think about. The business with discovering that Eastern had been the one spying on me. I hadn't found out much more than that from her. Though our aborted conversation had confirmed my previous impression that the New Moon Corporation was a little on the flaky side. And not in any benign sense of the word. They had started out with me by talking about murder; if that's your square one, then the potential for damage rolling all the way across the rest of the board is pretty good.

The cigar's coal was dying to dirty red. I flicked off the ash and gave the wet end a puff. The orange flare outlined my knuckles.

Even if I hadn't gotten any—the other any—off Eastern, I could take some comfort in the deduction that she still had some vestigial regard for me. Enough to lay the unneeded warning about New Moon on my head. And to get all pissed about what a jerk I was being. Even when the two of us had been an item, laminating ourselves together from ankle to breath on a daily basis, that had been a major component of her spoken exchanges with me.

Those were other days, Jim . . . That reminiscing about them still brought a twitch in my crotch showed that it must've been love. That it didn't bring anything more than that showed that I was getting old.

The fact that Eastern and I had a history, that there was a past to get nostalgic about—in a zone like the Madlands, where your DNA was hostage to the dance in which Eddie the Make had fallen—that made it pretty conclusive Eastern and I had some essential quality in common. We were bound to get together on one level or another. We were brother and sister under whatever skins we happened to be wearing.

I had all kinds of urgent business to think about, but I'd already absorbed enough of a nicotine load—the dry wind had died, and the room's air had turned thick and smoke-blue—to sink into loose, undifferentiated musing.

A favorite daydream of mine rolled by. I got on and rode with it, watching the movie on the mottled ceiling.

I was dead in the dream—that was why it was my favorite—and people still talked about me. Everybody's favorite dream. So much so, that in my version there was a lecture hall, one of those steep-banked circling university numbers, every seat filled. Podium and blackboard down below, the point where every gaze focussed. The guy talking had my face, if I'd gotten old and wise.

On the blackboard, somebody—probably not the lecturer—has done nice portraits of Eastern and myself, with cross-hatching to show her dark hair and the shadows on my face.

The lecturer has a pointer about a meter long. He taps my face—the face on the blackboard—with it.

He speaks. "We come now to the subject of *d*-rangers." He has a whispering, sepulchral voice; the audience leans forward in their seats to hear him. "A controversial subject in the convoluted natural history of the Madlands. In terms of the emotional baggage attached to just the word, we have entered a dread-filled semantic landscape."

The pointer taps Eastern's face. "The very existence of these entities was a source of much rumor among the habitués of the Madlands zone. Some were terrified of them, certain that they were real. Others considered *d*-rangers to be a joke that wasn't very funny. Like talking about ghosts or vampires, if there were a large section of the population who really believed in them."

He turns away from the board and grips the podium, the ends of the pointer sticking out to either side. "*D*-rangers—if they existed, or could even be identified—could be considered to have been the infectious agents or vectors of the *n*-formation disease endemic to the Madlands. So it is easy to see how the term developed its associations of death, despair, insanity down to the cellular level. The *d*-rangers could be said to have been the factor that put the *mad* in Madlands."

The lecturer broods for a moment into a fist brought up to his lips. He speaks around his knuckles, as though he could chew the answer to everything out of the round bones.

"One question of interest is whether the *d*-rangers were

in fact mere vectors transmitting the n-formation disease, or whether they themselves were infected with it. The fact that the d-rangers did not suffer the terminal multi-cancer symptoms associated with the disease is not conclusive proof; the d-rangers' characteristic abilities—the body-swapping, et cetera—may actually have been a super-normal adaptation or immune-system reaction to the disease. If we use the viral model in our examination of the disease—and it may not be just a model; there may indeed have been a virus localized to this geographical area, a left-over from the biological weapons labs associated with the preceding war—then it may make sense as well to project a certain population section not only resistant to the disease's negative effects but also deriving a situational benefit from the infectious agent."

The audience frantically scribbles all this down in their notebooks. My head is singing.

The lecturer presses on. "Viewed coldly, dispassionately, the d-rangers' ability was a functional evolutionary adaptation to the circumstances of the landscape in which they operated. They survived, in their own peculiar way, not because they had a right to, or any particular claim to moral superiority, but simply because they could. Yet at the same time, it cannot be denied that a certain revulsion is triggered in the human observer by the contemplation of the d-rangers' actions."

Right, you bastard—my hatred for him burned up from my breastbone. They always go on that way, in my dreams and reality the same. First they absolve you with the right hand, then they damn you with the left.

"Much as from a purely biological viewpoint, a vampire—if one had ever existed—could be said to have been merely following the same dictates of hunger and survival that we all do, so also with the d-rangers. Their nature determined the way in which they made their living. And yet,

91

and yet . . . that very nature disgusts us, arouses a seemingly righteous ire in our hearts."

I could have wept, in the depths of my maudlin daydreaming. Perhaps my imaginary lecturer wasn't such a bad guy, after all. Perhaps he understood.

"The moral dimension enters into the geometry of diseases when an infected organism—consciously or unconsciously—*becomes* the disease itself, and in so doing, becomes different from his or her fellows. The organism—the man, the woman—becomes no longer human, but another thing, a thing that looks upon his former species as prey, as food."

That seemed to be putting it pretty harshly. I still loved all you people, as much as you could be loved. You were the brake on that process, not me. I assumed Eastern felt the same way.

"Food, even if we're still talking in terms of models and metaphors, and not actual digestive mechanisms. Something more metaphysical than that, though no less real." The lecturer nodded, appreciating his own good point. "In discussions of the *d*-rangers, assuming their existence, this human substance was usually referred to as *o*-positive. Let us define this substance as that which enables an individual to organize reality—and his or her existence in that reality—and to maintain the commonly shared perception of reality. This *o*-positive substance is thus exactly that which enables a human being to *stay* human, in the field of humanness. The lack of this substance is what causes the *n*-formation disease, and the resulting genetic dissolution and death from multi-cancer, just as the lack of vitamin C causes scurvy and all the physiological effects pertaining thereto. Though, of course, our topic of concern today is slightly more serious than that; bleeding gums don't quite compare to hemorrhaging one's existence away."

The lecturer put on an academic, wryly amused look at

92

this last bit from his own mouth, and the audience smiled collectively in return. What a cold, heartless bunch they were. This was a bad daydream, and I really only had myself to blame for it. I could have ended it at any time, but I didn't. I let it roll on.

"Very well—we have established the nature of this substance, the human vitamin, the *o*-positive. What, then, was the relationship of our supposed *d*-rangers to this substance? The engines of rumor and folklore in the Madlands had it that the *d*-rangers lived on *o*-positive, draining it from their victims' bodies and souls—the comparisons to vampires and bloodsucking are inevitable and obvious. Though nothing so crude as sharp teeth plunged into sleepers' necks, and tongues lapping up pulsing flow, was thought to have been involved; the feeding process was believed to take place invisibly, outside the shade of human perception. This, of course, made identifying the feared *d*-rangers much more difficult, if not impossible. Your best friend could have been one, and sat next to you on the couch watching television, and all the while your human essence was being siphoned off. The best parasites—best in terms of their own sleek survival—are the subtle ones. Who operate undetected, until it's too late and the damage to the host organism is done."

Well, yes—I nodded, both lying on my bed and sitting in my daydream's imagined audience. That was another good point. Nobody knew the advantages of essentially invisible operation better than I did.

The lecturer lifted his pointer from the stand, and swung it toward the figures drawn on the chalkboard. "How much *more* repellent people would have regarded the *d*-rangers, if they'd known the *truth* about this appetite-sustenance equation!" The lecturer bit the words off, the working of his jaw indicating a genuine fury on his part. "As long as it could be said that the *d*-rangers *ate,* that the ineffable *o*-

93

positive substance was their food, then the possibility existed that they could be forgiven, even in the hearts of the victims, as long as those victims had hearts and not just some squamous amoeboid cell material where the human bits used to be. But there would have been *no* chance of forgiveness, of absolution—if the *d*-rangers had wanted it!—if it had been known that the *d*-rangers' so-called appetite for the *o*-positive substance had been entirely a function of economics. Of commerce! The *d*-rangers were small-scale entrepreneurs, merchants in the airy glue and brick of the human soul!"

The bastard was ranting now, but effectively so. I touched my face—in the dream I did, or lying on my half-awake bed, I couldn't tell which—and found my cheeks wet with the tears of shame. I was glad that the others in the audience were hypnotized by the lecturer's oratory, and didn't notice me burning.

This daydream was completely out of hand now; it rolled over me like a train. At the same time, I was pinned to the tracks by its onrushing light, the light of unpleasant revelations. I had been here before, and knew what was coming.

The lecturer's face had darkened, his anger bottled and sealed behind his stormy brow. "In fact, or as much as facts pertain to the mythic natural history of our hypothetical *d*-rangers, the *o*-positive substance, the soul blood of their neighbors, that which enabled the Madlands' habitués to organize both their external and internal realities, that invisible substance was soaked up by the *d*-rangers and *sold*, ladies and gentlemen, *sold* to the one party who had particular need and use for the commodity. That party? The king, the ruling presence of the Madlands—Identrope. The *o*-positive substance, gathered and sold by the *d*-rangers to Identrope, is the source of his growing control over the Madlands zone. Identrope's ability to control the reality within the zone increases as the ability of others, the habi-

94

tués, the victims who come into the zone and the unseen mercantile system of the *d*-rangers, their ability to keep reality organized decreases as their reserves of *o*-positive are drained away, to the point of contracting the *n*-formation disease. In a very real sense, the mysterious and omnipresent Identrope derived a double benefit from this commerce. Not only did he, from the accumulation of excess reality-organizing ability, become empowered to turn the zone's innate chaos into a reality of his own choosing, the shabby *noir* landscape of a pseudo-L.A. dredged up from the archives, an urban landscape where he himself operated most efficiently as an archetype wired into people's thoughts and memories; but he also, from the depletion of others' reality-organizing ability, was ensured of a constant supply of recruits into his church, converts desperate to avoid the terminal multi-cancer stages of the *n*-formation disease. These converts, Identrope's flock, achieved their salvation by being incorporated into the expanded neural web of the very architect of their damnation. Identrope got it both ways, coming and going, as above so below. It was a good deal for him.

"What about the *d*-rangers themselves, the source of supply for Identrope? What did they get out of the arrangement? Undoubtedly, there was some financial compensation—money can also be thought of as a reality-organizing substance, that works both inside and outside the human soul. Identrope and the *d*-rangers could be thought of as simply exchanging one form of reality for another, whichever the other party found more convenient for his or her purposes. Thus it was for the first group of *d*-rangers, the *d*-ranger *alpha*. Unfortunately for them, the *alpha* *d*-rangers had short careers; deriving no direct benefit from the *o*-positive in which they dealt, they all eventually came down with the dreaded *n*-formation disease themselves. The obvious analogy is to ancient drug dealers of one stripe or another, who, through their constant exposure to their stock of illicit substances, wound up addicted themselves, and finally dead, the victims of their own commerce. *Sic semper d-*rangers *alpha;* they didn't have the smarts for the long haul.

"A simple matter of evolution brings us to *d-*ranger *beta.*" The pointer's tip rapped on the chalk sketches of Eastern and myself, up on the board. "Nature may or may not abhor a vacuum, but the realm of predatory merchanthood certainly does. Every appetite-related niche will eventually be filled by a creature tooled either by circumstance and Darwinian selection or by the cleaner scalpel of self-will. These two"—*tap-tap* on Eastern's sketched clavicle, then mine—"having brains and keen desire, fit into the latter category. They—and there might have been others as well—*became* the entities necessary to supply Identrope with the *o-*positive substance gleaned from the hapless Madlands habitués. Just as with the *alpha d-*rangers; but with this difference: these two gained a measure of control over the process sufficient to protect themselves from the *alpha* consequences. *Beta* gained conscious control over the mercantile relationship, *which exceeded that of Identrope.* To some degree, the poor bastard did not know what was going on in a sphere of activity of which he had previously been the master."

This struck me as being an unusually sympathetic note for the lecturer to hit. There weren't a lot of people who had ever felt sorry for Identrope. And since this person was imagined inside my own head, that presented me with an interesting readout of my own feelings for my employer. I'd have to think about that sometime.

The dream lecture was already rolling on, and I'd missed a few words. ". . . essentially, what these two—the *d-*rangers *beta*—accomplished was to inject a new element of subterfuge into the proceedings. Deception now prevailed on both ends of the transfer of the *o*-positive substance from the victimized source to the ultimate consumer, with only the middlemen truly knowing what was going on. If even they did. What enabled the *d*-rangers *beta* to pull this off was their newly acquired ability to shuffle bodies, to put their own consciousness in the driver's seat of another human form. In this, the *d*-rangers *beta* gained a measure of control over the *n*-formation disease itself; they had learned to use the disease for their own purposes. The ongoing presence of the disease in the Madlands created a *situation of slipperiness*. The zone's habitués were infected with the disease; so were these new *d*-rangers. But with this difference: the mutual state of infection enabled the *d*-rangers to slide in and out of other people's bodies, like putting on a mask; they could do this before the undesired *n*-formation symptoms, the lethal progress into multi-cancer, appeared. In fact, these two *d*-rangers put their own original bodies effectively on ice, operating exclusively thenceforth out of borrowed bodies, and thus reducing exposure and risk to themselves to a minimum. They could crash as many 'cars' as they liked; there was always an inexhaustible supply of new ones to shuffle themselves into. This also enabled them to operate in secret, concealing both their true natures and identities from their *o*-positive customer Identrope. Indeed, in the case of the *d*-ranger *beta* known to us as Trayne, the individual in question not only supplied Identrope with the *o*-positive substance drained off from various Madlands habitués/victims and sold to Identrope through a rotating bank of body guises, but also worked for Identrope in an entirely separate capacity, that of choreographer for Identrope's regular series of religious broadcasts. A perfect deception; Identrope apparently never realized—or if he did know, he never let on—that his trusted employee Trayne was working both sides of the street, operating both inside and outside of that extensive organization."

The dream lecture came over me in waves, hammering me into an enveloping, suffocating darkness. The cigar had gone out, and its ashy taste lay foul on my tongue.

I gripped the edge of my seat, and felt the bed's mattress yield under my fingers. My stifled cry, the rush of my dizzying breath, had attracted attention; all around me in the dream's auditorium, faces turned toward me.

The lecturer went on, shouting now.

"A perfect deception! A nice deal, a sweet setup! How wonderful for this Trayne, to have fooled everyone this way . . ."

I knew what was coming, I'd heard it before.

"But what of his soul? He was able to put his body in the fridge, but what became of that other part of him, separate from his slippery mind? Did that get lost along the way? Did he leave it somewhere, like a matchbook in the pocket of a coat given to the Salvation Army? Did he step on it and crack it open while he was looking for his keys? Did he, did he did he—"

The shout a roar now. But no one was listening to him. All the faces in the auditorium turned toward me. And the faces were all different, and they were all mine.

And none of them were.

Something new happened that had never happened before in all the repeats of the dream that I'd put myself through. The auditorium shook from a giant's blows, over and over, the walls and ceiling trembling.

I opened my eyes. The front of my shirt was covered with grey ash from the dead cigar.

The blows came again, not as loud as in the dream's magnification. There was somebody at the door, beating on it with a fist. Outside, in the dark streets, machinery snarled and rasped, circling the building like a wolf pack.

16

I went into the bathroom to splash cold water in my face. I felt stiff and weird, still entombed in sleep—at some point, my daydreaming had slipped into the soft iron of real dreaming, the straight uncontrolled stuff. Dreaming's a hard row when you know you're dreaming and can't do anything about it.

How much of my senses were still logging that bad nocturnal/neurological input, I didn't know. Somebody was still pounding on the apartment's front door, and there was all that snarling machine noise outside the building—maybe that was just dream hangover, taking a long time to ebb away. After all, I could still hear the voice of that lecturer with my face crying inside my ear. Echoes and ghosts; the world was full of them.

I decided to ignore the door-pounding for a little while longer. If it was happening in the real world, or what passes for it around here, whoever it was could goddamn well wait until I'd pulled my act together. It sounded as if the person really wanted to see me; let him earn the privilege. I turned on the cold tap full blast and bent over the gurgling sink.

Raising my dripping face, I leaned on the sides of the porcelain and gazed into the mirror. Past the layered clouds of soap film on glass; I didn't recognize the face I was wearing. I didn't even know where it had come from, unless the dream residue had totally polluted my optic processes, and the face was one from the lecture audience that had goggled at my transfigured weeping.

The pounding on the door was still going on, loud enough to make my toothbrush shiver in its holder. I was fully awake, unfortunately. The machines outside hadn't gone away, either. The combined noise was enough to jog my memory into gear.

I'd shuffled into this body last night—picked it up as it'd been strolling away from a liquor store on Pico, the kind of place that never rolled back the steel grilles over the windows. Luckily, the previous occupant had only started to get a buzz on—the paper-bagged bottle of Wild Irish Rose in his mitt had only had a few nips taken off the top. Most people walk around with their minds so blank, anyway, that walking in and taking over is like strolling through the unlocked door of an empty house. I rubbed a hand over my new face. I'd have to give it a shave pretty soon, but that could wait. Not too unhandsome, a little more Mediterranean than I generally cared for. I could feel a little jangle along the spine, probably the first stages of the n-formation disease that had given me access across the corporeal barrier. I'd have to rotate out of this sucker in a couple of months, but that gave me plenty of time to do what I'd planned.

It was all coming back to me. The dreaming had sat on me so hard that it'd temporarily blanked a whole section of short-term memory. Now I remembered why there was

100

somebody knocking at my door. And the machines outside. This was all stuff that I'd arranged. I toweled off the new face and headed for the front door.

Rasty Mike stood there in all his sweaty glory. I'd caught him in mid-stroke, pulling the door open just as his ham-like fist descended. The big-knuckled appendage, its ridges permanently stained black with thirty-weight and road-dirt, stopped in midair a couple of inches from my left ear. The bananoid fingers unfolded into what a grizzly bear's paw would look like if it could touch-type and dial a telephone. The wrist fur sprouting from the cuff of the ratty stained sweatshirt was thick enough to knit. You wonder why an ape like that wears clothes at all.

The machine noise came in louder with the apartment door open. The lugging cough of big-bore Harleys, mixed with the higher whine and rasp of a few vintage Triumphs and BSAs, flowed over me like the high tide of an ocean under offshore-drilling platforms, the air sweet with the aroma of gasoline and other petroleum by-products. The wind of the mechanical world that the rats out in the junk-yard would have extracted their human spines to live in.

"You the guy who called me?" Rasty Mike jabbed a tele-phone pole with a broken fingernail at the end of it toward my gut. "Said we had *business* to talk about?"

"That's me." Right off the bat, I couldn't remember what kind of pseudonym, if any, I'd arranged this rendez-vous under. That had been the whole point of my picking up a new body—and face—so Rasty Mike wouldn't know exactly who he was dealing with, and latch onto my game.

"This better be good." Rasty Mike, the L.A. biker king, lumbered past me into the apartment. He filled the front room as though I'd fired up a hot-air balloon in there, but some of the presence was mere body odor.

As the train passed before me, I saw the words and em-blem stitched onto the back of his sleeveless denim jacket.

101

"Stone Units" across his shoulder blades in big letters, in that corny Barnum & Bailey typeface with the little spiky bits that bikers all think is so classy-looking; matches the retro circus lettering on the gas tanks, I suppose. In the center a big piston, computer-diddled to give the image a granite texture. The rocker patch on the bottom read "Madlands L.A." They dug on this weirdness being their home turf.

Rasty Mike pulled up one of the windows, leaned out, and shouted at his entourage out in the street. "Hold it down, you fuckin' assholes! We're trying to talk in here!" The revving of engines ebbed for a moment, then climbed back up, punctuated with a few empty bottles smashing against the stucco. Rasty Mike didn't care about the noise, anyway; it had been a show for my benefit, to demonstrate that he could say rude things to a bunch of one-eyed murderers and other perpetual hard-ons.

He deposited himself in an armchair. His scraggly beard, marked with a few strands of statesman-like grey, folded over the mound of his gut. The section of sweatshirt riding over his stomach looked as if he'd had his breakfast bacon and eggs served on it. The guy exuded ugly street radiation, asphalt smegma. Like the machines outside, the Stone Units' rolling fleet: not pretty polished show Harleys, such as the ones that had already started cropping up underneath entertainment biz butts around Sunset and La Brea. But bad-ass grunge buckets, with frayed duct tape peeling from cracked battery cases and exhaust pipes rattling with an out-of-tune tuberculosis.

"How'd you get our clubhouse number?" Rasty Mike folded his hands over his gut.

I leaned against the wall. "I've got my contacts." Dialing straight in like that was what had gotten Rasty Mike to turn out for business talk; anybody who had their headquarters' direct number must be an important person. What he didn't know was that he'd given me the phone number himself, some time back, when I'd been wearing a different face. I'd done him and his jolly crew a favor.

Lucky for me, I hadn't let on back then where I lived. I hadn't told them my real name then, either. So I could invite the cheerful gang over, and they wouldn't make any connection. I had become my own third party, and not for the first time.

"So what's all this about?" Rasty Mike had what looked like little black holes for eyes, not the cosmic kind, but the kind like in the ocean where little tiny moray eels would come zooming out and rip off your face. There wasn't much about him that didn't look like bad news. "We were having a party—" Christ only knew what kind of bloodletting a Stone Units social event involved. "—you interrupted our fun." If you could gravel-line a three-year-old's pouting voice. "So what's the big deal?"

I gave a shrug, trying to counteract Rasty Mike's evil radiation with my own relaxed cool. "Nothing much. A little information I thought maybe you guys could use. Something maybe you could make a little profit on."

The moray eels spun around—I couldn't see them in there, but I knew that's what they were doing. Mention money, and it gets people's attention, always. And Rasty Mike wasn't so far gone into party mode that the magic word hadn't registered.

"Yeah? Lay it on me."

I smiled like a humorous sphinx. "Ever hear of a bunch called the New Moon Corporation?"

Rasty Mike's face clouded. "Do they ride out of San Berdoo?"

"No." I shook my head. "You're thinking of something else. No, this is like a company, you know, a business."

"Never heard of 'em."

The only businesses Rasty Mike and his friends dealt

103

with were tattoo parlors and a couple of chroming shops on the low end of Alvarado. I tried to enlighten him. "They're into like TV and broadcasting and stuff. Show business. That kind of thing."

"So what about them?" He wasn't impressed.

"Well, they've been doing some rooting around. Out in the junkyard. You know, all that old military stuff." I figured the Stone Units wouldn't have much interest in that antique machinery, either. Harley-Davidson had never done much Pentagon contracting. They might have some academic interest in weapons bigger than handguns, but not enough to motivate them to go looking around themselves, simple souls that they were. "Anyway, these New Moon people found something really, uh, interesting. They found an old satellite that they've been able to restore to full operation, and they've smuggled in a European-made rocket that they'll be able to put it up into orbit with. And it's a pisser. This pup's a flat-out rock-and-roll item."

"Yeah?" A flicker of interest.

Now that I had him hooked with a fragment of the truth, I could start feeding him the lie. "Yeah. What it is, this satellite's a major weapons system. It's got lasers, heat rays, particle beams, all kinds of shit—it's the Swiss Army knife of kick-ass technology. The war they were fighting back then must have fizzled out before this thing could be launched, otherwise it damn well would have been over pretty quick. This thing's that powerful."

Rasty Mike's thick fingers drummed on his gut. "Sounds wild."

"It is. You can believe me on this one. Now, here's the deal. The satellite's already been launched; it should be stabilizing and getting set up in its orbit sometime in the next twenty-four hours. But it's just dead metal sitting up there until it's activated. And there's just one guy that can do that. Some guy named Trayne."

104

"Trayne, huh?" Rasty Mike's functioning brain cells rubbed against each other, trying to make a spark. "Where've I heard that name before?"

I knew that none of the Stone Units watched the tube, so it was unlikely they'd be able to hook my name up with Identrope's broadcasts. "Beats me, jack. Anyway, this Trayne guy is the only one in the whole New Moon outfit that can turn this war satellite on and make it do its stuff. He had to have his skull opened up like a can of tuna, and special neural rewiring done, just so he could get in synch with this satellite's operating code. They slammed into his head a whole bunch of stuff that came in a little box with the satellite. So he's like the walking remote control for the thing."

"Good for him. What's that got to do with the Stone Units?"

I'd have to connect all the dots for this clown. "Don't you see? What if, instead of these New Moon guys running that satellite, it was you? Man, there wouldn't be *any*body who'd hand you any shit if you had something like that floating over their heads. You could kick ass all around town. Better: all over everywhere. You and your bunch would finally have some real clout, the kind of clout you *deserve*. The Stone Units would be able to roll right on out of the Madlands, and shake down the whole fuckin' world. Money and respect, man—you'd have it *all*."

The moray eels were hypnotized, and in the eels' eyes were even tinier eels, equally agog over these lovely prospects.

I rolled on. "All you'd need is to get your hands on this Trayne guy, and you'd be all set. Grab him, and you'd have control of the war satellite, and then everything's cake on a stick after that."

Rasty Mike grunted. "Yeah, right. They probably got this Brain guy—"

105

"Trayne. His name's Trayne."

"—they probably got him locked up tight. Like behind walls and guns and guard dogs and shit. They're not gonna let something that valuable out on the sidewalk where we could jump him."

My knowing smile floated up again. "Yeah, well, that's what you'd expect, isn't it? That they'd have this Trayne squirreled away in a steel bank vault. Unless something went wrong. Unless something happened to him. And he—*got out.*"

Another two dots hooked up behind Rasty Mike's forehead. He was starting to get the picture. "How could that happen?"

I shrugged. "All sorts of ways. Suppose—just suppose now—that some person who was in charge of looking after this Trayne got a notion to do something different. Suppose this person had a different agenda in mind. That the New Moon Corporation wouldn't exactly approve of. Suppose this person made the valuable Mr. Trayne disappear from where he was supposed to be, and reappear somewhere else. Somewhere real close by."

It was Rasty Mike's turn to smile, a big loopy leer in the forest of his beard. "Yeah . . . That'd be cool."

"All right." There weren't any dots left. "Let's quit screwing around. I got this Trayne sitting right here. You want to see him?"

I led Rasty Mike down the hallway to the back bedroom. Throwing open the door, I pointed to the trussed-up Geldt lying on the floor. "There's your man."

Geldt still had the gag stuffed in his mouth; he made noises around it, his eyes bugging out at the sight of me and Rasty Mike in the doorway.

Rasty Mike looked like an old lady at the bargain counter of the local butcher shop, sniffing at the suspicious merchandise on display. "This is the Trayne guy you were talking about?"

"Sure is." I prodded Geldt with my shoe. "I'd let him tell you for himself, but he's kind of a noisy bastard when you unplug him. I got neighbors to think about."

"What d'ya want for him?"

I had thought about hitting the Stone Units treasury up for a little cash in exchange for Geldt aka Trayne—you can never have too much. But had decided against it; the Units weren't inclined to pay for anything that they could just break your spine and take from you instead. And cash, at least at this stage, wasn't the point of this whole exercise.

"*Nada.*" I spread my hands, palms up. "Free, gratis. Take him, he's yours. Enjoy him in good health."

Rasty Mike's eyes narrowed into little slits. Definitely suspicious. "What's the deal, man? What do you get out of this?"

I gave Geldt a sharper kick in the ribs, enough to make him squeak. "Me and this guy go a long ways back. I got what you might call some long-standing grudges against him. He was getting entirely too cushy a deal from the rest of those New Moon guys, for my taste." Another kick. "It'd please me no end if Trayne here had to sweat and suffer a little, instead of having his butt kissed the way he thought it was going to be."

Rasty Mike bought it. He had two of his minions, trolls in greasy denim, come in and haul Geldt out. They tied him onto one of their bikes like a deer carcass from the woods.

Standing on the sidewalk outside the apartment building, while the Stone Units coughed and roared their way down the hill, I gave Rasty Mike some more advice. "Listen—that Trayne guy is a sneaky sonuvabitch. Believe me, I know him. The bastard's likely to say anything to get himself out of a jam. Don't let him feed you some line that

107

he's *not* Trayne. You got the right guy, so just lean on him until he does what you want."

Rasty Mike even shook my hand. "Thanks, man." He climbed on his bike and started it up. "Anything we can ever do for you, just let us know."

"Don't sweat it," I told him. "You're already doing me a big enough favor."

I listened for a while to the bikes' engines fading away, then went back in. All in all, it had been a good night's work.

17

NEW body, new face, new voice—or at least new to me. The last came in handy when I called up Harrison the next morning.

I worked my way through the New Moon switchboard and got the man himself on the line.

"Yes? Who is this?" Busy executive radiation coming over the wire.

"You don't need to know the name, Mr. Harrison." He hadn't recognized the voice—why should he? He'd never heard it before—and that was just the way I wanted to keep it. "Let's just say . . . a friend. All right?"

"What do you want?" Spooky radiation coming back at him had hooked his interest.

"Well, Harrison, it's more like what you want. I think you want to know what's happened to our mutual friend Trayne. Your new employee."

I could hear his spine stiffen way off in the distance. "I'm not sure I know what you mean." A pause, while the gears and wheels spun around. "There's nobody by that name working for us . . ."

"The fuck there isn't. He may not be on the official payroll, but he's doing a little job for you, isn't he? That's what the two of you were talking about just yesterday, wasn't it?"

"What do you know about that?"

I looked out my apartment window at the murky L.A. sky. "Let's just say I know enough. Enough to know that you'd be interested in hearing what's happened to Trayne."

"All right." Harrison sounded disgusted at the greed of the world. "What's this going to cost me?"

"Nothing at all. This is a freebie. Like I said, we're all friends, aren't we?"

"Maybe. So what is it you've got to tell me?"

"Your Mr. Trayne's gone bye-bye."

"What?"

I spelled it out for him. "Off the scene. Splitsville. And check this—it wasn't voluntary. He was carried out."

Harrison's voice jumped down the wire at me. "What the hell are you talking about?"

"Grabbed. Kidnapped. Bag over the head and hands tied behind his back. The Stone Units—they're like this local motorcycle gang—they busted into Trayne's place last night, wrapped him up, took him away. Into the night. I guess somehow they'd heard he was a valuable piece of merchandise."

"Is this some kind of a joke?" Harrison was full of questions today. "Listen—whoever you are—why should I believe you about this?"

I shrugged; he couldn't hear that, but it helped my voice go cold. "Check it out yourself. You've got the ways and means to do that. Hey—and don't forget where you heard it first."

110

I hung up on him and rubbed my ear—the bastard had been shouting toward the end. Which was a good sign, actually, as far as my plans were concerned. I wanted Harrison up and hyperventilating, scrambling around and quacking like a duck because of *his* plans unraveling. In any corporation there are always plenty of snoops and snitches, and I didn't figure New Moon would be the exception. I wanted word of the disappearance of "Trayne" getting out as quickly as possible—whether he realized it or not, Harrison was going to help me out in this endeavor. Eventually I'd let him off the hook—that was another part of my plans—but in the meantime he could sweat and scurry on my behalf.

I went out for coffee, hitting three Formica-and-vinyl dives along Sunset. Helping to spread the necessary word. The Madlands are so tight—it's that frontier mentality of clustering together—that it wasn't hard finding well-connected habitués who would pass the disinformation along. *Hey, did you hear what happened to Trayne last night? He got nabbed . . .* It wouldn't take long for it to reach all the way up to Identrope himself.

As for myself, once I'd gotten this body's caffeine levels adjusted, I went back to the apartment, packed up a few essentials into Geldt's Hudson, and shifted my base of operations to another part of town. Part of my monthly nut was paying the rent on three or four other shoe boxes I kept going under other names. It's a dumb fox that doesn't have two exits to his burrow; it's a smarter fox that keeps a string of burrows to move in and out of. I wanted Harrison's snoops, and any other interested parties, to swing by my previous address and find me utterly gone. Before I left, I messed the place up a bit, to make it look as if a pretty good fight had gone down before they'd been able to drag me away. I've got a reputation to maintain.

The new place was also where I'd stashed the body I'd

previously been walking around in—my real former residence. I stood by the bed, looking down at the sleeping, or just vacated, face I'd grown used to wearing for a while. Not seeing it in a mirror this time, but the right way around, the part in the hair over on the left side where everybody else had seen it. I wished the face would open its mouth and say hello to me. I get so lonely sometimes, when that high anonymous wind rolls off the desert.

I had time to kill, before I could segue into the next stage of my plans, so I fixed myself some lunch—I'd left a stash of saltines and canned chili in this apartment—then settled back to knock through the books I'd thrown into my traveling bag. Nice mint copies, the page edges not yet gone brown, of a couple Gold Medal Originals, Gil Brewer's *The Brat* and *Hell-bent for Danger,* by Walt Grove. That was one of the more pleasing parts of so much old stuff called back into existence from the archives—good stuff like these weren't fucking "collectables" you had to buy in those anal-retentive little plastic bags and fork out an extortionist's paycheck for.

By midafternoon I had nailed the Brewer and was halfway through the other one. Great stuff. The clock on the wall, if there had been one, would have told me that it was time to nudge my plans a little farther along. I shuffled back into the other body, so I could have my previous voice back, and made some phone calls.

First I dialed the rehearsal studio up at the top of Identrope's web. With my elbow on the windowsill, I could look up and see the dirigible burning against the sun. A phone was ringing up there.

Nora answered; I knew she did her own daily solo barre about this time every day. She had that authentic dancer's dedication.

"Hello?" She didn't even sound out of breath, though I

knew from past observation that the armholes of her leotard would be darkened with sweat.

"Hey, Nora—it's me."

She almost dropped the phone; I could hear her grab it
with both hands. "Trayne—oh my God. I thought . . . I
thought something terrible had happened to you. What I
heard, and everything. I thought you were *dead.*"

Typical dancer mentality: riven with grief, and still going
through her workout. Tears in her eyes, to go with the
sweat.

"Naw, I'm fine. Disaster reports are premature."

"But I heard—everybody did—that you'd been kidnapped, or something. Some band of maniacs came and
took you away, and there was all this gunfire and blood
and stuff. It sounded horrible."

Band of maniacs pretty accurately described the Stone
Units, though they had been on their best party manners
when they'd been by my place. *Gunfire and blood and stuff*
was the usual accretions that rumors pick up as people
hand them around. I'd expected as much, which was why
I hadn't done that embroidering myself.

"Yeah, well, all that's not exactly true." I played rubber
band with the curly phone cord. "As a matter of fact, none
of it is."

"That's great. There are a lot of people who are going
to be glad to hear that."

"No, there aren't." My main reason for calling
Nora—other than it always being pleasant to hear her
voice, even for a presumably dead man—had been to as-
certain that word of my "kidnapping" had reached Identrope. If Nora knew about it, then the buzz was
undoubtedly throughout Identrope's headquarters, up to
and including the big guy himself; the dancers were always
near the caboose on the rumor train. "Listen, I want you
to do me a big favor. I want you to not tell anyone that

113

you got this call. You haven't heard from me."

"I don't get it."

"You don't have to. At least not right now." I tried to make it sound less harsh. "I'm working on a little surprise for everyone. A joke. And they all have to think I've been taken away. By that band of maniacs. Believe me, it'll be really funny when it all goes down."

"You sure?"

"Positive. But you gotta promise me, okay? You haven't heard from me."

She promised. I knew I could trust her. She hadn't become so human yet that she had acquired guile.

"And so if anybody asks, you're just all grief-stricken with what you hear has happened to me." Something like that would be within her acting abilities.

"I guess." Her voice sounded small and even more distant, as though the perpetually burning dirigible had broken its mooring with the web and had started drifting out to L.A.'s sea of thin, deracinated clouds. "Trayne—are you sure you know what you're doing?"

I laughed, and in my own ears sounded like someone strapped to a roller coaster whose final dip ran through a deeply longed-for hell. "Don't worry about me, sweetheart. I'll be seeing you in a couple of days." I hung up.

There was more business to take care of, but it would have to wait until morning. The other body was on the only bed in the apartment, and it struck me that it deserved a peaceful rest more than some sharp schmuck like me. I compromised by pulling the pillow out from underneath the other body's head, and lay down on the floor.

If I dreamed, I didn't remember what it was.

18

I dropped in on Harrison, still in the body he'd seen me in before. I could have done this bit over the phone, too, but I wanted the pleasure of seeing him plotz at the sight of me.

The New Moon receptionist must have been in on the word about Trayne being kidnapped—maybe she and Harrison had a thing going, a little corporate pillow talk—because her mouth dropped open a foot or so when I walked in. She buzzed me right on in to Harrison's office.

"Jesus Christ!" Harrison jumped up from behind his desk, nearly toppling over his big leather chair. "Trayne—we thought you were . . . we heard that . . ." He came around and grabbed my arm, shoving his wide-eyed face right into mine, as if to verify I wasn't some kind of hallucination.

"Yeah, right; I know." I disengaged myself from his clutch. "I know just what you heard. You got a phone call

115

that said I'd been kidnapped by a bunch of bikers." I sat down in one of the smaller chairs and sprawled my legs out.

Harrison looked puzzled. "How do you know about the call?"

I started to say *I made it,* then changed at the last second. "I . . . was responsible for it. I had a friend of mine ring you up with that message." There was no point in complicating Harrison's head with the truth. A civilian like him wouldn't have understood, anyway.

"What the hell for?"

To dink with your sorry mind. I didn't say that at all, but just kept silent.

Harrison was back behind his desk, still shouting away. "Do you have any idea what's been going on around here? Because of that stupid phone call? The scrambling around we've been doing? We sent a team out to your place, and when they reported back that everything checked out, that you were gone and your apartment was all busted up . . . we've been trying to throw together a contingency plan, all because we assumed it was true—"

"You were *supposed* to assume that. That was the whole reason I had the call made."

"For Christ's sake, why? Trayne—I thought we had a working relationship here."

I let out a sigh. "Don't break your heart over this, Harrison. Everybody loves you as much as they ever did. It's just that I've got my little plans and schemes, and I'm moving them along. You want to have Identrope plugged? Fine—that's what I'm working on. The phone call to you was all part of that. I wanted the word to get out that I'd been kidnapped. That I was off the scene entirely. And it's worked. So far the word is pretty solid out on the streets that I'm out of the action for a while. And I've checked out what's been heard up in Identrope's headquarters. It's the same thing. As far as Identrope is concerned, his be-loved choreographer is gone."

Harrison spread his hands out on his desk. "I don't un-derstand. Why do you want people to think you've been kidnapped?"

A shrug. "I'm not going to be operating as myself. My plans for nailing Identrope call for me to be going around incognito. In disguise. So it helps if people are thinking that the real Trayne is nowhere around."

Harrison didn't look puzzled now; he looked as if he were starting to get pissed. "Would you care to explain a little bit about these plans of yours? A few details about how you're expecting to pull all this off?"

I shook my head. "No. You don't need to know."

"Then I'll tell *you* something, Trayne." A big dark storm had settled over his face. "Quite frankly, I think you've lost it. Maybe this wasn't such a good idea hiring you. The general perception is that everybody out there in the Mad-lands is a flake, but—we thought maybe you were the ex-ception. But now I'm beginning to think you're as screwed up as the rest of them. Trayne—why the hell do you think we wanted to hire you for this little job? Think about it. It's because you *are* Trayne. You've got *privileged access* to Identrope. You can waltz in up there anytime you please, in the middle of the night when there's nobody else around, if you want, and just see him. That was the whole point of your being added to this project. Now what use are you to us? You don't have any more access to Identrope than the average guy off the street. There's no way you can get to him now."

I tilted my head back and spoke to the blank ceiling. "Well, I think differently. I've got my own plans on how to do the job."

"Oh? Thinking differently, are we?" Harrison noisily rustled papers on his desk. "I'll give you some different

117

thinking. Consider yourself unemployed, at least as far as the New Moon Corporation is concerned. You're not on this job any longer. We'll find some other way to get done what we need. Using somebody whose brain is bolted down tight."

"You can't do that."

"What?" Harrison gave me one of those looks. "Trayne—we can do whatever the hell we want. It's our project. And if we want all flakes overboard, that's just what we're going to do. You got me?"

I shook my head. "You can't do it. I'll tell you why. First of all, your legal department is a lot faster and more efficient than is good for you. I checked this morning on our contracts. They've already been faxed and registered. That piece of New Moon's future revenues is in my name already, contingent upon my performing satisfactorily. And it's a strictly pay-or-play proposition. You try to yank me, it's all mine and I don't even have to do shit for it."

Harrison went white around the lips. "Contracts are made to be broken."

"Yeah, well, that brings us to my second point. Contracts are like eggs, Harrison; if you need a sledgehammer to break one—and you will, I can promise you that—then there's going to be quite a mess flying around. I got paperwork on you now. On all of New Moon. You try to *un*hire me, it's easy enough for me to go public with what you were originally hiring me to do. That's major bad publicity. Plus whatever legal ramifications; probably have the Feds sniffing around here. Maybe the FCC—killing off your competitors, or your competitors' programming sources, to be precise, might fall under unfair broadcasting practices. And you could kiss off any notion of actually being able to get Identrope anytime soon. He'd be warned; he'd button up the web and his headquarters so tight you wouldn't be able to slide a nail file in there."

118

Pieces of Harrison's face were twitching, as though they were about to fly off like Mr. Potato Head put together on a jelly grenade. "Are you threatening us, Trayne? Because if you are, I can assure you—"

"Simmer down. Don't think of it as a threat. Think of it as a prediction. Of all the shit that's going to come down if you get antsy and start doing stuff you don't have to bother with. Why get your ass in an uproar, Harrison? When it's so much easier to just sit back and do nothing. Just let it ride for a little while. The plans I'm pushing along aren't going to take that much time, for Christ's sake. A couple days, maybe a week at the most. You're in such a hurry, you can't wait that long? Practice a little patience. It's a virtue, plus you won't eat out your stomach lining. You might as well give me the play, and see if I pull it off. If I screw it up, then you can go to your Plan B."

Harrison's fury-laden eyes followed me as I stood up. "So help me, Trayne, if you're screwing around with us . . ."

"Don't sweat it. What I need right now is for Identrope not to know where I am. So if you'll keep a lid on it, about my coming by here, everything will be fine. You'll see." I turned and headed for the door.

I hadn't told Harrison all my reasons for wanting to disappear. He didn't need to know that part of my reason for operating on the sly was so I could have a free hand in going about another little investigation of my own.

I wanted to take a closer look at this whole New Moon setup. The more I'd thought about them, lying on my back and looking up at one bedroom ceiling or another, the more I'd become convinced there was something hinky about them. I didn't like the way they seemed to have popped up out of nowhere. They seemed to have some unusually complete sources of information, more than I cared to see anybody working with. With Trayne officially off the

119

scene, I might be able to get a clearer fix on Harrison and his friends.

On my way out, I winked at the receptionist. Her boss would put a clamp on her revving up the corporate gossip line; she didn't know that yet. So I still got a smile back from her.

19

I didn't know where to start—I have the attitude for this sort of thing, but not necessarily the experience—so I drove Geldt's Hudson back out to the junkyard. That seemed as good a place as any to do a little poke into this whole New Moon business.

Time was a major consideration for me. I didn't have a lot of it to screw around with, trying to read out what the real deal with Harrison and his buddies might be. My own plans, of which I had been bragging to Harrison, to off Identrope were my main priority. And the clock was ticking. If I looked into New Moon and the hole suddenly got much wider and much deeper real fast, I might have to curtail my interest to some more leisurely date, if that were to ever arrive. Or just learn to live with not knowing, ignorance being the standard human condition, anyway.

The Hudson crested a shallow sandy rise, a desert-blown asphalt strip bisecting the hill, and the car's rocket snout looked down on the military debris. All those bits and pieces of man's crafty enterprise and death-lust. The sun gleamed off metal like a glaze of luminous syrup.

I parked where I had before, right on the edge of the 'yard. The Hudson's tire prints from the previous expedition were still visible in the dust.

Somebody else was already there. Other than the 'yard rats, whom I expected to come slinking out at any moment for another hit off the shiny chrome and period styling I had come cruising in with. Somebody with a little more substantial claim to any human condition at all. I felt the tug inside my skull, a ripple on our mutually shared wavelength.

She was hiding, watching me as before. I scanned around the mute landscape. "Okay, Eastern. I know you're here. Come on out and say hello."

"You don't have to shout."

I turned and looked behind me. She was sitting on the Hudson's fender, her jeans polishing the metal. Her smile congratulated herself for slipping past me like that.

"Watching me again?" I put a foot up on the bumper.

"Don't flatter yourself. You've gotten to be way above my boredom threshold, Trayne." She leaned back, palms on the hood's curve. The residual engine heat seeping through was enough to arch her fingers. "No, I was out here already. Matter of fact, I'm somewhat surprised to see you out this way."

"I'm at least half full of surprises these days."

"Word is, you've been unusually busy. What with getting yourself kidnapped and all. And here you are walking around on the outs already."

"I wouldn't have expected you to buy the kidnap bit."

Eastern laughed. "I wouldn't have believed it if I'd seen it. I pretty much figured it was some tediously complicated maneuver on your part."

122

"How about doing me a favor and keeping your lip zipped on this one?"

"I'm not going to blow your cover, Trayne. Not without a real good reason. It's worth it just for the entertainment value I get out of watching you do this shit."

She jumped down from the fender and we started walking farther into the junkyard. A new silence nagged at me: the almost subliminal scratching and scurrying around of the 'yard rats was missing. It usually didn't take them long before they came swarming around, hidden behind the crumpled banks of ancient metal, their shaggy heads popping out to study any intruders on their world.

"What's going on?" I looked around as we walked. "Where are all the regulars?"

Eastern's smile pulled on a knowing cast. "The rats? They're around. I've even talked to a couple. But they got a scare thrown in them. Most of them are down in their burrows, just holding their breath."

"What scared them?"

"You'll see."

Several cars, nice new-looking ones from outside the Madlands, and a commuter van with the New Moon logo on the side, were parked in a clear space farther on. That suited me fine—a bunch of the corporation's employees had apparently turned out for work, tightening screws or whatever on the old wartime satellite. White lab coat types, no doubt. If they ran true to form, they wouldn't know who I was—tech drones usually kept their heads down and didn't concern themselves with the front office's shenanigans. I could ask a few strategic questions and maybe get a little closer to the inside dope on what was happening with their employer.

The same unbroken silence hung over the area, like a rain cloud painted on glass. I couldn't hear anybody working or even breathing in the building that Harrison had

123

toured me through. It wasn't too likely that everyone was taking a coffee break on the other side of the horizon—I didn't like the nonsound of this.

Eastern pulled back the big sheet-metal door, ripping the air with the sudden rattling noise. But I had already dug the toe of my shoe into a wet patch by the door's long sliding track, and the sandy dirt had come up red. A fly with iridescent green behind black hairs—the insect looked large enough to have a name and Social Security number—buzzed away, annoyed at my intrusion, then came back to feed on the sticky fluid. I knew what it was, and knew there would be more inside the building's darkness.

I wasn't wrong. Eastern looked over her shoulder at me, then led me in.

The white lab coat types were there, just as I'd anticipated. But they weren't working on the ancient satellite, or fine-tuning the rocket delivery system the New Moon Corporation had smuggled in from Indonesia. They were all sleeping with counselors and kings, facedown in spreading pools of red. The red was wet-shiny, forming mirrors in which the overhead ventilation equipment made little dancing crescents of sunlight. The only sound was the buzzing of other flies, the lucky ones who had found a way in to the great mother lode of fly-feasting. Plenty for everyone.

"So what do you think?" Eastern's smile was long gone. "A real mess, huh?"

"Shit." The air in the high-ceilinged building felt close and tight as a closet unopened for years. A little knot swelled behind the hinge of my jaw. I didn't like to see poor bastards like these, who'd never really done much wrong except find themselves in the way of the world's great sharp-edged gears, get it in the neck. It's called a slaughterhouse when things as dumb and wide-eyed as cows walk in but don't walk out. "Any idea what happened

124

here?" I pulled my foot back from a hand outstretched on the bare cement floor.

"Whatever it looks like." Eastern had wrapped herself in a cold front, sufficient to make bored-cop sounds. "That's what happened."

"Okay." I worked to swallow, and the knot became loose and sour. "When did it happen?"

"Beats me. I got here maybe an hour or so before you came rolling up, and the floral arrangements were all in place. As you see them."

I hated that flip crap. It all came from too many bad books and movies, where that sort of thing is considered cute. I should know, I had seen and read most of them, in or out of the archives.

I went over to the workbench. Harrison's satellite was still there, with all of its attendant equipment hooked up by black umbilicals. So getting hold of the prize egg hadn't been the point of this little exercise. If it had been, it wouldn't have been necessary to kill all the New Moon tech workers—it would have been perfectly easy, and a lot less messy, to lift the satellite out of their hands with just a few threats and a simple show of violence.

Which meant, if you followed the thread far enough, that killing all these people had been exactly the point. That spoke of a rigorous system of calculation, one where getting a lot of pawns off the board as quickly as possible was desired.

I turned back to Eastern. "So why are you here, anyway? Official capacity? Cop business, I mean?"

She laid the same cool look on me. "Would have been, but I'm not a line cop anymore. I've gone over to the private sector."

"Yeah? Who with?"

"Canal Ultime."

I expected as much. If she were going to quit the Feds,

it would only be to go with somebody just about as big. And CU had undoubtedly made her a good offer. She had the smarts and the experience to do a good job for them.

"So your new bosses sent you out here?"

Eastern shrugged. "I've got a lot of discretion on how I operate. Long as I don't fudge my expense account. I came out here because there's been a lot of rumors floating around about some new communications satellite being worked on. I thought I'd better check it out."

"I thought these people were keeping a tighter lid on things than that."

"'These people' being the New Moon Corporation?"

I nodded.

"Well, I got some sources in there, too. CU wouldn't have hired me if I only had the same stuff they did."

I pointed a thumb at the spread-eagled bodies. "So Canal Ultime didn't do this?"

A shake of her head. "I'd know if they had. No, my outfit's clean on this one."

She wasn't lying to me. There was enough of our old wavelength on the air for me to read that.

There was something else I could read, based on long experience and the cold look in her eye. She was only nominally working for Canal Ultime. Like me, once you got past the official, for-public-consumption allegiances, she was out for herself. An independent agent. Unless CU was even smarter—and corporations never are, it's not part of their nature—they weren't aware of what a snake they'd clasped to their collective bosom.

By mutual unspoken agreement, we left the building and went out to the open, where we could breathe without that butcher-shop aroma cloying on our tongues.

All that blood was making me reconsider my plans, or at least the most immediate of them. Those guys with their faces on the concrete might have already known what I'd

126

been looking to find out, even if it'd been just little pieces of that information, that I would've had to fit together like a jigsaw puzzle. And look what good it had done *them*. I still wanted to find out what the scoop was with New Moon, but not at the risk of waking up dead.

"You taking off?"

I was heading on a fairly straight line for where I had left the Hudson. My intentions would have been clear to anybody. And why hang around some place with this much bad news attached?

I nodded. "I got some business to take care of."

Keeping pace with me, Eastern processed my face and general aura through her microscope. "Trayne, you are up to something no good." She shook her head. "You walk like a man trying to deliver a time bomb on his lunch hour."

My keys rattled around the Hudson's door handle. "I don't have a lot of surplus time, if that's what you mean." I pulled the car door open and slid in behind the wheel.

Eastern leaned on the sill when I rolled the window down. "You wouldn't have any little, uh, *secrets* that you'd want to ease off your heart?"

"It's my burden." I hit the ignition. "I wouldn't want to lay it on you."

She stood back from the door. "Trayne—be careful. There's a lot of ravens up there that'd just love to peck out your eyes."

I slipped into gear. "Thanks. I'll look both ways when I cross the street."

Then I drove off.

20

I had to get cracking, if I was going to get anything done.

As the pseudo-L.A. rolled over the horizon toward me, I tried to work out in my mind what I was going to do next. My brain refused to cooperate; suddenly, inside my head there seemed to be vast empty landscapes, as though the dry desert hills had seeped through the curved bone and established themselves in the soft tissue at the center.

The steering wheel sweated in my hands. I still felt woozy and sick from all the blood out at New Moon's junk-yard work site. Dimly, I wondered if Harrison and the rest of the gang back at the corporate headquarters had heard yet about what had happened. Or when they did, if it would make any changes in their plans. They still had the satellite; screw those guys in the white lab coats . . .

My thoughts, what there were of them, went along in this descending spiral until I had to pull the car over, open the door, and lean out. My gut heaved until it was empty.

I wiped my mouth and spat to get rid of the sour gastric taste.

I drove on, heading for the last apartment I'd been in. I suddenly felt the need to be inside walls that were at least marginally familiar and safe.

Part of my feeling sick was due to not knowing just what I was going to do next. I'd been lying to Harrison when I'd told him I had my plans all figured out, that all he had to do was sit back and give me my shot. The truth was, I had had some vague notions about what would be a smart way to go about killing Identrope, doing it in such a way that I was exposed to the least risk and the most chance for living long enough myself to cash in on my slice of the New Moon pie. The trouble with vague plans is that from a distance—when they're way off in time, out there on the horizon—they look as solid and substantial as well-thought-out ones with all the bolts and screws tightened down. It's only when they come up close with the earth's inevitable turning that you see all the holes and pieces stuck on with masking tape.

I parked the Hudson down the block and walked. A night wind, hot and choking, swirled around me. Now my knees felt wobbly, the bone workings replaced with a loose pudding. I leaned against the door for support as I waggled my key in the lock.

This was more than just getting the shakes from close-up death observation. Standing in the middle of the apartment's front room, I looked around at the walls and windows receding from me on waves of nausea. I felt deep cellular dismay, little fires and ice cubes. I laid a hand on my forehead; a sweating fever licked my palm.

"The flu." I muttered the words aloud. "Goddamn it." I had probably picked it up out in the junkyard, if not from this last visit—a little bit too fast an incubation period for that to have been the case—then from the previous time

129

I'd gone out there. Those greasy 'yard rats were all a bunch of germbags, sniffling and sneezing on every centimeter of exposed metal. You can't hang out there without catching something eventually.

Lucky for me—as soon as my brain ground around to remembering it—I had the sure cure waiting for me in the bedroom. Lying in the bed there was a nice, uninfected body, the one I had been using before and then had left there when I'd shuffled back into this one. All I had to do was go in there, shuffle back into *that* one, and I'd be healthy again. Or as healthy as I ever got; at least in operational condition. After that, it might be a good idea to dump the empty body out on the street or something, before it shed too many viruses around my temporary living quarters—it'd be a hassle to swap again if I felt another sniffle coming on.

I walked into the bedroom, leaving the overhead light switched off. Sometimes it took a little while for the new body's eyes to adjust, and I hated coming to with a big glare dazzling in my face. I looked down into the blank face I had already worn before, relaxed, and did the thing . . .

Something was wrong. I was dreaming again, and knew I was, and I didn't remember that ever happening before when I shuffled bodies. Always before, I was in one, then I'd be in the other, with no perceived gap in time. Now I was in one of those clockless gaps without time at all. The lecturer with one of my faces was there, recycled from my old daydreaming; I was close to him, not sitting up in the banked rows of the audience, and he smiled as he tilted off gravity's axis. He rapped the pointer on the blackboard beside the podium, only there was no *tap-tap* sound, just silence. And the blackboard wasn't a blackboard, but the great dark night sky. Faint laughter sounded, like the bells of invisible churches. I floated past the lecturer—"Mr. Trayne," he whispered, "are you leaving us so soon? We've barely started"—and then through the blackboard's frame, and then I was above L.A., the real one or the pseudo—I didn't know. I swam in slow motion, black air in my hands, muffled stars wheeling in their scattered alphabet. I turned and the heat of the sun basted my chest and thighs. But not the sun; it was Identrope's burning dirigible, big as the sky now, let loose from any tie to the earth. It sailed piratically toward me, the stars flickering in the churning backwash behind. I spread myself wider, and the white flames boiled my palms away, leaving the machinery of bleached bone. I saw Identrope then, leaning over the bow, reaching for what was left of my hand. But already my flesh streamed away in ribbons, the fire unraveling me. My heart and lungs squeezed like party balloons through my rib cage, and danced and bobbed away, trailing red string. Identrope reached for me, but he'd be too late; I knew it as I fell, the dense bone running spineward to earth, no flesh of wind to bear it aloft . . .

I woke up—or the dreaming stopped, at least—and things were still wrong. I was on the floor, the back of my skull throbbing with each pulse of my blood, instead of lying on the bed's soft mattress. Wincing, I got my legs under me and stood up.

The dregs of the night dream filled my head. Night and stars and the burning dirigible, Identrope's reaching hand. I could have still been in the dream, except for the heaviness that hung anvil-like on my body. I dragged myself into the bathroom. My leaden hand couldn't raise itself high enough to flick on the light switch, so I leaned on the sink in the semi-dark and fumbled on the cold water.

The symptoms of the flu, or whatever the hell it was, clotted around this body, too. Nausea and the sweats. My slow brain tried to figure it out. I lowered my face to my cupped hands, splashing the cold water and drinking the little bit left in the hollows of my palms.

I looked up to the mirror. Light spilled down the hallway from the apartment's front room. I looked and saw myself, recognition ticking like a watch squeezed inside a fist. My face . . .

My spine kicked straight. Close to the glass, my fingers touched the cheekbone and ocular orbit that I looked out from. The skin, through the cold water dripping toward the throat, felt dense, as though woven from soft steel that couldn't be torn.

"Shit—" It was the same face that I'd had before. That I'd been wearing when I'd gone into the bedroom to shuffle bodies with the empty one lying there.

I didn't feel feverish or nauseous anymore. A quick bolt of fear burned away those sensations. I turned away from the mirror and sprinted for the bedroom, banging my shoulder against the bathroom doorway.

My brain raced as I looked down at the body on the bed. It was the same one that had been lying there when I'd first come into the room.

That was why I'd woken up on the floor, with my head whanging from where it had hit. The shuffle hadn't gone through. I was still in the same body.

Now my sweat went cold, my skin prickling chill.

I looked up from the bed, to the window on the opposite wall. A night not even as hospitable as my dreaming lay over the city's lights.

Right then, I knew I was in deep, deep shit.

21

SOMETHING was happening to me, and I didn't like it.

I didn't know what it was, either. That was the scary part. You can sleep with all sorts of boa constrictors and puff adders, as long as you know that's what they are. It's the not knowing that eats up your guts.

Oddly, mine had settled down a bit. The fluish nausea and fever had been somewhat purged; I was able to work my way through most of a pack of saltines, chewing them down dry in a mouth that seemed lined with cotton. After those, I sat at the table in the apartment's kitchen, drinking bad instant coffee, and tried to figure out what was going on.

I hadn't been able to make the shuffle between bodies, to exchange the one I was wearing for the nice empty one I'd left before on the bed. I tried one more time, and nothing at all happened. The complete *nada*. Not even the stupid dreaming this time. I stood there looking down at the

133

empty body, feeling like a fool. I felt like somebody standing in front of a combination lock that he's forgotten the numbers to, and he's pawing through his wallet and all of his pockets looking for the little slip of paper he wrote them down on.

Another couple hits of the acrid coffee didn't seem to help much. Whatever the reason for this sudden blockage—beyond the combination lock, constipation metaphors came to mind—it would undoubtedly screw up my plans, vague or otherwise. For the time being, or maybe the rest of my life if I didn't regain the shuffling capacity, I was stuck in this body, with whatever advantages or disadvantages that entailed.

I was still set on course to kill Identrope. The New Moon Corporation and I had a contract, and the big paycheck was in their hands, waiting until the moment I pulled it off. That welded my immediate motivator into place.

In terms of actual operational ability, I at least had the element of surprise on my side. Identrope had gotten the word that Trayne had been kidnapped, and so was somewhere off the scene. Identrope hadn't had any reason to suspect me of having murderous intentions before, so now he'd be doubly unguarded against my actions. If I could get to him in his headquarters at the end of the web, I shouldn't have any problems getting close enough for a lethal encounter. But, as Harrison had pointed out—not that I hadn't thought of it myself, long before that—the surprise bit had its flip side. Working anonymously or under a pseudonym, I didn't have that golden privileged access to Identrope that I'd had when I was his choreographer walking around in the open.

This was going to take some doing. I'd have to think about it.

There were some other things that I definitely didn't want to think about. Even if I knew I should. Like what this sudden inability to shuffle bodies really meant.

Maybe it meant that I'd finally hit the wall, reached the limit of my exposure time in the Madlands. All the time I had thought only other people suffered the bad effects of hanging out in this zone too long, and I had complete immunity; all that time, maybe it had just been a matter of relative scale. What they all came down with sooner, I was coming down with later. The big *n*.

The memory of finding that squid puddle on the floor of the other apartment . . . the mess with Eddie the Make's name still attached to it, like the price tag on a wax candle that had been left out in the sun, a label on that from which all form had fled. That was entirely too scary to think about.

Maybe it wasn't any flu I'd been feeling. The onset of symptoms, the sense of riot in the tiny cellular bastions—maybe no virus at all, not in the ordinary sense, but something even less filterable and identifiable.

Was this what Eddie had felt coming on? The slip, the loosening of genetic bonds, the warp and woof of his humanness peeling away from the frame? His future as a jellyfish come dancing down the tracks toward him? No wonder he'd felt grim and doomed. This was the deep dark lottery ticket, the one with the big prize where it cashes *you* in.

Or maybe it was just the flu, a twenty-four-hour bug that I'd already worked most of my way onto the upslope. I comforted myself with that notion and the lukewarm dregs in my cup.

One way or another, the time factor had ratcheted on a few notches more. If I were clean, uninfected by the *n*-formation disease, I'd better get my ass in gear and do whatever I was going to do about Identrope. After all, I was now walking around again in the face by which quite a few people could recognize me as the supposedly kidnapped Trayne. If I were going to cash in on that element of surprise, I'd better do it before what little anonymous cover I had was blown.

If, on the other hand, I was in the first stages of n-formation, I had *really* better get moving. The disease was directly related to exposure to the Madlands—that was one of the few sure things known about it. That didn't help most people; your usual run of Madlands habitués were so addicted to the pleasurable side of the equation that they no longer gave themselves the option of leaving the zone when they felt themselves coming down with the condition. Either they let themselves go all squamous, with the endorphin centers still romping in whatever was left of their cerebroneural systems, or they checked in with Identrope at the last possible moment, and got salvation and a cessation of their symptoms by being incorporated in the web.

Neither of those alternatives sounded that good to me. I wanted my soul and brain to stay in the same shape they already were in. That meant I had to finish up my business here in the Madlands—the business of killing Identrope—and get out before any more exposure to the zone left me scrambled as Cuisinart contents.

How much time that left me exactly, to do my job, I didn't know. From what I'd observed, the onset and progress of n-formation and the resulting multi-cancer varied from individual to individual. In some, it poked along for years, and all their friends got to watch and comment on their slow devolution. In others, it went on a much steeper ramp, hitting the takeoff slope of a geometrical progression almost overnight. Look at Eddie the Make: one day human, the next he looked like a rubber novelty item.

The strict dictates of intelligence, of survival smarts, told me that I should just bag the whole notion of killing Identrope, and get the hell out of the Madlands before I went irreversibly down n-formation's cellular anarchy route.

136

What good was collecting a slice of the New Moon Corporation's gross revenues if I didn't have a spine or hands to do fun things with the money? I'd have to hire a couple of guys to carry me around in a plastic bucket. They could take me to the movies and drop popcorn into whatever I'd be using for a mouth. That sounded keen.

No, something beyond mere greed was keeping me from just piling a suitcase of my underwear and socks into the Hudson, and lighting out for the real world with my skin and other organs intact. Something nearly as powerful, maybe more so.

Call it nostalgia. Of the preemptive sort. The homesickness that hits you before you leave.

This was my *home*. Turf, territory, stomping grounds. Thin as cardboard, water-soluble, not even real in the first place, and nobody pretended it was. An imitation of an imitation. A photograph of a mirage. The real, long-ago L.A. had been a place whose every street name had been written in the water, and the water itself had to be pumped in from someplace else, someplace real even in its dehydrated death. When the water stopped and the wars started, and after that the sand blew over the asphalt and concrete . . . then the only thing left had been the images, locked down tight in the archives. And in people's heads, those dreams that came spiraling up from wordless memory.

It just showed that dreams and images were realer than anything else.

So that when reality got loose, and the Madlands' crazy field needed something to pattern itself on . . . then all those false-front buildings and ready-made lives popped right back up, as though they had been mounted on springs buried in the sand. And this silly-ass pseudo-L.A. could roll right into production again, as real as the real thing had ever gotten.

137

I'd been making my way through this irreal urban landscape for years now. I'd hate to leave it.

If nothing else, it seemed shabby to pack up and depart without finally hitting the big number on the board. I owed the place that much, to go off a winner.

Plus, I wanted the money. The real world outside wasn't known for its sympathy toward busted types.

That pretty much settled it. Whatever amount of time the *n*-formation gave me—if that's what it was; I wasn't even sure on that point—I'd use it on nailing Identrope. If I became a rubber squid in the process, those were the breaks.

I pulled on my jacket and headed out the front door. Night outside, and that suited me fine.

22

I pointed the Hudson toward the low-rent district.

Even lower-rent than the usual areas I hung out in. I had a plan finally cooking in my head, going from the general intent of killing Identrope to the specific details of how to go about it.

There was always a heavy recruitment by Identrope going on in the Madlands' entrance subzone. Basically, the flophouse district of the pseudo-L.A., the crumbling industrial outskirts of the city; it was where people hit when they were first making the transition from dabblers in the zone's pleasurable effects to full-fledged habitués, unable to tear themselves away. Also your basic wino zone, except instead of sluicing their brains away with fortified Mad Dog and Wild Irish Rose (though there were plenty of empty short bottles of those littering the gutter, too; it came with the territory drawn up from the archives), the down-and-outers were the ones who had already stayed too long in the zone and were just about to go under the *n*-formation tide.

As a matter of course, Identrope's enticements went over big with this subject population. You got your old-timers who were coming to the end of their string in the Madlands, and who needed to check into the web quick; plus a certain percentage of the relative newcomers would suffer a collapse of bravado as soon as the first *n*-formation symptoms showed up, and these would go hotfooting it immediately to the sanctuary of Identrope's embrace. This wasn't even counting all those from outside the Madlands, who'd caught Identrope's show on the air and came straight to the zone to dive into the salvation. Naturally, the low-rent district on the city's outskirts would be where these faithful types would first be spotted.

The notion I was working on was that I could blend in with a small group of converts who were about to make the trek up the web. If I stayed in the middle of them and kept my head down, there was a good chance that Identrope or any of his minions wouldn't recognize me—these mass altar calls were usually handled like running a sheep-dip. Once I was up there, I could slip away and get into the headquarters, and wing it from there.

It wasn't much of a plan, but it at least had the virtue of simplicity. And if I had to abandon it at any point along the way, I wouldn't be giving up much.

The only other preparation I had made was to dig a little 9mm out of its hiding place, duct-taped to the back of the toilet in the second apartment. It was a short-barreled piece, so long-distance accuracy was not one of its virtues. But I figured I'd be working up close with Identrope when the time came. If I needed to, I could put the muzzle up to his head.

The 9mm hung in my inside jacket pocket; I could feel

140

the weight against my heart whenever I cranked the Hudson's wheel around to make a corner.

Out on the streets, the low-rent types were doing their usual listless promenade. Little clusters of them hung around the dirty windows of flophouse lobbies, peering in to see the flickering TV screens in the dark corners, past the old rummies sprawled on sagging couches. The blank faces all looked to see if Identrope had come on yet; that was what they were waiting for.

Those were the newcomers or the true believers. The zone habitués touched with the first signs of n-formation did a zombie shuffle up and down the cracked sidewalks, stumbling off the curbs into the strata of yellowing trash in the gutters. They wandered across the streets without even looking to see if there were any cars coming along to flatten them.

This was a depressing, dead-end territory. What didn't smell like piss smelled like fried food, dark grease soaked right into the brick walls. My heart didn't sink so much as draw back in my rib cage, looking for the nearest way out.

There were some likely candidates for my concealing herd of sheep. I'd have to park the Hudson down some alley, and get out and walk around. Enough people looked ready to go, to make the trek to the promised land—I could organize them easily enough myself, and get them heading toward the web's downtown anchor point.

Through the windshield, something caught my eye. A face different from the others. It didn't have that blank, waiting look, that vacant expectation of either disaster or salvation. The face had the normal human qualities, ideas, and dreams moving behind the eyes. And sharper than usual; those eyes had hunger in them, too.

I only caught a glimpse of the face; not enough to make a positive ID. One of those flashes, a blur, as though seen in a car zipping by in the opposite direction. The milling crowd on the sidewalk swallowed up the face.

Like trying to remember a dream, when there's only a little piece of it left in your head when you wake up. And you can't get rid of that piece; it just keeps rattling against your skull as you tug and tug on a piece of string that goes nowhere.

I pushed down against the steering wheel, raising my butt off the seat, the top of my head brushing against the Hudson's roof liner—just so I could try and see over the crowd, to spot this guy again. No luck.

An open space at the curb—or there would be if one of these wandering assholes would get back up on the sidewalk. I nudged the geek with the nose of the car, and he barely noticed. I had to goose the accelerator hard enough to shove him sprawling onto the cracked concrete.

I parked and got out. Craning my neck, I looked around for that face I had spotted.

"Hey—"

An aggrieved voice howled behind me. I turned and saw the guy I'd knocked over with the car. Unshaven, smelling like three weeks on a flophouse mattress, with pink infected eyes. He lifted up his hands, the palms abraded raw by his landing on the sidewalk.

"Hey—" Louder; it seemed to be the limit of his vocabulary.

I pulled a dollar out of my pocket and thrust it at him. "Buy yourself some Band-Aids."

The dollar fluttered to the guy's greasy shoes. He was still waving his stigmatized hands around as I pushed my way through the other shuffling figures.

The crowd parted before me, closed up behind. I thought I saw him, the face, up ahead.

Hands grabbed the front of my jacket and pulled me around. "Wanna buy a parrot?"

142

"What the—"

A bearded face this time, a real beard, not just somebody with no use for a razor. Salt-and-pepper, foliage thick. A hat with a grosgrain ribbon around the crown.

"A parrot!" The bearded guy had a seriously demented look in his eye. "Doesn't talk! You don't want a bird that talks!"

"Yeah, you're right about that." I didn't want any goddamned birds at all. I tried to unclamp his boulder-like hands from my jacket, but failed.

He let go of his own accord, so he could pull open his sweat-stained shirt. A big yank, elbows out; he threw his head back, with his chest swelling up.

At first I thought he had an extensive tattoo job. Birds, green feathers glistening. Then the tattoos moved.

This was an n-formation development I hadn't seen before. A new twist on cellular anarchy. The man's body was changing into another species, fragmenting into several different individuals. A riot of tropical birds, compressed beneath a thin transparent membrane that looked ready to split open at any time. The birds would burst into the city sky, screeching their sudden freedom. His bones would be left maybe, ribs like denuded tree branches.

A beady eye, near where his clavicle had once been, looked at me. I turned and fled, diving into the crowd's yielding mass.

Now I didn't want to find anything except the Hudson again. I'd gotten turned around by the bird guy—one of the more baroque manifestations of the n-formation disease's humorous approach to reality—and couldn't tell down what street I'd left the car. The business about finding the face I'd spotted—that had been a whim, I told God under my breath. Just one of those momentary brain spurts. Just let me find the car and get *out* of here. I was having an open-

143

air claustrophobic reaction—the dread of other people's bodies close up to mine.

I bumped straight into somebody's chest, the impact nearly knocking both of us over. The man grabbed my arm to keep himself from falling backward. I looked around at him and saw the face.

This close, I knew immediately where I'd seen it before. A million times.

It was my own face. The one that I'd been born with. That I'd left sleeping blankly up in its hiding place in Identrope's web.

And here it was, walking around on its own, my original body attached beneath it.

"Watch where you're going, why don't ya?"

My face didn't recognize me.

23

I took him someplace to get a cup of coffee.

Didn't even know what his name was. Or what my name was—I mean, what name that original body of mine was operating under. Or whatever.

He eyed me—with my eyes, whoever was walking around behind my face—with deep distrust, when I came on friendly toward him.

"I don't exactly know what it is you're after, mister, but why don't you just fuck off? I don't think I'd be very interested."

Where'd that shitkicker persona come from? The way he talked intrigued me even more. He sounded like he came out of some museum of cracker mannerisms.

"Hey—" I laid a carefully gauged hand on his sleeve. "Don't get into a sweat over it. I just want to talk to you for a couple minutes. All right? No big deal." I pulled on his arm—my arm, formerly—and gave him a salesman's smile. "Come on. What's it going to cost you?"

I let go and took a few steps away. I looked back over my shoulder and saw him standing there on the sidewalk, the liquid crowd swirling around this stone. His face, my old face, was a study in doubt. Then he shrugged and followed after me. I could read that one easily enough: he didn't have anything else to do, or place to be.

A couple blocks away, I steered him into what looked like the coffee shop of the dead. There were as many flies on their backs as doughnut crumbs under the counter's plastic domes. We grabbed the only booth that didn't have somebody sleeping in it, facedown on folded arms. The coffee the waitress brought us had been simmered to kerosene.

The guy with my face gulped down half his cup, the chemical taste notwithstanding, and eyed the decrepit, age-cracked pies in the cabinet behind the counter. It didn't thrill me that somebody walking around inside my body was that desperately hungry. I ordered him a slice of whatever looked recently edible, and watched him wolf it, head lowered to his shoveling fork.

He was halfway through a second piece before he slowed down, possibly to take a breath. I sat across from him, arm draped over the back of the torn plastic seat, watching him. He looked up at me as he wiped his mouth with the back of his hand.

"See?" I nodded toward the one and a half empty plates. "I told you it'd be worth your while."

He studied the constellation of crumbs on the table, as though they spelled some important message in code.

"Been a while since you ate?"

His turn to nod. "Yeah. Sometimes I forget."

"Sure. We all do, fella. It's the pace of modern life."

My old face darkened with anger. "You shouldn't make fun of me, mister."

146

I raised my hand in a pacifying gesture. "Sorry. Didn't mean to." I'd had a little time to study him. My suspicions were starting to gel. "What's your name, fella?"

Silence. I'd expected as much.

His walking around in my original body went a little way in clearing up some mysteries. Such as what I'd observed a few times before when I'd been sneaking around Identrope's web, and had thought I'd found signs of the body having been tampered with. No third party had done it; it seemed obvious now that this guy, the mind inside the body, had been doing it all along. Unplugging himself and climbing down the web to go for a little stroll, then going back up and tucking himself in. The only problem with that explanation is that it didn't cover what he was, that he could do something like that. And where he'd come from.

"You don't have a name?"

A shake of the head. "Not rightly."

"What do people call you?"

"Don't call me nothin'. I don't talk to folks much."

That seemed obvious. The guy used his voice like somebody who'd never driven a car trying to figure out how the pedals worked.

I tried a different tack. I'd been catching a familiar radiation from him, something darker and even more personal than just seeing my own face. "What do people call . . . people like you?"

His head jerked up as though he'd gotten an electric prod in the spine. Eyes wide in alarm, then narrowed in suspicion, trying to decode the message in the face across the table. "What do you know about that?"

I smiled at him. "I know all sorts of things. Like what people talk about. Or what they whisper. Things they're afraid of. That's why you have to be careful, isn't it? So they don't find out."

147

He watched me with a wordless, animal-like apprehension.

Looking over my shoulder, I saw that the place had gone empty, as if on cue. Big vacant spaces wrapped around us, the walls and Formica counter being wheeled silently away. I turned back around and leaned over an empty coffee cup, my current face close to my original.

"I know what that word is. That you hear all those people saying, out there on the street."

His hands twisted together, squeezing the knuckles bloodless. "What they call me . . . if they knew . . ." A blue vein ticked at the corner of his brow. *"D . . ."*

He wanted to say *d*-ranger, but he could only squeeze out the one syllable, the single letter.

I eased up on him. "So they'd call you D. If they knew. That must be your name, then."

He looked at me with desperate gratitude, his face studded with sweat. "Yeah . . ."

"Okay, D." It was as handy as anything else would be; I had to call him something. "You come from up there, don't you?" I used a tilt of my head to point upward.

"Up there?"

"The web."

He nodded. "There's this big burning thing all the time . . ."

"Yeah, right. What happens? I mean, when you're up there."

A shrug. "I don't know. Sometimes I just . . . wake up. Hungry, like."

He couldn't mean *hungry* in the ordinary sense; when I went on my usual maintenance visits to the web, I always made sure he was hooked up to Identrope's nutrient lines.

D read what I was thinking. "Not hungry for food. Something else."

"And this is where you come for it?"

He nodded. "Yeah. I can find it here."

"What is it?" I didn't figure he'd know the term *o*-positive; I wanted to hear how he'd describe it.

"It's . . . stuff." His gaze drifted away from me. "You can't see it. But it's there. It's inside . . ." He gestured toward the dive's door and the street beyond. "Them. It's like glue, or something. It's what keeps all those people out there from falling apart. Becoming . . . other things."

That was an adequate definition of the *o*-positive substance's reality-organizing ability. The guy inside that old body of mine wasn't stupid, at least. I would've hated for a complete moron to have been walking around with a face that used to be mine.

He went on talking; I didn't have to prompt. As though he were making a confession to me.

"I don't hurt them. I just take a little bit at a time. They can spare that much, can't they? And I don't take it all from one person. I spread it around, just a little sip from a whole bunch of people. So's they don't even notice it missing. That's all right, ain't it?"

"Sure." I nodded sympathetically. I'd done worse in my time.

D looked at his hands spread flat on the booth's table. "I'd be lying to you if I said it was just 'cause I didn't *want* to hurt 'em. I don't care about 'em one way or the other. Some of these people, you see 'em out there, you can tell they want to be dead or something, but dead some way so they'd know they were; like sleeping, but different." He shook his head, human complexities opaque to him. "So it's not that; it's just that I *can't* take too much of that stuff from them. 'Cause I'm sick. But not really. Not sick like them. It's all complicated, mister."

I knew what he was trying to say. Complicated sicknesses were my specialty.

D's problem was that he was infected with the *n*-formation disease, but had found a way to live with it, just as I had. More than that: *n*-formation had enabled him to *be* in the first place. In a true way, he was a creature of the disease, as though a virus had learned to walk like a man. I had tried to keep that original body of mine infection-free, but the Madlands' effect had seeped in despite my efforts. Maybe from the proximity of all those other infected bodies on Identrope's web; maybe from some deep underlying perturbation in the reality field. At any rate, I was sitting across from the result.

A precarious balance had to be maintained by this D fellow. I could see his situation right from the get-go. He wasn't tapping off the *o*-positive substance from the Madlands habitués and selling it, the way I had been; he was living off it. On a food-versus-merchandise basis, that put him on a moral level above me. I didn't mind. But D's life—such as it was—was also dependent on the *n*-formation disease that he carried and that enabled him to tap the *o*-positive. Consequently, he had to be careful not to tap too much of the *o*-positive, or he might actually cure himself of the disease, or at least throw it into remission, and then he'd starve to death, unable to get any more *o*-positive. At the same time, he couldn't tap too little of it, or the disease might blossom into full-fledged multi-cancer, and then his little ass would really be fried. The guy was on a tightrope made out of razor blades.

My analytic mode, sitting across from D and taking him apart with my eyes, kept on rolling. It suddenly struck me where the guy's cornpone personality came from, or at least where I had first encountered it. D's manner and appearance was a dead-on take of that ancient 1930s Dust Bowl refugee Tom Joad; not the precise Steinbeck character, but Henry Fonda in the movie of *The Grapes of Wrath*. With my expertise in rooting around in the archives, I should have spotted it sooner.

150

I wondered where he'd gotten that kind of stuff fed into his skull. Maybe there was some kind of residual connection between what was going on in that original skull of mine and whatever one I was currently using. Maybe he'd come awake, his mind blank, when I'd been watching that old film, and the Joad business had just zapped right in there. Then again, that Okie stuff was part of ancient Southern California mythology; the Madlands, in its constant re-creation of that world, might have just called some Joadoid personality into existence, using D as a convenient carrier. Whatever the explanation, it didn't matter much. The guy was walking around with my face and a repertoire of shitkicker moves.

D was obviously doing some heavy-duty analysis of his own. I could see it sparking around behind his eyes.

"You know . . ." He rubbed his chin as the words drawled out. "You do seem kinda familiar, mister. Somehow. The more I look at you, the more I seem to remember you from someplace. But I don't rightly know where."

"Don't sweat it." I tapped my fingernail on the rim of my cup. "Maybe it'll come to you."

D shook his head. "It seems crazy like, but . . . it's almost like I remember you from a long time ago. Like you were my long-lost brother or something. But I don't know if I even ever had a brother. Not like you, at least."

He was catching a piece of that odd kinship radiation. He could look at me and see a mirror, but with somebody else's face in it.

"Well, D—" I gave him my kindest smile. "Maybe we *are* brothers."

Another shake of the head. "My only kin is . . . up there."

It took me a moment to figure that one out. "You mean Identrope?"

D nodded, looking both a little embarrassed and defiant at the same time.

"You think Identrope's family to you?" Now I was starting to talk like him.

"I don't think it, mister. I *know* it. In my gut. If I could just get across these crazy parts around here, and get to him . . . He'd recognize me. And he'd help me. That's what kin are for."

A wild longing hope had broken in D's voice. Not the same lust for salvation that Identrope's usual be-doomed followers expressed, but something darker and more powerful, a yearning for union on the subatomic level. Family business.

"Maybe . . ." D reached over and touched my hand. "Maybe you could help me."

He didn't have to say what; I knew what he meant. Maybe I could get him to Identrope, somehow.

The edge of another plan entered my thoughts, with Identrope's death at the inevitable still center.

I gave D a bigger smile. "Maybe . . . we can both help each other."

24

I had to hand it to Geldt. I had grievously underestimated the little fucker.

Not until later, after all kinds of shit had happened, and bits and pieces were still raining down, ashes floating in the air, did I find out what Geldt had managed to pull off. Reports came filtering in to me from the various parties involved, and I lined up the various jigsaw edges until I got the big picture.

Geldt was, I thought, off the scene and no longer an active player, due to my own machinations. Rasty Mike and the rest of the Stone Units had taken him off my hands; they could feed and water him for a while. That while might be a short one or a long one, depending upon how obnoxious Geldt made himself. The Stone Units had been known to drop screaming parcels off an overpass onto the hard concrete bed of the Los Angeles River, said packages being people that the Units had decided were on the tiresome side. I'd figured there was likely some learning curve for Rasty Mike and his crew, at the apex of which was the realization that they'd been sold the old stiff one, and that Geldt was not the valuable property they'd been led to believe. Geldt's disposal lay on the other side of that curve.

Though no longer on the scene as a player, his own scheming interrupted by my maneuver, Geldt was paradoxically having a greater effect as a passive participant. Once I'd convinced Rasty Mike that Geldt was actually this mysterious entity known as "Trayne," Geldt at that time became transfigured into a new state of existence. Here were all these people paying attention to him, who wouldn't have deigned to piss on him before. He should have regarded that as a net improvement of his lot in life. Plus, his having been subsumed into "Trayneness" furthered my own scheming, giving me a new anonymity in which to operate.

All in all, I'd figured that Geldt as Trayne was a pawn whose position on the Madlands board was nailed down, no longer subject to his own calculus of greed and spite.

I was wrong about that, as it turned out.

He must have been listening up pretty sharply while I'd been handing my own line of bull to Rasty Mike. Maybe he'd managed to wriggle over to the door of the room I'd been keeping him in, and plaster his ear to it; at any rate, he had the whole scoop on exactly what I'd told Rasty Mike, about him being Trayne, and, even more importantly, all the business about him being able to control the satellite the New Moon Corporation was planning to send up. Behind his bugged-out eyes—and how much of him being scared pissless, I came to wonder, was also an act designed to keep me thinking I had everything cooled—and his bullet-sweating face, his brain must have been racing, every little cell firing as he figured out his own moves.

The way I see it, rolling the movie inside my head, Rasty

Mike and the rest of the Stone Units took the trussed-up Geldt straight back to their funky clubhouse. I've seen the place, down in the middle of the warehouse district. The main decorating *motif* is black engine grease, as though they'd actually tried to paint the walls inside and out with Pennzoil thirty-weight. Lots of bike parts lying around, machines in various stages of dis- and reassembly, most of them looking like the bones of chromed sabertooths mired in the tar pits. Broken down Salvation Army sofas, shiny and smelling of sweat. Bootleg Mexican biphets and bennie cartwheels, trodden into white powder in the muck. And various women, the Stone Units' girlfriends, of some species that had started out only vaguely human and thus didn't have much to lose by hanging out in the Madlands.

The Stone Units probably dragged a straight-back wooden chair out from the clubhouse kitchen and tied Geldt into it, hands behind the chair's back, right in the middle of the club's main room. The Stone Units had seen enough movies to know that was what you did with your prisoners, especially if you were going into heavy interrogation mode. Was Geldt still sweating then, or had he gotten his spiel worked out in his head, all ready to fire?

Rasty Mike, in my head movie, whipped off the gag from over Geldt's mouth. Looming up big and dangerous in front of their captive—*Vee haff vays,* et cetera. Except Rasty Mike was already being steamrollered, before he could open his own hairy mouth. Geldt was off and running.

"It's about fuckin' time!" Something like that would've been the first words out of Geldt's mouth. Geldt was just enough of an animal psychologist to have known that you can't show them fear. He would've called up whatever secret reserve of guts he kept underneath his stomach, and gone for the big show of bravado. "I was about ready to eat that goddamn rag, it'd been in my mouth so long. What the hell were you assholes waiting for?"

Rasty Mike would have been rocked back on his heels a bit. My spiel to him had led him to think that Geldt, in this incarnation as Trayne, was some spineless corporate drone, deep in the pockets of the New Moon Corporation's boardroom directors. He wasn't expecting someone to come up chewing bullets and spitting out shrapnel blood.

"Whuh—?" Some brilliant comment like that from Rasty Mike.

"You heard me." Geldt would have narrowed his eyes down to razor slits. "Come on. We've got work to do. Untie me, for Christ's sake."

By then, even Rasty Mike's brain would have managed to get back into gear. "Hey. Wait a minute. Don't go telling *us* what to do—"

"You want to be rich? Powerful? Kick ass and sleep in late? Get blown by beautiful women instead of these douche bags you got flopped around here?" Geldt's full-out salesman pitch. "Then get these fuckin' cuffs off my wrists. Christ, I can't even feel my fingers anymore. If I get gangrene waiting for you guys to pull your thumbs out of your butts, I'm going to be major pissed. And then I'll have a good mind to just shut up, and you won't get all the candy you want in this life." A lift of Geldt's eyebrow. "So what's it going to be, hair ball?"

By that time, all the rest of the Stone Units would have been clustered around. Rasty Mike's underlings had missed everything I had pitched to him when he'd been in my apartment. All they would have known was that Geldt/Trayne was a figure of some kind of strategic importance. So Geldt's talk of money and getting laid would easily have fired off their greed and lust circuits—in these guys' neural systems there probably wasn't much else left. They would have started bouncing up and down, and climbing over

156

each other's shoulders in sheer salivating excitement.

That kind of excitement is contagious for the weak-minded. If he'd been by himself, Rasty Mike might have resisted it. But surrounded by the hyped-up microcephalics he called his brothers, he undoubtedly gave in.

"That's better." The straight-back kitchen chair would have been a throne then, all eyes upon the seated man, Geldt rubbing circulation back into his chafed wrists. "Now we can talk."

What did Geldt tell them?

I know he didn't waste time denying that he was this thing called Trayne. Fate, in my person, had dealt him that hand, and he had spotted a way of filling the inside straight. Better a Trayne with something these murderers wanted than some schmuck named Geldt that they dispense with like something they'd stepped in on the dirty sidewalks outside the clubhouse.

The business about the New Moon satellite being some kind of ancient super-weapon had already been planted—by me—in Rasty Mike's head. It would have been easy enough for Geldt to spread it into the rest of the Stone Units' thinking, such as it was. It's also easier to build on top of lies with more of the same, rather than trying to refute them with anything close to the truth.

Next would have been to confirm that he, "Trayne," was capable of controlling the New Moon's killer satellite. Another already-implanted notion—all of this would've been cake for anybody, let alone Geldt with his back to the wall.

Finally, the third leg of the tripod, something of his own creation.

"All right, you guys—" More movie talk, even if Geldt didn't know that was where he was getting it from. By this point, Geldt would've been sprawled out in the chair, maybe even tipping it back a bit to give that air of easy command. All the Stone Units, including Rasty Mike,

157

would have been under the sway of his words. "That other guy's a punk." He meant me. "We don't need him. He sucker-punched me when I wasn't looking. And the only reason I was hanging out with him was because I was trying to put together a crew for this action. Somebody had told me he was a righteous type, and he turned out to be a weasel. You can't trust people like that. I should've come around here and recruited you guys, since I was looking for right-on criminal accomplices."

A murmur of approval from the crowd. Geldt was singing their song.

Rasty Mike, if he'd had any sense at all, would've tried to hold on to at least a bit of his leadership role. Rubbing his chin through the thatch of his beard—"Just what kind of action you talking about?"

"Come on." Geldt would have continued to lay it on thick. "I was dummying up all along with those New Moon people. I'd been putting up with their shit for years, scheming and waiting to get the control implants for the satellite crammed into my head. Soon as the satellite went up, I split on 'em. That puppy up there is mine now. I can do what I want with it. Fire and brimstone, major bad news raining down. Only thing is, I need some help on the ground. Right? A group of like-minded people to handle all the details. Such as piling all the loot up in one handy place. All the better to divvy up shares. That's where you guys come in."

"Wait a minute. That was *our* plan. Except you were supposed to be working for *us*."

"Get real." Geldt would have glared at Rasty Mike. "You think if I've got some ancient war satellite up in the air, loaded to the gunwales with instant death, I'm going to stand around and take orders from somebody else? When I can just fry their asses on the spot? No way, dickbrain."

I don't know if Geldt came up with a convenient expla-

158

nation of why he hadn't rained fire on *my* ass, back when I'd had him trussed up in my back room. Fortunately for him, the Stone Units' brains were built for speed and not for logic.

"Let's face it, guys. Either I get some official clout in this organization, or you're all dead meat."

The upshot of Geldt's verbal footwork—as it was reported to me later, by those who should know—was that Rasty Mike retained his head-honcho position with the Stone Units. That was considered fair; after all, he knew everybody's name. But Geldt, or "Trayne" as he was being called now, instead of being the Stone Units' prisoner, the way he'd started out, was elected by acclamation to commander in chief of Rasty Mike's battle council. He'd made it; he'd talked his way into their good graces.

What happened after that, Geldt had no way of foreseeing. He was improvising on ice, as it was. He'd bought himself some time and maneuvering room, but at a price he'd have to scramble just to service the compounding interest on.

If he'd thought the Stone Units were an ugly bunch before, he hadn't seen at that point what they could be like when they found out they'd been fooled.

25

IF I'd known what was going on with Geldt, all his cutting and maneuvering while my attention was elsewhere, I might have been better prepared for the other changes that were about to roll my way. If Geldt's worm could turn that much, from prisoner/hostage to biker subchieftain, then I shouldn't have been surprised by any other transformations roiling just under the skin of the world.

I took my new pal D to a hole-in-the-wall bar, the kind of place where the woodwork was stained black with the tears of alcoholics and a flotilla of dead men's cigarette butts drifted in the urinals. One, I was tired of that stomach-peeling coffee; two, I wanted to get this D guy feeling even chummier toward me, and going down the line with a few beers and shots seemed like a good way to accomplish that. And three, I needed to make a phone call.

The bar had a little alcove by the men's room door, a pay phone with whores' numbers scratched into the black enamel. I could keep an eye on D, sitting hunched on a stool and knocking his first one back, as I fed in a dime—it was an old phone—and dialed up Harrison. The city was wrapped in deep night, but I had the feeling I'd get Harrison in his office, anyway.

I was right about that.

"Trayne! For Christ's sake!" His voice yelped in my ear. "Thank God you called me. You heard about it, didn't you—"

"About what?"

"Jesus, Trayne—they were all killed! It looked like a fucking slaughterhouse out there!"

The penny dropped. "Oh, yeah . . . right. Out at the junkyard." I had almost forgotten about the carnage scene I had stumbled onto out at the New Moon Corporation's work site. All that blood soaking through white lab coats, death's own Rorschach. I was a little dismayed at how cold my heart had grown over the years; all those poor bastards facedown in the dust, and, after my initial gut reaction, I had barely managed to register them in memory. "That's a real shame, all right."

"Shame?" Harrison screamed over the line. "Are you out of your mind? Something like that happens, we have absolutely *no* corporate contingency plan for it, we don't have the slightest idea how it's going to affect our operations . . ."

Yadda yadda yadda. I let Harrison run on for a while, holding the phone an inch away from my ear to avoid catching any of his flying spittle. The guy was both cold-hearted and overexcited, a bad combination.

"Harrison?" I eased in when the man stopped to pant for breath. "Are you through for a moment?" I didn't wait for an answer. "It's not going to help, running around flapping your wings like a kerosened chicken. Take deep breaths. Now, have you done anything at all about this situation?''

He gulped air, then spoke in a small, strangled voice. ''We've secured the area. Where the missile and the satellite are. We've sent in a new crew of technicians—''

I wondered if the New Moon Corporation had bothered to clear away the previous, now dead, tech crew before sending the new ones in. I couldn't see how it would do much for employee morale to be walking around in pools of your predecessors' blood.

''—and we've got them working on a rush basis, trying to get the satellite wired up and ready for launch. We pulled in an outside security agency to maintain the area's perimeter—''

''Really?'' I had a hunch. ''Who's in charge of that?''

''What is her name . . . real sharp woman, used to be a line cop for the Feds . . .''

''Her name wouldn't be Eastern, would it?''

''That's right. You know her?''

''Yeah . . . she's the best. You won't have any problems now.''

I had to admire Eastern's operating skill. Now she was working for everybody, Canal Ultime and New Moon, with none of them knowing about the others. And at the same time, she was working for no one. No one but herself.

Harrison's voice pleaded at my ear. ''Can you think of anything else we should be doing?''

That was the problem with rooting around in the junkyard, looking for keen buried treasures. Just like in the old fairy tales, every magic treasure chest came with interesting curses attached. I could have warned Harrison and the rest of the New Moon Corporation, but I doubt if they would have listened to me.

I couldn't resist, anyway. ''You know, you should have thought about this, and been a little more careful, before you went out there dicking around with this stuff."

"Trayne, what are we going to do?" He sounded desperate.

"You're asking me?" That proved how desperate Harrison was. "Here's my advice. Don't do anything. Just sit back and enjoy the show." I hung up on him.

D was holding down the fort, with a couple more empty glasses arranged before him on the bar. The old face of mine that he was wearing now looked slightly flush and loose from the alcohol percolating within. A lock of hair dangled in front of unfocussed eyes. He looked like he didn't get drunk too often, but when he did, he went all the way down the line, to that place called oblivion.

I sat down on the stool next to him and took a sip from the half-empty glass I'd left when I'd gone to the pay phone. The bedraggled face turned to look at me.

"I just *know* it." Not mumbling, but picking each word out carefully, like soft diamonds from a pile of ashes, the way drunks do when they're trying to hold on. "I just know he'd help me. We're kin. Real kin. I just know it."

D was still rambling on about Identrope. That was fine by me. As long as this stayed an obsession in the guy's head, I might be able to use him. I'd have to start putting together an exact plan. Maybe there was some way I could work it so that D killed Identrope. If D got rebuffed by Identrope, this longed-for help not forthcoming from Identrope—I still wasn't clear on precisely what kind of assistance D was hoping to get—D could very well flip. Even if he could just be fooled into thinking that was the case, that his kinfolk had turned him down. D obviously had that primeval shitkicker sense of morality, of blood justice, where he could whip out a piece and blow away a snake like Identrope. It was a possibility. If that was the way I decided to go, there were still a lot of logistical problems to work out, like getting D within firing range of Identrope. I'd have to think about it.

"We'll get you there, pal." I pulled bills from my wallet and laid them on the bar. "That's a promise." The bartender, polishing a glass with a damp rag, looked over and barely nodded, indicating that sometime in the near future he'd ooze over and pick up the money.

I steered D out onto the sidewalk. He wobbled as if someone had cut his bones loose at the joints. He hadn't had that much to drink—either he was the biggest lightweight going, or his brain wasn't wired anymore for taking hits of any intoxicant other than straight *o*-positive.

"You're my real buddy." D's arm flopped around my neck. "You ain't like them other shit-heels. Me and you—we gotta stick together."

"Sure thing." I looked around, trying to figure out in what direction I had left the Hudson. The street had gone deeply dark, the streetlamps missing as though they had been sucked back down into the concrete. "Through thick and thin." The bar's vinyl-padded door closed behind us, and the dim light that had spilled out around our feet vanished, leaving us in total black.

All the people had gone as well. The street was empty of its usual crowds. An idiot wind stirred the paper in the gutter, a whisper of the desert rolling loveless behind the hills.

I looked up and saw dragon clouds eating the stars. My skin became the envelope of a corpse, eternity in the wet canyons of my gut.

D had left my side and gone to the wall to shout out all the beer's barking names. He staggered back with a luminous sober face, shaking hand rubbing the white spit strings from his lips.

We're in trouble now. My eyes had adjusted well enough to the dark that I could see the city's buildings had become

164

low squat shapes, the towers kneecapped into a small town's drugstores and five-and-dimes. A single main street set apart the shuttered windows.

I could see the Hudson now, at the end of the street. Dust hazed the fender's gloss, the chrome pitted and tarnished. Hubcaps gone. The car hunkered down on wheels fitted with age-shredded whitewalls. A headlight had been smashed to leave a blind socket, and the windshield was starred with a spiderweb of shattered glass.

Something big and bad had happened, while D and I had been in the bar. The world had turned, or at least this part of it. It didn't look good.

I glanced over at D standing beside me. And I saw it in his eyes, that world written small, a seed in two stones of fire. And I knew.

He was home now. This was his world.

"You know—" I looked at him, but he didn't look back at me. "I don't think we're in L.A. anymore."

26

WHERE we were, we were in the middle of downtown
Shitsville, USA.

I saw that more clearly in the morning, when the sun
came up. We spent the night in the rusting hulk of the Hudson, D curled up snoring on the backseat—easy enough for
him; this was all coming home as far as he was concerned—while I slumped behind the steering wheel, hands
tucked inside my jacket to keep my fingertips from freezing
off. I'd been thrown enough by this change in territory not
to feel like wandering around in the dark. The whole landscape looked like the butt end of the universe; I didn't want
to chance coming across any of the hairier parts.

I'd already thrown away my 9mm piece. It hadn't come
through the transformation any better than the Hudson.
The gun I'd pulled out of my jacket had looked as if it'd
been buried in an alluvial slump, the workings rusted and
obviously inoperable.

166

The sun rolled bleak and red over the low horizon, pulling long shadows out of stubby prairie weeds. The Hudson was parked right at the edge of the town, so I could look across the earth's raw surface. What I saw was blight and dust, a true God-hated geography. One narrow road cut into the distance, bordered by sagging wire fences.

I let D go on sleeping. I got out of the Hudson and stamped my feet to get the blood moving in them again.

The small town was revealed in all its malignant glory. What had been the big sprawling city when D and I had stepped into that bar the night before had now shrunk down to a pokey main street fronted by one- and two-story buildings. The windows had old-style gilt lettering, with striped awnings tattered at the dangling edges. If a place like this had existed in any L.A. I had ever known, it would have had to be on a studio lot where they had been doing a period piece, something along the lines of *Andy Hardy Meets the Great Depression*. Even the spire on the little white church at the end of the street looked bent out of line, as though it had given up trying to stand straight.

I looked back at D sleeping inside the Hudson. That sonuvabitch walking around inside my original body—I blamed it all on him. That Joad miasma he carried around—somehow he'd managed to blow away the world I'd come to know and be comfortable in, my shabby pseudo-L.A., and put in its place this Dust Bowl relic, some Okie farm town that had seen all its hopes, money, and topsoil go sailing away on a grey wind. This place was curling up to die. Anybody still left here would be a ghost walking around in the cemetery of its own life.

This was going to make my job a lot harder. There was no getting around that.

If we'd still been in the Madlands' pseudo-L.A., I would have known how to get to Identrope, or where to find him, at least. It would have been a straight shot to the web tethered onto the ground at the edge of the city, and then climbing up to Identrope's headquarters underneath the burning dirigible. But out here in the middle of nowhere . . . it was going to take some major navigational skills to get where we needed to go.

And there were larger, more unsettling questions to be addressed. Such as how exactly we'd gotten here in the first place. It was one thing to blame D; it was another to figure out what that meant.

Obviously, D had some unusual relationship with the Madlands, something I hadn't encountered before. The Madlands' amorphous, chaotic nature had all along been pulling things into existence, such as the pseudo-L.A. itself. In a sense, the Madlands had always been creating itself out of bits and pieces from the archives, pasting together an existential collage of image and dreaming. Anybody who wandered into the zone just had to get with the program, either consciously or as another ego-submerged bit player.

That's what I'd thought was the deal with this D. That the Madlands had pulled up the Tom Joad persona from the ancient film racks in the archives, and stuck him with it. But now I had to consider the possibility that D and the Madlands were in some kind of two-way love affair. The Madlands had created him, so to speak, but he was changing the Madlands in return, drawing a big chunk of it into his 1930s, *Grapes of Wrath* world. In effect, the Madlands had created an entity with a power equal to its own.

The big question now was whether D's power exceeded the Madlands'. Whether D could pull all the zone into his own bleak, dusty world. At the moment, I was assuming that L.A. was still out there somewhere; it was just a matter of getting to it. But if D's power was rolling on unchecked—as though he were some walking manifestation of the n-formation disease itself, my original face the disguise for D's part in the Masque of the Grey Death—then the city, and the web and the burning dirigible, all of that, might be obliterated, replaced by this dilapidated shitkickerdom. And if that happened, I could pretty much kiss good-bye to any chance of getting at Identrope.

Even worse would be getting to that point and discovering that there was no longer any way out. What if D, without his even trying to, made a spatial loop out of his grimly revised Madlands, the edges of the zone rolled back into its center? You could walk into this world, but you wouldn't ever walk back out.

These were the dark meditations working through my head as I leaned against the Hudson's crumpled fender, and watched the sun come up over the flattened earth. Mornings are always the cruel wedge on my clock.

I opened up the car and gave D a poke. "Come on, you weird sonuvabitch. You're the one who got us into this mess. I'll be damned if you're going to sleep through it."

D raised his groggy head, red-gummed eyes blinking. "Huh? What's going on?"

"The end of civilization as we know it. It got canceled due to low ratings."

"What's that, mister?" D shoved his slack face around with the palm of his hand.

"Forget it. We got work to do."

We found some stale doughnuts and a working water tap in a diner halfway down the main drag. Crumpled newspapers in the stove and a match enabled us to boil up coffee.

We didn't find any other people. Either this place had come into existence without any, or they'd all had smarts enough to leave.

D spoke the words inside my head. "We gotta get going." He pushed crumbs around on the diner counter with his finger. "We gotta start out for Los Angeles. Right away."

169

I swallowed coffee brack. "Fine by me. The only problem is, which way is it?"

He looked at me, amazed at such ignorance in human form. "Jesus Christ, mister. It's west of here. It's as far west as you can go. Everybody knows that."

"West?" It showed how long I'd been living in the city. Geographical references didn't have a lot of meaning for me.

"For shit's sake. The sun comes up from over there." D pointed. "So we gotta go thataway." Another point. "Right where that big old highway heads out."

That big old highway turned out to be a stingy two-lane strip of asphalt. We started walking, the rising sun at our backs. Before we left, I'd checked out the Hudson once more and had found it stone-cold dead, a corpse of a car. Lifting the hood had revealed only rust and dry-cracked hoses. The Hudson wasn't going anywhere.

"Got any idea how far it is?" I was already sweating. I didn't get into long-distance pedestrian mode very often. "I mean, how long we're going to be walking?"

D shook his head. "It ain't far." He was laying them down, a chin-first pilgrim's expression set on his face. "Can't you smell the water?"

A cool breeze drifted toward us. I couldn't smell anything, but could almost imagine the ripple of currents over rounded stones.

D went on striding along. "We'll get there," he said, "when we get there."

Hours of silent walking went by. The noon sun battered the landscape and the brains simmering inside our skulls. The river, wherever it was, didn't seem to have come any closer.

Up ahead, the highway was greased with shimmering mirages. At the side of the road, I spotted a figure standing. When we got a little closer, I could see the person had a

170

thumb out in classic hitchhiker pose, waiting for a ride. The person would have a bit of a wait; I hadn't seen a car or truck on the highway the whole time D and I had been walking its length.

We kept walking, and finally got close enough for me to see who the figure was. In my surprise, I called out: "Nora!"

She looked at me with a blank, puzzled expression, as I stood right in front of her. "Am I supposed to know you from somewhere?"

"Nora—it's me. It's Trayne."

She shook her head. "Mister, I don't know you from Adam."

Was I in the wrong body, one that she wouldn't recognize me in? For a moment, I couldn't remember. And then I saw that it didn't matter. Somehow, she had become part of this new/old world, pulled into D's Dust Bowl sham reality. She had on a period dress, a cotton *schmattah* that came down to mid-calf. And those clunky shoes women wore back then, and a cloche hat. She looked as if she'd stepped right out of those ancient early thirties.

D came up to us; I'd left him behind a few paces when I'd spotted Nora. He nodded politely to her. "Howdy, ma'am."

"You fellas heading to California?"

D nodded. "We're going to Los Angeles."

Nora's small face lit up. "That's where I'm going!" She dug into a little purse she was carrying. "I got a job waiting there for me, and everything." She extracted a matchbook and handed it to me. "See, that's the place I'm gonna be working."

I read the words on the matchbook. It was an advertisement for a dance hall; it promised "Lovely Hostesses." She was on her way to be a taxi dancer in some dive in L.A., the whole dime-a-dance routine. It probably sounded glamorous to her; she still radiated the innocence I remembered from her previous incarnation. At least it would be somewhat in her natural line of work.

Nora shook her head when I tried to hand the matchbook back to her. "No, you keep it. Then you'll know where to find me, and you can come see me. You look like nice fellas. And you're from round here, ain'tcha? Folks like us should try and stick together." She stepped past me, closer to the side of the road. "Now, if you'll excuse me a moment . . ."

I heard the distant sound of a car approaching, and looked over my shoulder. A rolling dust cloud had bloomed on the horizon, and was heading for us.

Nora got her thumb out. D and I hung back, watching her. I wasn't surprised when the roadster came to a stop right beside where she stood. I only got a quick glimpse of the driver, nothing that I could recognize, before Nora climbed in. She waved out the window to us as the roadster sped off.

D wiped his brow with his sleeve. "Them pretty girls get all the breaks."

"Yeah, well, that's why we're still standing out here, isn't it?" I gave him a push. "Come on, let's get walking. We've got a ways to go."

27

"IT'S not far now." D announced this as he scanned the landscape, a hand shading his eyes from the afternoon sun. He stood at the crest of a low rise, looking into the western distance.

I finished wringing out my socks, wet from fording the river. The smell of water in the desert air caressed my back. We'd come a long way fast. Either that, or distances around here had taken on aspects of their ancient celluloid origin, the dull parts getting edited out. I reassembled myself and climbed up to where D was standing.

"You see?" D made a gesture, somewhere between Daniel Boone and Moses, toward the horizon. "Look out there."

We'd been traveling through dust and dry rock. The river splashing along in the middle of the bleak territory had been the first bit of motion other than scuttling lizards and the sun crawling overhead. But on the other side, what lay before us was different.

I'd half expected to see the city, my old pseudo-L.A., sprawled out, the grey buildings and streets subduing the earth beneath. That would have been convenient; we could have gotten right down to the business of finding Identrope. What we got instead was green, neat rows of orchards marching along. More of D's world: these were the fabled orange groves that every Joad had longed to see, the promised land next to the Pacific. From up where we stood, the trees' leaves looked like dark green leather, with a few gold specks of ripening fruit. L.A. was out there somewhere, beyond the groves and before the ocean. We still had some walking to do.

"Come on." D headed down the slope, loose gravel sliding under his feet. I followed after.

We found another road, a two-lane job, better kept-up. The shade from under the distant orange trees stretched toward us. In the world I came from, the one that was generally thought of as being the real reality, the groves had been stripped out of this area long time before, replaced by concrete, asphalt, and despair. The feeling that one had found one's beloved, only to have participated in her gang rape with power tools. Where I came from, the bones were buried so deep that people mourned without words, not knowing why they woke up with tears on their faces.

It was good to see the trees. I owed D for that much, for his having given me the chance to turn my face toward green that I'd only known before from the black-and-white sections of the archives.

"Where is everybody?" I shaded my eyes, peering forward to see if I could spot a farmhouse or any other sign of life beyond the trees. I wasn't sure if I sensed the presence of other people nearby or not.

D shrugged. "Beats me, jack. Didja think there was going to be a welcoming committee?"

He must have been feeling good, getting flip with me like

that. Probably in anticipation of his family reunion with Identrope, or at least the one for which he was hoping.

"I don't know." Despite the sun pressing down on my neck, a rash of gooseflesh tingled over my arms. "I was expecting *something,* at least." Maybe the explanation was that D's reality was so low-rent it couldn't afford a full complement of extras to fill out the scenes. Maybe the only ones moving around in this landscape were the featured players. Right offhand, I didn't know whether that would make plugging Identrope more or less complicated. I trudged on, thinking about it, as the first dropped leaves from the orange groves blew against our feet.

As it turned out, we did get a welcoming committee. I heard them before I saw them. A rasp of motorcycle engines, nicely tuned and muffled, sounding more like the voices of authority than Rasty Mike and the Stone Units' rolling TB ward.

The motorcycles—whoever they were; it only sounded like a couple of them—were heading our way. As they got closer, they definitely sounded like cop bikes. A little *frisson* of apprehension sank small teeth into my heart. I remembered now, from my rooting around in the archives, that there could be some unpleasant encounters with officialdom in the Joad world.

My apprehension paid off in black chips. Soon as I saw the cops come around the next bend in the road, astride classic old Harley-Davidsons with sprung seats and every surface that wasn't chrome painted black or white, I knew we were in for a bad time.

The police motorcycles sputtered to a stop right in front of us. Dust settled as the cops pushed their goggles up onto their foreheads. They didn't have on helmets, but old-style peaked caps with their department emblem over the visors. Their high boots, polished obsidian under the road grime, looked like standard Third Reich issue.

175

"You boys been walking awhile?" The lead cop squinted at us as he peeled off his heavy gloves. He didn't have a happy face on. "You look kind of tired."

I nodded. "Yeah, we've covered a little bit of ground." I glanced over at D standing beside me. His face looked heavy and dully resentful, eyes narrowed down to slits. I turned back to the cops and smiled. "We started out this morning."

The lead cop's partner leaned over his motorcycle's handlebars. He looked like the type who was born with jowls, the baby who just got uglier as he grew up. "So you're not from around these parts, then?"

D spoke up. "Nope." He pointed a thumb over his shoulder toward the hills and the bleak territory beyond them. "We come from way yonder."

That got a grisly smile from the lead cop. "Boy, we don't care where you're from. If you're not from here, none of you tramps is much of a pile of shit far as we're concerned."

This conversation wasn't going well. "Uh . . . look, Officer. We're not really planning on staying around here. We're really just sort of passing through. We've got an appointment in Los Angeles. And actually, we're late for it already. The only reason we're walking is that our car broke down." That much was true; the poor old Hudson had been broken down in every part when we'd left it behind. "So if it's all right by you, we'll just be on our way. And you won't see us again."

The grisly smile vanished, along with the lead cop's eyes behind glowering folds. "Son, there ain't nothing all right by me. At least not from a couple trashy Okie 'boes like you two."

"Officer . . ." I held my hands up, palm outward, the usual placating gesture. "We don't want any trouble . . ."

They both laughed, sounding like red-eyed dogs behind

176

a fence topped with barbed wire. The lead cop smiled wide enough to expose tobacco-yellow teeth. "Listen, shit-for-brains. You already got trouble." Wet spots appeared at the corners of that lipless mouth, as though he were sinking his discolored teeth into a raw steak. "You got trouble soon as you came over the state border. We already got enough of you Okie *dee*-generates taking a crap out in the woods and making cock-headed rude remarks to women coming out of church, to suit us. We don't need any more of your kind around, especially when it ain't even gonna be picking season for another month or so. You boys should've gone on up to Salinas with the rest of your raggedy-ass kinfolk to work the cotton."

D's face was dark enough for thunder. He spoke in a low voice. "You got no call to be talking to us like that . . ."

"Well, that's where you're wrong, boy. Wrong *again*. That's exactly how we're supposed to talk to trash like you. Folks around here pay us to give you trouble. Trouble enough that 'boes like you will think twice before you come through these parts again, looking to steal chickens and rape sweet little girls."

I spoke before D could say anything to make it worse. "Officer. Let's be reasonable about this." I didn't have anything to prove with these jerkwater small-town cops. I just wanted to get around them and keep on heading for L.A. Save whatever hassling I could engineer for Iden-trope. "We're not here to do any of that shit. Like I said before, we're just passing through. You blink, and we'll be gone. You won't even see our backs." All the time I was laying out my spiel, I was trying to spot a fallen tree branch or anything else I could use to get a lick in on these bas-tards, in case sweet-talking them didn't work. Leave it to that jerk D to call into existence the absolute worst aspects of that whole Joadoid milieu. Why couldn't he have pulled up something like a roadhouse with cold beer on credit and

177

a jukebox stuffed with only slightly anachronistic Hank Williams songs?

The lead cop smiled at me. "That's the way it really is?"

"No question about it."

The smile soured. "Shut up. The only question we got is just how far my boot's gonna fit up your ass, you sorry sonuvabitch."

From the corner of my eye, I saw that D had balled up his fists hanging by his side; he squeezed them so hard that the knuckles looked as though they'd burst through the skin. He spoke through clenched teeth. "Mister, I'm telling ya . . . don't talk to us like that . . ."

Both cops smiled as they got off their motorcycles. The lead cop's partner pulled out a nightstick from a holder bolted underneath the tank, and slapped it across his palm.

I could see how this was shaping up. I stepped backward, debating in my head about when to break and run. The trick would be to find some place in this flat territory where these guys wouldn't be able to catch up with us on their machines. Catch up with *me,* if I couldn't grab D and get him to come along with me. He looked pissed off enough to take the cops on, but I couldn't give him very good odds. If he got past the nightsticks, the cops still had the pieces strapped to their hips.

That was the last thing I wanted, for these two redneck enforcers to whip out and start firing. Getting the shit kicked out of me was one thing; I might always regain my power to shuffle bodies, and find a new one that still had most of its teeth and wasn't pissing blood from fractured kidneys. Getting shot was a whole other matter. Out here, where nobody could see them, the cops could do what they wanted. If they wanted to tack up our perforated corpses on the nearest fence post as a warning to other transients, there wasn't anyone to stop them.

The second cop grinned and advanced on me.

178

"Officer—I think there's been a terrible misunderstanding here . . ." My heel caught on a tree root and I fell backward, landing hard against my shoulder blades, knocking the wind out of me. The cop loomed up huge in the dancing black spots of my vision.

"Hey!" D called out. "Get away from my buddy!"

I heard the lead cop's sneering voice. "Just who the hell do you think you're giving orders to?"

Pushing myself up on my elbows, I was able to raise my head; I raised my forearm, expecting the nightstick to come crashing down on it. Instead, I heard a strangled cry. I lowered my arm and saw the cop pawing at his suddenly bloodless face. His fingertips curved in as though he were trying to dig through to the bone underneath. His eyes were wide with fright.

I looked to the side and saw D standing rigid in place, head tilted back, the tendons in his neck straining. His wild gaze was locked on the second cop.

"Jesus fucking Christ!" The lead cop's shout broke the silence.

Something with tiny barbs dropped on my hand. I saw a black beetle crawling across the skin and convulsively flung it away.

Another beetle crawled out of the corner of the cop's mouth. I watched it hang on his lip, before a flood of more insects swarmed over his tongue.

The cop dropped to his hands and knees in front of me as I scrabbled away. He lifted one hand to claw at his face; the flesh came apart like rotting cloth. His exposed teeth broke, splintering out of his gums.

His gut heaved as he vomited up more creatures, segmented worms writhing in the scattered pool of crawling things beneath him. His stomach hollowed back to his spine as the last of his internal organs blossomed in new scuttling forms from his mouth.

179

The cop rolled onto his back, hands fluttering above his half-skulled face. The lidless eyes watched as the fingers cracked at the joints, the tendons drawing into their own blind life.

A mercy when the eyes dimmed, the crest of his skull breaking open. Something crab-like peeked out, then scuttled back into the dark protection of the crumbling shell.

The empty uniform fluttered on the ground, as the last small creatures scurried from the sleeves. The leaves beneath the orange trees rustled as the beetles dug into the moist earth.

Over by D, the lead cop stood transfixed, his jaw locked open, his gaze frozen in horror.

I looked at D; his teeth were still clenched, his breath coming hard. He'd finished sucking the *o*-positive from the second cop, the one who'd made the mistake of pushing me around. All the cop's reality-organizing ability had been consumed; his body hadn't been able to maintain its encoding. It had been the *n*-formation disease's multi-cancer stage compressed into a few seconds.

D had done that, and I'd never seen anything like it.

Everything I'd thought about him would have to be revised. It wasn't a matter of whether he was powerful or not. It was a question of how powerful.

28

WHATEVER the extent of D's power, there was definitely a limit to it at the moment. He'd gone pale and trembling, swaying as though he were about to pitch over.

The lead cop's brain seemed to snap back into position. Whatever had happened to his partner, he knew who was responsible. "You fucking sonuvabitch—" He fumbled at the leather flap of his holster.

D made no attempt to defend himself. He turned an anguished face toward the cop, as though he would welcome the bullet in his chest.

That might have been fine by D, but I knew that once the cop started firing, he was likely to take out every living thing in range. And that included me. I was still kneeling a couple of feet away from where the second cop had dissolved into bugs; I dived for the holster hooked to the belt encircling the empty uniform.

The lead cop's gaze snapped toward me as I came up

with the revolver. Before he could swing the muzzle of his own gun around, I squeezed the trigger. The first shot hit him square in the breastbone, lifting him from his feet and sprawling him backward on the ground.

Blood bubbled from his mouth as I stood over him. I pumped in another round to make sure, then stepped over the body and walked over to D.

He didn't look too good. He'd squatted down, head lowered as though to keep from passing out. His breath was heavy and labored.

"Hey, D—" I poked his shoulder with my empty hand. "How you doing?"

He glanced up at me—a little color had started to creep back into his face—and shook his head. "That was bad." A low, mournful voice. "That was the worst it's ever been."

"Well, it's over now." I watched him sucking in one hard breath after another. He had dismayed himself with his own power. This must have been the first time he'd let it all out, his whole *d*-ranger ability; he'd sucked the one cop bone-dry of *o*-positive, and the result hadn't been pretty. Complete cellular anarchy, all reality-organizing functions of the subject individual gone, while he'd still been alive and healthy—no wonder the bugs and planarians and other organisms he'd broken down into had been crawling around so fast. They'd still had a lot of life-force left in them; it just hadn't been all stuck together into one human being any longer. I wondered if the cop's crawling fragments had remained bugs and stuff, or if once out of sight, they'd broken down further into ants and sand fleas, then on into protozoa and microbes, germs and viruses. Maybe right at that moment there were preorganic molecules with the cop's name written on them, wriggling through the leaf mulch and topsoil.

"It ain't over." D rubbed his pallid face. "Long as I'm alive. It'll never be over."

182

I left him to his dark mumbling and walked back over to the dead cop. It would have been a lot easier for us if D's power hadn't crapped out before he could have nailed this one, too. I stood looking down at the body. A corpse is always an inconvenient thing to have around; a police corpse is the ultimate in that respect. And this was one I had drilled myself. He was bound to have lots of buddies who wouldn't be swayed much by my pleas of self-defense. They'd climb over each other to get a chance at blowing me away, and saving the local taxpayers all the expense of a trial. Cop-killing was traditionally a matter of instant justice, especially in a rural locale such as the one D and I had wandered into. If only D had been able to suck out this one's *o*-positive as well; then there would have just been another empty uniform on the ground, and I'd have been off the hook.

I dragged the cop's body off into the nearest stand of orange trees, and covered it with dry leaves. The other cop's empty uniform I wadded up and stuffed into an irrigation pipe. Two motorcycles; I could handle one, but I was reasonably sure D wouldn't know how. I rolled one into the orange grove and toppled it over.

The police-issue revolvers were another matter. Good to have a working piece handy again. Hard choice as to which of them was the more incriminating: the one that had belonged to the corpse under the trees or the one I'd killed him with. By the time I thought of that, though, there had been so much shuffling around that I'd lost track of which was which. For a moment I considered giving one of them to D, then decided against it. He was already enough of a loose cannon without piling on more firepower. I looked over my shoulder to make sure he wasn't watching, then pitched the extra gun into the trees.

"Come on." I pulled D up by the arm. "Let's get going."
The motorcycle's seat was big enough for both of us, if

183

I sat all the way forward. The engine coughed into life on the third kick. I shouted over the sputtering roar for D to climb on; he looked dubious for a moment, then did as he was told. I paddled the bike in a wide circle onto the road, then gunned it, heading west. D wrapped his arms around my waist, locking his fists together against my stomach.

We made good time, the miles rolling beneath us. But I started to get worried. The road led into increasing signs of civilization. The orange groves clustered thick to the asphalt's edge were interspersed with telephone poles and a few entrance gates with mailboxes, dirt lanes leading back to houses of varying sizes. We hadn't seen any cars or other vehicles yet, but we shot past one old woman weeding a knee-high garden with a hoe. She gave us a fish-eyed examination as we went by, then dropped the hoe—I could see her in the bike's mirror—and headed toward her house. Probably to make a call, which meant trouble.

It was the motorcycle, I realized. With me and D on top of it. The black and white Harley-Davidson with the police department emblem on the side of the tank was a dead giveaway. It struck me now that I should have peeled the uniform off the dead cop—the other's uniform had been already empty and ready to go, if it'd been given a shake to clear any remaining bugs out of the trousers—and disguised myself and D in them. Nobody would have taken much notice of two uniformed motorcycle cops flashing by, even riding double the way we were.

We'd have to ditch the bike. I hated to do that, but if the old lady had put the word out on us, it'd have to be done. And soon, before we got into whatever small town lay up ahead of us. We'd probably also have to get off the road, where we could be spotted. I didn't relish the notion of trying to cut cross-country, on foot through the orange groves, but I didn't see any other choice.

Just as I was getting ready to slow down and stop, I spotted the solution. Some distance away, a freight train was moving along parallel to the road. I found a cutoff and went bouncing over the rough ground, D holding even more tightly to me, until I'd gained the smoother right-of-way alongside the railroad track. Gravel stones pinged against the motorcycle's underside as I matched speed with the train.

"Listen up!" I shouted over the combined noise of the bike and the train engine up ahead. D craned his head forward so he could hear what I was saying. "Here's what you gotta do. See the freight car next to us?"

I had pulled the bike alongside an empty car rattling along. D glanced over at it, then shouted into my ear. "Yeah—"

"I'm going to get as close as I can to it. You're going to have to let go of me, then reach up there and grab those iron handholds by the door. Then pull yourself up and swing on inside the car."

"What—? You're out of your fuckin' mind, fella!"

I jabbed my elbow back into his ribs. "Just do it. If you want to get your ass out of here—it's the only way." I swerved the bike closer to the train. "Goddamn it, get up there!"

In the bike's mirror, I could see D reach for the lowest handhold. The bike tilted, nearly falling under the train's wheels as D shifted his weight. With a sudden lurch, he sprawled himself against the side of the car. He kicked and managed to swing his feet up into the open door. He let go of the handholds and rolled into the car's darkness. A moment later, he crawled out to the edge of the opening. "Now what?"

I took one hand from the bars and reached toward him. "Grab my hand. When I say, you pull me in. And don't let go!" I stood up on the bike's pegs. "Okay, now!"

D had one hand around my wrist, the other clamped

185

above my elbow. As I kicked the motorcycle away, he toppled backward, dragging my ribs across the splintering edge of the doorway. For a few seconds, I was half in, half out, the graveled right-of-way streaming dizzily beneath me. Then D dug in with his heels and hauled me the rest of the way. I sprawled facedown on the floor of the freight car.

I raised my head to look over my shoulder, just in time to see the riderless motorcycle take a flip at the edge of the gravel, tumbling end over end into a drainage ditch choked with high weeds. It wouldn't be found for a long time in there.

"Jesus Christ." D sat with his forearms across his knees, still looking scared around the eyes. "That was the absolute sorriest thing I've *ever* done."

I was busy picking splinters out of the front of my jacket. It seemed pretty obvious to me now, if it hadn't before, that this was a reality based on old movies. In any existence more realistic than this one, a stunt like that wouldn't have been possible.

"You boys going far?" A voice spoke out of one of the freight car's dark corners.

"Shit!" D scrambled backward, away from the voice.

A grizzled vagrant slapped his thighs, laughing. I could see now the little nest he'd made for himself, a rope-tied bedroll and a canvas sack with his various necessities. His grey beard and sparse-toothed mouth made him look about eighty, a sun-withered gnome.

"'Cause if ya weren't going far before, ya are now! This train's got a ways to roll!"

"That suits us fine." I looked out at the landscape sliding by. "We're real traveling types."

The tramp dug into his beard with a dirty claw of a forefinger, then studied his black nail. "I'm glad you boys came along. Now we can take turns watching out, and I can get some sleep for a change."

186

"Watching out for what?"

"Yard bulls. Railway cops. They got some mean sonsa-bitches on this line. Like to knock ya out with their big ol' saps, then leave you lying on the tracks. If you come to before the next freight, then all you got is a cracked skull. If you don't, they'll be pickin' up pieces of ya with a rake all the way to the next town."

This on top of everything else. "All right. We'll look out for them, then."

The tramp nestled back against his bedroll. "You don't have much to worry about, at least until the train starts to slow down. Then we'd better all move our butts, and jump off. There's a bridge right before the next yard, where they don't like to come looking. We'll be all right there." He closed his eyes and in a few seconds started to snore.

D stood at the other side of the doorway, leaning his face out into the wind. "At least we're still heading west."

"There is that." I sat down with my back against the car's rough board sides. "Wake me if anything that looks like L.A. comes along." I folded my arms across my chest and closed my eyes.

29

FROM under the bridge, we watched the tail end of the train roll off. The noise of its passage gradually faded away in the deepening twilight.

Jumping out of the freight car, I had hit the ground wrong. I kneaded my ankle, hoping that I hadn't sprained it. The ache lessened under my hand, and I rotated my foot experimentally. It seemed all right.

"We'd best be going." The old tramp lifted his pack onto his shoulder. "Can't spend the night here."

"Why not?" D looked around the low space. "Seems all right to me."

The tramp shook his head. "Too close to the freight yards. Sometimes the bulls, if they don't catch anybody aboard the train, they come down and see if there's anybody to roust out. You don't want to wake up to getting your head thumped." He started walking along the sandy bank of the creek that ran under the bridge. "Come on. I know a good place around here."

We followed after the tramp. After a half hour or so of walking, we climbed up from the creek into a thick cluster of trees. A small campfire burned in a clearing a little way in; more ragged shapes of men were huddled near it.

A couple of the men nodded in recognition to the tramp. They were all obviously of the same wandering breed. Our tramp pointed with his thumb toward us. "These fellas are pretty decent types."

They made room for us around the fire. One of the men ladled out watery beans from a blackened can; I dug in, but D wouldn't touch them.

"Where you fellas heading?"

I wiped my mouth with the back of my hand. "Los Angeles."

The tramp nearest me shook his head. "That's a right mean town."

"Yeah? How so?"

He shrugged. "Things have really tightened up there. Tighter'n a mallard's ass. Something's got hold of those folks."

"You ain't shittin' about that." Another one chimed in. "I just headed outta that burg. Couldn't take it no more. That whole bunch is weird as white crows. Nervous, jumpy, don't know what they'll do next. You ask 'em for a sandwich, they're as likely to give you a million dollars as a shotgun full of rock salt. Started making *me* nervous, so I cleared out. I'd just as soon be back in Sioux Falls, where I can at least starve to death with people who know how to act normal like."

This was strange news. I picked at the beans left in my tin plate. "Any idea why they've started acting that way?"

The whole circle shook their heads. "Seems like they're fixin' for the end of the world." That was from the tramp who'd been on the train with us. "They all spend too much time listening to some fool stump preacher on the radio.

189

Got their brains all fucked up." He poked at the fire with a stick. "Course, maybe the world *is* about to end, in which case they got a call for gettin' excited. Me, I don't care much one way or the other."

Preacher sounded familiar. "Is that Identrope you're talking about?"

The tramp nodded. "He's a big deal in L.A. now. Bigger'n Aimee Semple McPherson ever was. People tune him in every night. They get all fired up, send him all their money. Can't fathom that, myself. If I had money—and it'd be the first time in my life if I did—I wouldn't send it off to some oily jabberjaw talkin' fire and brimstone all night long. Especially if I thought the world was gonna get wrapped up anytime soon. I'd have a better use for the dough."

Another tramp nodded vigorously. "Amen to that, brother."

"I'd build myself a house outta empty red dog bottles, and I'd wait for Jesus Christ Hisself come knocking on my door. And then I'd say, Mister Jesus, I got two full bottles left, one for you and one for me; why don't the two of us go on down the line tonight? We can go over to the roadhouse, put our mitts on the asses of other men's women, and get the holy shit kicked out of us. So why would anybody want to go to Heaven, when they can have that much fun right here?"

They all went talking on into the night. None of them put much effort into trying to dissuade us from going to L.A.; it was part of their basic tramp credo that every man had the right to screw up in his own way. They unloaded on me—D wasn't listening, but just went on staring into the dying fire—all their advice on the best routes for getting there, and how to avoid the cops along the way. We weren't, in fact, far from the city; a good day's traveling, if we got an early start, would get us there.

190

The company of tramps retired to their bedrolls, leaving me and D sitting by the last red embers. D had something on his mind; he kept biting his lip and working the hinge of his jaw, grinding his teeth. His eyes were wild, touched with reflected sparks.

"That was bad . . ." He wouldn't look at me, but spoke to the ashes. "That was real bad."

I leaned back, watching him. "What was?"

"What happened back there. With those cops."

"Yeah, well, it's never too good an idea to get into trouble with the law."

He shook his head. "I don't mean that. Trouble's no big deal. There's always trouble. I mean what I had to do. To that one cop fella. The way I made him come apart like that. I did that. I ate up all that stuff inside him, like glue or something, and then he just . . . *changed*. Like he couldn't hold on to himself anymore. He couldn't just be what he used to be. It all let go, and all the little bits went flying like."

"Creeping, actually."

He shot me an angry look. "This ain't nothing to joke about. I'm being serious. Whenever I did that before, taking that stuff outta people, I was real careful not to take too much. I didn't want to hurt 'em. But that cop fella—he made me mad. I tried to warn him, but he just wouldn't listen. So I had to do it."

"*Sic semper tyrannis.*"

That went right by him. He was deep into his musing. "I gotta be *careful*. I can't let that happen again. There'll be more trouble if it does."

I didn't see what he was so worried about. After all, I was the one who'd actually shot a cop. I was more likely to get nailed for that; a prosecuting attorney would have a hard time convincing a jury that D had turned the other cop into a collection of bugs and worms, microbes and shit.

191

If nothing else, D had solved the perennial murderer's problem of disposing of the body. You couldn't dump someone into a vat of acid and get rid of him better than that.

"Take it easy," I told him. "We've put a pretty good piece of ground between us and where all that happened. As long as we keep moving, and keep our noses clean, there's not much chance people will be able to hook us up with it. Nobody's going to find out what you really are. I'm the only one who knows, and I can keep a secret."

"It's not people finding out that's got me scared. It's worse'n that. Bigger trouble. If it happens again—if I get mad, and let it come haulin' outta me, and *do* that to somebody again—there'll be hell to pay. Bad things, that I don't even know *what* they'll be. I can just feel it, though. I felt it then, with them cop fellas, building up inside me. Right here." D laid a hand on his chest. "But if it happens, it won't be just inside me. It'll be everywhere." The hand gestured at the night world around us. "Like them fellas were playing up about, Jesus coming back and all that. Only it won't be like that. It'll be something bad."

I didn't say anything, but just leaned back and watched his hunched-over form by the dying fire.

He turned and looked over his shoulder at me. "That's why I won't be able to help you again. Not like that. If there's trouble with cops or anybody else. I won't do it. I can't."

"Fair enough." I nodded. "That kind of thing happens again, it'll be every man for himself." I had the cop's gun; I could create my own kind of trouble, if anybody tried to hassle me.

I left him still sitting there, and went off to lie down and catch some sleep. If we were going to hit L.A. tomorrow, I wanted to be ready.

192

30

WE pulled into L.A. just as the sun was going down in smoke. The palm trees nodded behind buildings several stories lower than I remembered them.

D and I had caught a ride from an old C-cab truck hauling a half load of crated tomatoes out to a canning factory in San Pedro. We'd bounced hard-tailed on the truck's worn-out leaf springs, while the driver had bent our ears about how the load was hardly going to cover his gasoline costs, and then he'd have to deadhead the empty truck back up to the Central Valley for another pile. He wanted somebody to bitch to, more than anything else; I dozed off at least once, and woke to the same complaint going on. The guy could hold the truck steady on the road with his wrists at the top of the steering wheel, his hands busy rolling another cigarette from a pack of Riz La papers and a flat red can of Prince Albert. The truck cab smelled like hell's ashtray. We could have walked to L.A. as fast—the driver barely got up enough speed to blow away the flies walking around on the squished-open tomatoes—but it felt good to get off our feet.

The truck driver let us off near the produce district warehouses. For a moment, he looked as if he were about to hit us up for a share of the gas, then decided against it and drove off in a rattling cloud of black exhaust.

We headed for downtown, picking our way over the rows of rail tracks. The whole ride here, the truck and its driver, had been a piece of D's shabby Joad world. Now I saw that the city, as I'd been anticipating—or dreading—had been subsumed into that reality as well.

Not just a matter of the buildings being shorter, sucked down into some earlier stage of urban existence. The miasma of bad economics slunk through the streets, like a cross between greasy low fog and the last quarter inch of brown in a nameless bottle. D and I passed by a shuffling soup line, the watery kettle staffed by Sally Anns with tambourines and the old-style hats with the big ribbon bows on the side. The grey men hunkered down on the sidewalks and ate with heads lowered, as though they were going to dive into the wisps of steam and drown.

"Looks like hard old times around here." D walked along with his hands shoved in his empty pockets.

I nodded. "Hard times everywhere." At least in the Madlands.

"Well, that don't worry me none. I got kinfolk in high places."

He meant Identrope. D's attitude had improved in general since we had reached this bleak L.A. He was obviously anticipating that it wouldn't be long before Identrope—on whatever family basis D was so sure of—would help him out. Whatever that meant.

High places—that had me a little concerned. As we'd hit the outskirts of the city, I'd started looking for that familiar sight, the burning dirigible with Identrope's headquarters

194

suspended beneath it. The L.A. I had known before had always been tinged with the lurid colors of those inexhaustible flames. A big reason why this Joadized city looked so grey was that that fire was missing from the sky. When night fell, it was complete. If Identrope was still around, he'd either changed the nature of his operations or moved them somewhere outside the city. In either case, it was going to be harder than I'd anticipated to track him down. That is, in person; I'd already heard his radio show coming from the speakers of old Atwater-Kent radios near people's open windows.

I had one lead. One connection to that other pseudo-L.A. I remembered. I fished the matchbook out of my pocket and read the address on it. It was walking distance from where D and I had drifted, if there hadn't been too much more geographical distortion in this area.

"Remember that little lady, out on the highway?" I held the matchbook up to D's gaze before I dropped it back in my pocket. "I think we should go look her up, first thing."

D frowned. "Why?"

"She seemed like a pretty smart cookie." I pitched it to him in language he could understand. "Kind of girl that hits the ground running. I'd be willing to bet she's got the local scene pretty well scoped out already. Probably be able to give us some straight advice on what to do next. Besides—" I shrugged. "Have you got any better ideas?"

He didn't. We headed for the taxi-dance establishment.

The place's only sign, at least on street level, was two hinged boards out on the sidewalk; both sides promised "20 Beautiful Girls—Friendly and Clean." An arrow pointed to a narrow stairway set into a brick building front.

"This must be the place." I nodded toward the stairs. "Come on, let's go on up and see if we can find her."

D hung back, wearing a look of deep distrust. "You go up. I'll wait for you down here."

"Suit yourself." I figured it was some ingrained shitkicker puritanical streak surfacing in him. Dens of iniquity, flesh-pots of the soul, brazen painted harlots. He hadn't gotten it from me. "Don't go wandering off, okay?" I started up the stairs.

Two flights up—there were more arrows painted on the walls to guide me—I found the dance hall. An empty band-stand at one end of the big room, with a rick-a-tick snare drum, string bass laid on its side, and a piano whose key-board was beginning to sag in the middle. If the musicians were as old and decrepit as the instruments, they could have been the original Muzak on Cleopatra's barge.

The wood floor had once been polished, but now was scuffed to the point of splinters. Too many sailors with twenty-four-hour passes, farm boys with the egg money sto-len from their mothers' cookie jars. The walls were still vibrating with unrequited hard-ons.

A girl in a beaded-fringe dress sat backward on a chair, reading a movie magazine. "We're closed, mister." She didn't look around at me in the doorway. "Come back in a couple hours. The band'll be going then."

"Nora—it's me."

She looked up from an article about Deanna Durbin's love life. For a moment she didn't recognize me, then her face brightened into the knockout smile she'd always had. "It's that fellow from out on the road. That's right, ain't it? Where's your buddy?"

"He's outside." I pointed back down the stairs. "Having a shy attack."

"Wait a minute." Her forehead wrinkled. "How'd you know my name? Did I tell you?"

At this point it wasn't worth trying to explain everything to her. "You sure did."

"I must have really thought you were a nice guy, 'cause I don't usually do that. Tell men my name, I mean. Not my

196

real name. They don't even know it here. I'm supposed to tell the customers my name's Sugar. That's really stupid, in my opinion."

She pulled out another chair from the ones stacked against the wall. "Can I get you something to drink? I mean, there's some coffee left, behind the bar. All the girls drink a lot of coffee here."

"No, I'm fine." I sat down and looked at her. They'd cut her hair, or she'd done it; she didn't have the *chignon* anymore, but more of a Louise Brooks bob. "You getting along all right here in the big city?"

"Pretty well. You meet a lot of people. Some of them are real nice."

She was lying to me. Smiling and sounding sad at the same time. "Yeah, I've met some of them, too. Real lot of churchgoers, most of them."

"I don't know about that." Nora tilted her head. "There's that radio program they all listen to . . ."

I'd hit it, right off the bat. "That's right. What's that guy's name?"

"I think it's Identrope. At least, that's what they say on the radio."

I nodded. "You know, I heard about him before. Before I ever got to L.A., I mean. He's a real famous guy. Even bigger than Billy Sunday."

"Oh, yeah?" She looked at me wide-eyed. "I'd never heard of him before I got here."

"Matter of fact, that was one of the big reasons I wanted to come to the city. So I could go to one of this Identrope's revival meetings. You know, where they do the radio broadcasts from? I heard he had a great big church. Only now I can't find where the place is at."

"It's not here any longer. One of the other girls told me all about it. They closed up shop and moved out of the city. 'Cause of it being a sink of depravity, and all."

My heart ticked over slowly. "Did he go far away? This guy Identrope, I mean."

"No, just a little south of here, is all. To some big piece of land the church could have all to itself. They've got—at least, what I've been told—their own regular amusement park and all down there. I guess that's for the kids, or something. So the kids would have stuff to do while their folks are busy getting their souls saved. Seems a little strange to me, though."

That was all I needed to know, in what direction lay Identrope's place. I figured that once I got close to it, I'd see the dirigible burning up in the sky.

I could have buttonholed anybody out on the street and found out the same information. It struck me now that all I'd really wanted to do was talk to Nora, even if she didn't remember who I really was.

"Gotta get going." I stood up from the chair. "I just came by to say hello, is all."

"Are you going to go down there? To that Identrope's place, I mean."

"I thought I would."

She reached out and touched my hand. "Why don't you stay here a little while longer? With me."

A note of concern had sounded in her voice. "Why? Is there something wrong?"

A shake of the head, but she wouldn't look me straight in the face. "No—it's just . . . I don't know. It makes me feel funny, when I think about it. Like you shouldn't go there. But I don't know why."

I gave her hand a squeeze. "Don't worry about it. Tell you what. I'll come by here again and see you, soon as I'm back in town."

She smiled, but didn't look happy.

I went back down the stairs and hit the street.

There was nobody waiting for me on the sidewalk. D was gone.

198

31

A rummy sprawled on the sidewalk, his back against the brick building, a dead Tokay bottle between his legs.

"Hey, buddy—" I had to give him a slight kick to get his attention. "There was a guy out here a little while ago. You see which way he went?"

The drunk gave me a leer and a wink. "*They* went along there." He pointed a wobbling finger toward the other end of the street.

I saw what he meant when I hit the corner. D was a couple of blocks away, arm in arm with a young woman. She was dressed in Joad period costume, the black lines of seamed silk stockings vertical on her calves. The little purse gave it away, though; that's always been such a traditional hooker's emblem that I could tell her profession, and her interest in D, right off. She smiled right up into his face, and he gave her the john's usual shit-eating grin.

They didn't see me. I followed them to the expected

cheap hotel. I waited down on the sidewalk, watching until a light appeared in a window up on the third floor. Their silhouettes moved against the cheap curtain, then disappeared.

I hung out in the shadows down below for close to half an hour. Then the woman appeared at the window by herself, smoking a cigarette, a thin flowered wrap pulled around her. She looked sufficiently postcoital for me to head on up.

She opened the door when I knocked. And smiled at me.

"Hello, Eastern," I said. "How've you been?"

"Fine, thanks." She tilted her head. "Come on in."

I had known it was her, sensing her presence through the hotel room door, and had suspected as much from down in the street. Her taking on an appearance suitable to this period—I couldn't tell if she'd shuffled herself into a new body here, or had just been pulled into this reality's way of doing things—wasn't enough of a disguise.

She offered me a glass of something brown and evil. "Want some?"

"I'll pass. Where's D?"

"Is that what you call him? Over there."

D lay in a broken-back bed, sleeping the sleep of the wildly oversated, in more ways than one; the alcohol she'd fed him flushed his cheeks with simmering blood. This farm boy walking around in my original body never knew what hit him. She'd always been good that way.

I sat down on the edge of the bed. D's clothes were piled untidily on the floor. "Any special reason you put the moves on him?" I sniffed at an empty glass on the bedside table.

She shrugged. "Old times' sake, maybe. I've got some fond memories of you back then. The body's in pretty good shape, considering how long ago that was."

"I've kept it on ice."

200

"Besides—it might've actually been you in there. I knew you were somewhere around in this territory. So I thought I'd better make sure." She looked wistful. "It would've been nice if it had been."

"Yeah, it would've been." Eastern always got sweet and slightly declawed afterward. She came over and sat down next to me. "There some reason you're in these parts?"

"There's no other parts to be in right now. Hadn't you noticed? This *is* the Madlands for the time being. There's some strange stuff happening these days."

"I thought it was just me."

She gave me a half-sad, half-exasperated look. "Trayne—I don't know what the hell you're up to. But you'd better get with the program."

I held out the empty glass. "Why don't you tell me all about it?"

She poured me a finger. "About what?"

"All the stuff you've been finding out lately."

A finger for herself. She sipped at it. "Why should I tell you?"

"Like you said. For old times' sake." I pointed to D still snoozing away. "He got one part. I'll take the rest."

Eastern drained her glass. "Like the girl in that old joke says: 'Not 'til now, you sweet-talking sonuvabitch.'" She shook her head, smiling. "All right. Just to keep our track record complete."

What Eastern told me—

While D and I had been hoofing it across the Madlands, Eastern had been pursuing her own investigations out at the New Moon Corporation's work site in the junkyard. Since she had been put in charge of security, hired for that purpose by Harrison and the rest of the New Moon brass, she had complete access to all areas. Behind the barbed wire they'd hastily thrown up, and the armed rent-a-cops

201

doing their perimeter patrols, she got busy snooping. That was also something she was good at.

Much as I'd figured, the bodies of the murdered New Moon technicians were still out at the work site. A medical crew had been brought in to run some preliminary autopsy work on the cadavers, so Eastern didn't have to mess around with little knives and drill bits herself; all she had to do was call up the rough-draft reports on the in-house computer system.

Some interesting things right there, stuff that she had a better handle on than the autopsy team. The CAT scan readouts showed a particular cancer-like patterning in the brain cells of the murdered techs; Eastern was able to recognize it as a precursor state of the *n*-formation disease. That was *very* intriguing to her. These New Moon employees had started to suffer the usual symptoms of exposure to the Madlands' reality field *without being in the field itself.* Somehow, the Madlands had reached out and touched them, long-distance calling. Eastern had never seen that happen before.

"Strange stuff," Eastern said, as we sat on the bed and rolled our glasses in our hands. I had to agree.

Some more snooping; Eastern had decided to check out all the electronic gear in the New Moon work site. It had taken her a while, but she'd found another interesting thing, well hidden but there nonetheless: a closed-circuit link between the site in the junkyard and some other unidentified point. A little network tracing established the link's other terminus, a dedicated hook in the Madlands zone, somewhere around the tethering point of the web going up to the burning dirigible and Identrope's headquarters. Pretty obvious that Identrope hadn't been using the line for calling and checking on the weather in the outside world.

The closed-circuit line was still connected and active.

Bingo City, as far as Eastern had been concerned. This was what she did best, getting in through these back doors that people had left unlocked. Basically, the cat burglary equivalent of stealing clothes off a line. A tap on this line would give her access to whatever data bank files Identrope was maintaining up there on the web. All his little secrets would be hers.

"Except it didn't work that way." Eastern poured herself another finger. "It just didn't work at all."

"What happened?"

"Nothing. That was the strange part. Exactly nothing. There weren't any access codes to hassle with, no encryption, no nothing. It should've been just like walking into somebody's kitchen and raiding their refrigerator. But it didn't happen. The closed-circuit link just . . . *resisted*. It was just . . . balky. Slow, and stubborn. And finally it just stopped. But all the circuitry showed that the line was still active. It just wasn't cooperating." She took a sip from her glass. "The weirdest thing was that I started to feel like I was dealing with a living thing. Not on the other end of the line. But like the line itself was alive."

I held my glass out for a refill. "Did you test this out any?"

Eastern nodded as she screwed the cap off the bottle. "I put a readout device on the line about twenty or so meters from its terminus in the New Moon work site. Then I sent an innocuous signal along the line; it came out fine, completely unaltered, at the readout point. But when I sent any kind of signal that could've accessed or manipulated other areas hooked up to the line, like Identrope's data banks, the signal didn't pass through the wire even to the readout point, or else it got there scrambled, neutered sort of. Whatever was affecting operations on the line was *in* the line itself."

We drank to the mutually agreed weirdness of this. I had

already drunk enough to start feeling toasted. The alcohol translated from my empty stomach into my bloodstream with enough raw heat to flame my ears. Behind us, D went on sleeping, emitting a gentle snore as he slept off his load.

Eastern's voice circled around me as she told me what had happened next.

She got hold of Identrope himself. Live, and on the line.

She hadn't been trying to. She had still been trying to shove her signals down the rock-stubborn wire, when that recognizable voice had come over the audio band of her equipment.

"What'd he say? I mean, after hello."

Eastern hesitated a moment. She gazed at the room's wall. Then: "He said he loved me."

I shrugged, unimpressed. "He loves everybody. He says so on his show all the time. It's all part of his Christ-like demeanor."

She glanced at me. "Yeah? He said he wanted to marry me."

"That is new." I rubbed my sweating brow. I almost expected to see blood on my hand, my brain having given such a lurch against the inside curve of bone. "Elaborate."

She did.

Apparently, Identrope had been impressed with her efforts at getting through on the closed-circuit link. Nobody else had ever gotten that close to him; that had been the way to whatever heart he had all along.

More than that. This was not some simple, flesh-and-blood marriage proposal. Identrope had something else in mind.

It must've been love, or something close to it. Identrope, like a teenager crooning over the telephone, revealed to Eastern everything he'd accomplished. And his ultimate plans. He laid out the whole bit for her. He was going to sweep her off her feet, one way or the other.

204

"The web," Eastern told me. "It's all in the web. He's not *in* there, somewhere. He's *there,* period."

Identrope's web was, in more senses than one, a brain in the process of constructing itself. (This information was his heart bared to her, the ultimate engagement ring.) The web, when completed, would be different from the human brain that it was modeled upon. Identrope's web would have a consciousness capable of perceiving and comprehending totally unfiltered "white reality." It would be the brain of God, perhaps—Identrope told Eastern this, laying it on thick—omniscient and omnipotent in a reality that included all other possible realities, including those beyond mere human comprehension.

"What a deal." I drank and listened.

There was more.

If the web was becoming a brain, then Identrope himself would be its central cortex, the thinking ego part. He'd gained a unique control over the actual physical material of the web, the wires linking all of his subsumed disciples together. All metal is crystalline in structure, the crystals more or less rigidly bonded to each other depending upon the exact alloy content. Simple metallurgy, so far. But with Identrope, the crystalline nature of the wires had become the equivalent of synapses in an organic nervous system. That is, each metal crystal in the wire passed on or modified an electronic signal just as the synapses in a human brain pass on or modify a bioelectric signal to the next cell in the neural pathway. (I thought that was what Eastern told me; a lot of these explanations were getting fuzzy around the edges, alcohol-eroded.) That was how Identrope had been able to build a defense against any penetration into the web, such as Eastern had attempted from the closed-circuit terminus out at the New Moon work site. The metal "synapses" had identified and rejected her signals. Identrope had, in effect, caused mere metal to take on hu-

205

man characteristics at the atomic level. His power went down that far.

I lay back across the bed, feeling D's shins under my shoulder blades. "Go on," I murmured. Through half-closed eyes I watched the water-stained ceiling slowly rotate.

"You know about all that 'white reality' stuff, don't you, Trayne?" Eastern leaned on one elbow. "I know you do."

"Sure . . ." If I closed my eyes, I could see the stars beyond the ceiling, the gearing of any handy universe.

"Everything . . ." Eastern's voice sounded a little sleepy and blurred, a page where the ink had dissolved and run. "Every tail in every mouth of every snake . . ."

Where Identrope had been. She had told me that, what Identrope had told her. Now where he was going.

That wished-for white reality was growing closer with every formerly individual human consciousness that Identrope added to his web. He wanted Eastern to join him—to "marry" him—on this ultimate project. Not as another sucker to be merely absorbed into the system, but as an essential buffer between himself in this new grand state he'd have achieved and the commonly perceived reality of the world outside the web.

"Sheesh." I shook my head; the booze had put me in the mood for making my own pronouncements. "You know, this isn't anything new. This is an old story, just written on a slightly more . . . egomaniacal scale." The big words came flooding out of me, as I waved one hand about. "It's the same old thing where you have your *great men,* all lost in their profound and abstract thoughts, depending upon the faithful little woman, the usual practical-minded wife, to maintain the petty details of their . . . um . . . physical existence." The spiel left me slightly breathless. "The same old kitchen melodrama of the intellectual classes. Karl Marx ran his household that way, for Christ's sake."

206

"Maybe so." Eastern's gaze drifted away from me. "But I don't think Mrs. Marx ever got what Identrope promised me."

"Yeah? What's that?"

The ultimate argument. Identrope had given her a taste. Of the almost unfiltered reality he had already achieved inside the web he controlled. Right through the closed-circuit link to her head; Identrope manipulated the living wire into an exact sympathetic parallel to Eastern's nervous system, so she could get the full bang.

She wasn't able to describe it to me. More than words failed her. Thought and concept failed.

Something like a kaleidoscope of overlapping realities, all the possible ways that possibility itself could be. The sensation had been so intense and multiplex that Identrope had had to yank the plug before Eastern's unprepared nervous system had burned out.

"You don't know what it's like, Trayne." She looked at me with a frightening clear gaze. "If you knew . . . you'd understand."

"Understand what?"

"Why I agreed. To the marriage proposal. It's worth it. Whatever it takes . . . it's worth it."

"Aw shit." I had raised myself up a bit to listen to her, but now let myself fall, heavy and sodden, back against the bed and D's legs under the blanket. "Just tell me where to send the flowers. I don't think I'll make the wedding."

"You see? You don't understand. That's the whole point." The bed creaked as Eastern stood up from it. She started to pull on her clothes, slipping the period dress over her head and letting it slide down. "But you will."

"That's what I'm afraid of." I checked the bottle on the table. It was finally empty. "So is that why you're here? In the Madlands, I mean."

She nodded. "I'm on my way to meet him. To hook up with him."

"How romantic. I take it the territory's a little different from what you'd expected?"

She looked puzzled. "Yeah. I don't know what's going on here. What happened." She looked down at the Joadoid dress. "I don't know what's happened to *me*."

"Strange stuff." I wasn't going to bother trying to explain all about the sleeping D to her. "Maybe we'll all understand someday."

At the room's door, she turned and looked back at me. "Take care of yourself, Trayne."

"Whatever. By the way—" I tilted my head toward D. "How was he? I mean, I have a personal interest in this. It's my body he's using."

Eastern smiled. "Trainable. The raw talent's there." Then she was out the door.

I stretched out across the bed, hands clasped behind my neck, trying to make myself comfortable. And had my own smile going.

Eastern had underestimated how much I knew, how much I understood. She'd forgotten, or else never really known, how close to her I was, how much I could read out from her.

Somewhere, in all the stuff she'd just told me, she'd been lying.

And I didn't think it had been that last little bit.

32

D kept a shamefaced silence for most of the way, as we headed south.

Trust an old farm boy like him; his shitkicker code of morality was locking in big time. Torn between lust and self-loathing. I should have known as soon as we'd hit town that he'd be looking to do a swan dive into the fleshpots. Whatever hellfire Bible-thumpers were loaded into his memory from the archives' files, they'd programmed him into viewing any city, and especially this one, as Sodom and Gomorrah on greased wheels. He'd lucked out by getting picked up by Eastern in her classic hooker transformation; she'd obviously shown him a good time without warping his mind onto some *Of Human Bondage* plot line.

After Eastern had left, I'd managed to rouse D with a cold wet rag from the bathroom down the hall. He'd opened up eyes that'd looked like cherries boiled in milk, then had rolled onto his stomach, hung his head over the side of the bed, and spat on the floor. Then he'd gotten dressed in silence, exuding the sullen radiation of someone who'd gotten kicked out of the Garden of Eden for too many parking tickets.

"Are you going to be like this the rest of your life?" We'd been walking for a couple of hours, and I was getting bored with the gloom routine. "Or what? Because if you just want somebody to kick your ass for being a bad boy—if that's what'll make you happy—then just bend over. Don't give yourself a hernia trying to do it yourself."

He glared at me, puritanical murder in his own heart. Then he smiled, looking abashed. "Well, shoot. I guess it ain't the end of the world."

"No, that's coming up later. You got your ashes hauled; that doesn't exactly qualify you for the mark of Cain on your crotch."

D mused on this as we walked. "She *was* a right pretty thing."

"Heart big as all indoors. You did yourself proud, you bold buccaneer. Or something like that."

Ironic that he got that little strut in his walk, his pleasure at having made his mark in the big city, just as we got to the outskirts. The Joadoid pseudo-L.A. was considerably smaller than the one I was used to. I supposed that was historically accurate. The concrete and brick thinned out, and we were on the side of a two-lane highway cutting through the ubiquitous orange groves.

I already had bad memories of territory like this. This brand of landscape was where we had been hassled before. I kept an ear cocked for the distant rasp of police motorcycles. If I heard as much as a whisper of decently tuned Harleys, we were going to dive into the underbrush.

Deep evening had set in, when D turned to me and said, "I saw a ghost."

"Just now?"

210

He nodded, stopping in his tracks and grabbing my arm. "Over there." He pointed to the trees some distance from the side of the road.

I looked, and saw a flash of something white moving around. Not a ghost, but worth investigating. I didn't want anything sneaking up on me.

The two of us crawled through the orange groves' fallen branches and thick mulch of dead leaves, until we could see over the top of an irrigation embankment into a small clearing on the other side.

"Holy shit." D's muttering was heavy with disgust. "It's them dumb motherfuckers."

"Keep your voice down." I reached over and pushed him flatter to the ground. "You want them to know we're here?"

D's ghosts—there were more than one, probably close to a dozen in all—stood around a small fire, drinking beer, telling jokes and laughing with big guffawing voices. All dressed in white robes that came down to the middle of their shins; the cuffs of their trousers were visible beneath. The robes' pointed hoods were pulled back, dangling like used condoms behind the men's necks. Their beefy red faces shone with excited sweat.

"Goddamn Klan assholes." D sneered at the gathering. "There ain't enough trouble in the world, these dickbrains gotta go lookin' to cause more."

I didn't have to explain to D who the men were, or what they were doing out here. He knew all about them; in his world, the place and time he'd come from, they weren't ancient history. I knew about them from all my rooting around in the archives. I'd gotten far enough into the subject to know that a bunch of KKK troopers were entirely appropriate for Joadoid Southern California. The mistake most people made, when they had any kind of handle on The Grand History of Cretinous Behavior, was in assuming

211

that the Klan had been necessarily a racist, anti-black organization. An assumption like that made it hard for people to believe that there had been any Klan activity at all in California in the thirties, when there just hadn't been that many blacks out here to begin with, at least not enough for even the worst black-hater to get hot and bothered about. Why bother dressing up in pointy-headed ghost costumes to get on blacks' asses when there weren't any blacks around? What people forgot, or never knew—and D did know—was that the Klan's original function had been as a terrorist organization supported by rich landowners to keep poor farm workers in their place and prevent them from agitating for better pay and working conditions. Naturally, in the American South after the Civil War, this meant that the KKK mainly went around knocking in black skulls with axe handles, and it had made a big appeal to the white population's racism for support of its clandestine activities. But in the orange groves and cotton fields of California, the KKK popped up again, happy enough to fuck with the poor Okies and other Dust Bowl refugees who'd fled West looking for work. There'd been plenty of local historians who'd tried to suppress this ugly history—I'd come across their worthless puff-piece books, all sunshine and gold rushes—but I'd seen the contrary proof down in the archives, ancient black-and-white photographs of Klan rallies that filled the streets of the pokey farm towns around here.

Those old photos flashed through my head while D and I watched the Klanners having their party. Amazing how much it proved the dictum that if you've seen one asshole, you've seen them all.

I gave D a nudge. "Come on—let's get out of here." I kept my whisper barely audible. Parked at the edge of the clearing was a mud-spattered pickup truck; in its bed was a full complement of discolored baseball bats and other unpleasant articles. I could see a lot of reason for not letting these yahoos know that we'd been spying on them.

We backed down from the ridge of the embankment, until we were sufficiently far away that we could stand up in the grove's darkness and not be seen. The dead leaves crackled unnervingly under our feet. We finally reached the road, and picked up the pace, resuming our progress southward.

The stars overhead were our only light. Both D and I were tired enough by this point that, once the adrenaline pump of spotting the local Klanners having a good time had passed, we could almost drift asleep as we walked. More than once, one of us caught the other, stumbling off the side of the road into the dry weeds.

I came up from one semi-drowse to see our shadows stretching out before us, the silhouettes of our legs normal-sized and sharp, the shapes of our heads magnified and blurring into the darkness. That wasn't right, but it took a moment for my leaden brain to figure out why.

There were headlights behind us. My spine snapped straight as I looked around and spotted, beyond the double glare, the shape of the pickup truck barreling toward us.

No time to say anything; I plowed into the drowsy D beside me, clutching him around the shoulder and toppling him off his feet. The two of us went sprawling hard into the strip of gravel at the road's edge, just as the truck steamed past.

"What the—" D pushed me away. He lifted his head and blinked dazedly, then saw what was happening.

The brake lights lit up as the pickup truck slammed to a halt several yards farther on. Out of the headlights' glare, I could see the white-robed figures piling out of the cab; the ones who had been riding behind vaulted over the tailgate. They started passing out the baseball bats to each other.

I dug the police revolver out of my jacket pocket. If

213

these rednecks thought they'd come across a couple of helpless fruit-pickers, somebody they could stomp into the ground as an object lesson to whatever migrant workers might be in the neighborhood, they were set for a surprise. I didn't have enough ammunition to take them all—there were only five bullets in the revolver's chambers—but I figured I'd only have to plug a couple before the others hightailed it out of here. Even if they only left long enough to fetch reinforcements, or weapons like the usual shotguns and .22 rifles found in farmhouses, D and I would still have time to make an escape cross-country.

My pocket had torn open on a sharp rock when we'd hit the ground; my full weight had scraped the revolver in the dirt. The chamber wouldn't rotate until I'd rapped the gun across my other hand a couple of times. The hammer mechanism ground back through a layer of grit as I cocked it.

"What the hell ya gonna do?" D looked at me and the revolver in alarm.

"Just be quiet." We were both flat on our stomachs; I raised my head and sighted the revolver through a fringe of weeds. "When I say so, we pick it up and run."

The Klanners, spreading themselves out along the road, came walking toward us. One fat one—his gut tautened the front of his white robe—seemed to be in charge. "Them shit-heels oughta be right around here somewhere." He looked from one side to the other, bat in hand. "They couldn'ta gotten very far away."

I aimed at the man's gut—it was the easiest, most obvious target. The stub barrel wavered, then locked onto the joggling white expanse. I squeezed the trigger back.

The revolver blew up in my hand.

"Shit! God*damn*!" I howled, clutching my wrist. A wet spatter of blood from my torn palm oozed under my fin-

214

gers. The jammed revolver had spun to rest in the dirt in front of me.

One of the Klanners shouted, "Jesus! Bastard's got a gun!"

"Come on—" D yanked me to my feet. "We gotta get out of here."

We stumbled into the orange groves' depths. My forearm still tingled with an electric buzz, but I could flex the fingers of my bleeding hand. We crouched down and tried to see what the Klan guys were doing.

Out on the road, silhouetted by the truck's headlights, they gestured excitedly to each other, waving the bats around. We could see them, but not hear what they were saying.

"They're really pissed now." I squeezed my wet hand into a fist. "They really want us now."

D pointed to the activity. "That bunch there's gonna try and circle around us." A group had split off from the others. "We better make tracks."

We ran at an angle slanting away from the road, until I grabbed D's arm. "There's something burning." The sharp odor of smoke drifted under the tree branches. "You can smell it—"

A wind gust raised distant orange-red sparks dancing in air. The smoke was visible now, billowing close to the ground.

"They're going to burn us out." The dry leaves mounded under the trees made perfect tinder. "Come on—"

The smoke clung choking in our lungs as we ran. The fire ran faster; we could see it lunge up ahead of us. The strip of road at one side was the only sector not aflame.

We made no plan, other than to dive as quickly as possible into the open and sprint for the other side.

For a moment, I thought we'd made it, gotten ahead of our pursuers. My eyes stung and blurred from the smoke.

215

I didn't see any white ghosts, so the blow that caught me behind the ear seemed as though from something invisible. I sprawled across the road, my torn hand ripping on the rough surface.

I rolled onto my back and saw the man, his Klan robe stripped off, standing over me. He grinned and hoisted the baseball bat over his shoulder.

My head throbbed and clanged with each pulse. In my wavering vision, I saw D a couple of yards away, pinioned by two more of the disrobed Klanners.

I reached toward him and shouted. "D! Go on! Do it! *Do it—*"

They jerked his arms behind him; a grimace of pain stretched his neck and jaw taut. But he heard me; his eyes squeezed tight, he shook his head in refusal.

"Shut the fuck up." The man above me let fly with the bat once more.

33

THE last time I'd seen the face that came swimming up before me, it'd accompanied a baseball bat slung over the owner's shoulder.

That'd been in the dark, out on the road. But I was still able to recognize the big, loose smile and the little, fat-swaddled pig eyes. It was brighter here—I blinked at the glare of an overhead light bulb—and I couldn't smell the acrid smoke of the fire burning through the orange grove. But the man's smile promised just as much gleeful violence, the whole aria of kicking someone else's ass. Probably mine.

"Well, I'll be switched. You *are* alive." He laughed in some space behind his waddled chins. "We were afraid the county was gonna have to plant you, and we ain't got any trustees to do the diggin' right now."

The only reply I could think of was along the lines of *Eat shit,* and I didn't think it was worth it. The bat and the

217

guy's friends might still be somewhere nearby. I opened my eyes a little wider and felt the glare ricochet inside my skull. The pain bloomed like a red flower, and I had to struggle against falling back into unconsciousness.

Now I saw where I was. Walls blank except for encrusted dirt, and words and dates scratched to the ancient white-wash beneath; one wall of grey-painted metal bars. Some kind of jail cell—I was lying on a sagging cot that folded from the wall on two short lengths of chain; on the other side of the cramped space, I could see D on another cot. He lay unmoving, his face turned away from me.

"Now we won't have to go to all that trouble. At least, not yet." The man stood up; he'd been sitting on a splinter-ing wooden chair in the middle of the cell. His bulk blocked enough of the light spilling in from beyond the bars that I could open my eyes all the way without being blinded. The Klan robes were long gone. Now he had on a khaki shirt with a deputy's badge pinned on. He threw a wet rag at me. "Here—clean yourself up. There's some-body wants to talk to ya."

The cell door clanged shut behind him. I watched him walking down the corridor past the empty cells; then I picked up the rag. It turned pink, with darker bits of dirt and crusted blood, when I ran it over my face. Somebody had wrapped a grey strip of cloth around my injured hand for a bandage. Red had soaked through in the center of my palm.

I sat up, bruises singing as they slid over the bones be-neath. I creaked over to D's cot. "Hey—" I nudged his shoulder. "You okay?"

He looked like shit, face puffy, one eye swollen shut. He groaned when I ran the wet rag over his forehead; one fee-ble hand tried to brush the rag away.

"Goddamn piss-ants." He rolled over and spat some-thing red on the cell floor. "Coulda taken 'em . . . if they'd

218

come at me one at a time . . ." The words came around his thick tongue with difficulty.

The last glimpse I'd had of him, out on the road, he'd been going down under a half dozen or so of the Klanners. With that many so tight around him, they hadn't been able to whale away at him with the bats as freely as they would have otherwise—that was probably the main reason he was still alive, without his brains scattered all over the asphalt.

"Yeah, well, when it's their bats, and their field, they get to make the rules." I was having trouble staying standing up; I dragged the wooden chair over and flopped down on it. "And we're not just dealing with amateurs here, you know. Our friends happen to be the local law, it seems. The bed sheets and pointy hats are just something they do on the side."

"It don't surprise me." D managed to get himself upright. He winced as he ran a hand over his ribs. "When folks are that mean, they're sonsabitches all day long."

We weren't able to talk anymore; the smiling deputy came up to the bars. He pulled out his keys on their leather lanyard and unlocked the door. "You there—" He pointed at me. "Get your ass out here. Time to go for a little walk."

The deputy led me to another section of the jail, away from the cells. I contemplated jumping him, but decided against it; I could hear others nearby.

"You know, I could make it worth your while." I kept my voice low, confidential. "Say, maybe to leave the back door unlocked. Some little . . . accident like that. I mean, you've already had your little fun with me and my friend. And we've learned our lesson. You let us go, and we'll be long gone before you know it. And we won't come back."

"Shut your mouth." His smile vanished. "I ain't interested in listening to some Okie trash like you. Put a sock in it, and keep on moving."

219

I got shoved into a straight-back chair in front of a desk. "Here he is." The deputy closed the office door behind him.

The man on the other side of the desk lifted his gaze from what he'd been reading. Big-knuckled Lincoln hands laid the papers down, and I found myself looking straight into Identrope's face. "Hello, Trayne." He smiled at me.

It took a moment before I found my voice. I nodded, feeling my hands sweat, the salt stinging the one bandaged palm. "Hi," I said. "Fancy meeting you here."

"It is strange, isn't it? Not anything I'd ever have expected." His smile faded. "Not from you, Trayne."

I'd had a chance to study him now. Identrope had evidently been pulled into D's Joadoid universe as well. His appearance had changed, getting with the period. The razor-cut silver hair, his televangelist 'do, had darkened and flattened, slicked back with brilliantine and parted high on one side. A stiff, tall shirt collar with a gold pin, and a stodgy three-piece suit, a gold chain draped over the vest front. He'd pushed his chair back from the desk, so I was able to see the whole effect.

"What can I say?" I scratched my chin. "These things happen. Around here, you can never be sure where people will wind up."

"That's not good enough." Identrope, leaning back in his chair, thumbs hooked in the armholes of his vest, leveled a dark gaze at me. "I expected more loyalty from you, Trayne. Either that, or more intelligence."

I shrugged. "Loyalty's a difficult commodity to come by these days."

Identrope shook his head. "Your brains, then. You could have at least used those. Did you really think I didn't know what was going on? From the beginning? All your little scurrying around, and plotting and scheming—did you

220

think you could do all that behind my back, and I wouldn't know about it?"

"Yeah." My mouth had dried to ashes. "That's exactly what I thought."

"Trayne . . ." Just that one word, the name, ached with an infinite sadness. "My son. That's how I thought of you. There was so much I wanted . . . for you. But there was blindness here. Not mine, but yours. You thought I didn't see. But my eye is never closed. My back is never turned. In this world, you can't hide these things from me. You cleave the apple, and I'm there. In your mouth, in your breath, the hairs numbered upon your head. You should have known."

I didn't say anything. I was waiting for *him* to tell me something I didn't know. A burning knife leapt out of my heart with each pulse, aimed at his throat. What had that *my son* line been all about? But I knew already, and the wordless knowing battered inside my skull, so loud I could barely hear the voice on the other side.

"And what was it for? What good did it do you, Trayne? Tell me that. Every step you took away from me, you lowered yourself. From the highest to the dust under my feet—you've gone to each in succession, and carved away your own soul in doing so. All of your little dealings on the side with that toad Geldt . . . that was how it started. You indulged in that, and it left you weak and open to that Harrison creature. You weren't able to see what he was, that he invited you to treachery and deceit, and those things had already become your bread and drink." Identrope's face grew sterner, distaste consuming him. "And where has it brought you, Trayne? Treading through streets of dust with some ignorant rustic, a fool, a thing of no consequence. That is your last companion, Trayne. Nothing at all."

221

I raised my face and looked at Identrope. "You've seen him?"

"Why should I have?" Identrope shrugged. "These small things are of no importance to me. They're only the things I use, pieces I fit together in the great design. But not you, Trayne. I didn't use you. I loved you." He looked down at the papers spread across the desktop. "But that was somewhere else, and another time."

That was when I knew. That I knew more than he did. I knew who D was.

The door opened behind me, and the deputy came in. Identrope gestured toward me. "You can take him away now."

The deputy grabbed me by one shoulder and pulled me out of the chair. "What do you want we should do with him?"

Identrope didn't look up. "Whatever you'd like."

An ugly smile turned toward me as the deputy shoved me toward the door.

I got pitched back into the cell, landing on my hands and knees. D sat on the edge of his cot, watching as the deputy slammed the bars shut.

"Don't go away." The smile paraded yellow teeth. "Me and my buddies got some stuff we'd like to talk to you about." The deputy turned and headed down the jail corridor.

D grabbed my elbow and got me to my feet. "What's going on?"

My bandaged hand had started leaking blood again. "I think our friends want to finish off what they started."

I was right. In a few minutes, the deputy and the same crew of Klan uglies had showed up outside the bars. They all laughed and waved the ball bats around while the deputy unlocked the door.

"You're the little turd who had the gun." The deputy led

222

the crowd into the cell. Two of them picked me up and pinioned my arms behind my back. "That wasn't a smart thing to do, at all." The deputy brought his smiling face right up into mine. "If you'd been nice and cooperative, we might've just roughed you up a mite, and then let you go. But since you decided to be a fool about it, we're just gonna have to teach you a real lesson." He poked the end of a bat into my stomach.

From the cot at the other side of the cell, D called out. "Hey, leave him alone! We didn't do shit to you guys—"

The deputy glared over his shoulder at D. "Shut your face. We'll get around to you in a little while. But first . . ." He hoisted the bat.

I saw the bat's thick end come swinging around in a level arc. Nicely timed: the two men let go of me right at the moment of impact. I went flying, and crashed onto the empty cot.

The deputy and his friends had obviously had a lot of practice at this kind of work. The blow had been enough to daze me, but not so much as to kill me outright with a skull crushed egg-like. This was going to be a long night before they were finished having their fun and I'd be put out of my misery.

I slid onto the floor, my fingers clawing across the cot's thin mattress. A second passed before the pain caught up with the trauma; then it surged over me, fire radiating from my jawbone.

"Give him another, Jake! Har dee har har!" The ones in the back of the crowd started making animal noises.

Through their legs, I could see D on the other side of the cell. He sat trembling on the cot, white-knuckled hands gripping the edge, his face just as bloodless.

I caught a boot in my mouth. I tasted blood as the leather volley began on my ribs.

"D—" I managed to stretch a hand toward him. The

223

bandage had torn loose, a red trickle running down to my elbow. "Help me—"

They let me crawl. It struck them funny, my reaching toward D. They howled when his trembling hand moved, drawn toward mine.

The tips of our fingers made contact. I saw the spark fall spinning inside his eyes. He knew, without words. Who I was, who he was.

D jerked his head from side to side, the tendons in his neck now knife edges around his windpipe. His eyes were naked creatures webbed in blood.

The men stopped beating me when they heard him scream.

A bat dropped and bounced on the cement floor. They turned as one and stared at D.

The scream's rage filled the cell, making every atom of oxygen a razor with a single word on the blade. D clutched the sides of his head, fingers tearing at the sweat-darkened hair. His tongue curled backward, as though to taste that sound, swallow it back down into the battered crypt below his belly.

Silence for a moment, then words.

"I told you! I told everybody!" D's hands swayed his head in a wobbling circuit, as if he could work it loose from the lock of his breastbone. "I told you to leave me alone—but you wouldn't! You just keep pushing and pushing, and then it happens *and I warned you*—"

He rose from the cot, stepping past me as I collapsed across the floor. I rolled onto my back, and saw him through a red haze, as he reached for the deputy.

Another scream, a weak, empty thing. The deputy's chest heaved with the draining of his lungs. D's hand caught the deputy's face, fingers digging into the jowls below the small eyes.

I felt the *d*-ranger power break against the walls of the

224

cell, slapping the other men back. The deputy's knees gave way as though the voiding bladder above had washed away joinings carved of sugar. D's hand squeezed, then jerked back.

The deputy's face was a rag in D's fist.

The intricate bone crumbled under D's other hand. From the round box of skull, D pulled out a grey rat, its fur slick with blood, its hindquarters a knobbed rope running back into the dying man's spinal column. The rat squirmed in D's grasp, the red eyes fragments of the deputy's, weeping with the same fear. D clenched his fist to a rock, and grey clotted bits leaked between his fingers.

The other men clawed their own faces, or dropped to their knees and scrabbled at the shivering metal bars of the cell.

I was going under, but not before I saw the stones of the walls become glass, then air, then stone again, darker than the hearts of mountains. They trembled and sparked, then exploded.

The floor opened up beneath me. I fell into a new universe, where the darkness kissed me hard.

I awoke at ground zero.

I raised my head from a charred stone, my hands full of ashes and blood.

Where D's power had gone off—the *d*-ranger ability, the cataclysmic drain of reality-organizing function—the world had imploded, set fire to itself, chased a radiant tail down a small black hole. The landscape around me was flattened and singed.

The scorch marks on the earth radiated from where the jail cell had been, a few yards away from where I lay. A shallow hole looked like a bomb crater. Under a roiling yellow sky, I got shakily to my feet and stumbled over to the spot.

D was there, what was left of him. His face—my old face, the original one—had blind red sockets. His hands were smoke on the ground.

Bits of the deputy and his Klanner friends were scattered

about, mixed in with the small rubble of the jail. Some of the pieces still looked human, others had been caught dead halfway through a transformation into strange, scrabbling forms.

The ruins of a familiar piece of machinery hunkered nearby. The pickup truck that the Klanners had run us down in squatted on melted tires, the paint on the fenders bubbled and blackened. I leaned against it, a residual heat seeping into my palms, and looked up. Ghosts floated in the immediate sky, the empty Klan robes, tattered around the edges, drifting lifeless to the earth.

I poked around some more, turning over both hard and soft scraps with the point of my shoe. I didn't find any trace of Identrope. There was no doubt in my mind that when the place had gone up, he'd been far away. That was his style.

Before I left, I dragged D's body—it was his now, for good—into the shallow hole, and kicked in enough stones and scraps of metal and brick to cover it. I turned and headed toward what looked like the low silhouettes of a small town on the horizon.

The town was similar to the hole-in-the-wall that D and I had started out from. Only brought up a couple of decades, to maybe the early fifties, Eisenhower and the Korean War. D's Joadoid world was either evaporating or had been thrown into fast forward. The same as with that other small town, the people were all gone; I walked through abandoned streets. Maybe when D's ability had overloaded and gone off, they'd all thought it was the Bomb, the great bowel-clenching fear of those days, come knocking at their doors, and they'd all scurried off to the nearest fallout shelter.

I found the window of a furniture store, with televisions, neat old Philco Futuras—brand-new here—with the picture tube sitting spacily on top of the box. The sets were all

227

switched on, tuned to the same channel. A news program, in flickering black-and-white; a silver-haired announcer—I looked closely to make sure it wasn't Identrope—sat at a desk and read from a sheaf of papers in his hand.

"Here's a cutie for you." The announcer winked and smiled. The screen cut from his face to a live-remote view of a big sheet-metal building, the front crumpled and blackened by fire. I recognized it: the New Moon Corporation's work site out in the junkyard.

"Seems there's been some rowdy action out in the countryside!" The news announcer's voice boomed through the glass as I leaned my hands and face against it. The angle turned and I saw dead bodies splayed out on the ground, toppled-over motorcycles, and, in the distance, the uprooted barbed-wire fence. "A local motorcycle club—police sources tell us that many of the organization's members have lengthy arrest records—called the"—he glanced at the top paper—"Unified Stoners . . ."

"No, no," I murmured. "The Stone Units."

". . . attacked a corporate operation in a remote location. Probably to steal power tools, or drugs from the first-aid kits. But the motorcycle thugs got more than they bargained for! You can say that! Seems the company—the Nude Moon Corporation, headquartered right here in the Southland . . ."

"New Moon."

". . . seems the company, for reasons of its own, had a full complement of armed security personnel on the premises. That's what those crazy motorcycle types ran right into! You have to admire their pluck—they sailed right in there regardless, even once the firing started."

I gazed blankly at the television screens on the other side of the window. This was the first indication I'd had of what Geldt had been up to since I'd fobbed him on the Stone Units. Later, when the dust finished settling, I'd get the

228

whole story pieced together, but for now my tired brain was dumbfounded.

The news camera panned over the corpses on the ground. There was Rasty Mike, his forehead caved in around a small black hole in the center. His lips snarled back to show his gnashed-together teeth. He was right at the New Moon building's rolled-up freight door, probably because he'd led the charge through the downed fence.

Geldt was there, too, about midway in the pack of dead bikers. Maybe he'd been caught surprised by the security forces New Moon had hired, and been popped before he'd had a chance to pull his usual sneak-away number. Or maybe he'd been caught up in his role as the bad-ass Trayne, the number he'd improvised for the Stone Units' benefit. That high-stakes criminal, looking for a good crowd of accomplices to hook up with. I never found out which it had been, Geldt or "Trayne," who had gone down with the bikers.

The news announcer rattled on, a fast counterpoint to my own crippled thought processes. "Whatever these boys were looking for, they'd probably agree now, it wasn't worth the trip! And here's the strangest part. Seems there was some kind of rocket setup on the premises; the company's representatives have so far declined to make any comment about what this was to be used for. But it was apparently fueled and ready to go when the motorcycle club made their ill-fated break-in attempt. Imagine their surprise when the thing took off!"

Mine was about equal. The window glass sweated under my hands as I pressed closer.

"Apparently the motorcyclists inadvertently triggered a preprogrammed launch sequence. Indications are that a low-level satellite has already been released; its exact trajectory and function have not yet been determined. Turning to sports, it's a big day for—"

I stepped back from the store window. So the New Moon satellite had gone up—I couldn't calculate yet what effect that would have on what I had to do. I had a deep suspicion that the timetable had been stepped up another notch by this event. If I was going to carry through on killing Identrope, I'd better get my ass in gear.

That whole project—Identrope's death—was obviously complicated by the fact that he was aware of my intentions, and had been all along. I had two factors on my side: one, if omniscience was one of Identrope's goals in constructing his web and achieving "white reality," he hadn't gotten there yet; he hadn't known who and what D had been. Identrope apparently hadn't even known that he'd been pulled into another whole pseudo-real universe, D's Joadoid world. So Identrope still had his blind sides; that gave me room to operate. And further on that, factor two: by now, Identrope would be sure that I was well and truly off the scene, killed by those fun-loving Klanners. The element of surprise was mine once again.

At the town's edge, I spotted a fire burning just above the horizon. I couldn't make out the tapered shape of the dirigible, but I knew it was there. I started walking again.

First I heard the music, the carnival pipes. It took me a moment, but then I remembered. What one of the tramps, back when D and I had gotten off the freight train, had been talking about. Identrope's new operation down here. A whole amusement park underneath the burning dirigible.

Night had fallen by the time I came within viewing distance of the place, bringing the colored lights up sharper. Now I saw where all the people had gone; they were here, crowded in around the carousels and giant Ferris wheel. The wooden framework of a roller coaster creaked under the hissing of the cars' wheels against the curved rails.

I worked my way through the parking lot and toward the entrance. The milling crowd's faces were flushed and overexcited, as though they were here for some candy-filled apocalypse. Small children screamed as though gripped by sudden fever. A sailor in uniform bent a woman nearly double in his embrace, his kiss all-devouring.

The crowd's tidal pull caught me and dragged me into its midst. The current drew me under a sign of a million blinking light bulbs—I couldn't see what the letters spelled—and spat me out stumbling in the park's center.

"You don't need a ticket, mister! Not tonight!" A teenage kid dressed like an elf with a hormone problem grabbed me and shoved me into a cart on tracks. Another elf slammed a lever over, and I rattled into a papier-mâché and chicken-wire cavern.

"Trayne!" a woman's voice shouted at me in the darkness. "Over here!"

My eyes hadn't adjusted. I looked around blindly. "What?"

"Just get out of the cart. Don't worry about it—"

The cart swiveled around a curve in the track as I jumped off. I landed on my hands and knees in a rubble of discarded paper cups and food wrappers.

The woman helped me to my feet. A blue-tinged light behind a Styrofoam rock allowed me to see. I found myself looking into Snow White's face.

"Hello, Eastern." I slapped dust from my trousers. "I like the outfit."

"What can I say." She raised her hands apart as she looked down at herself in the costume. "These things happen. I wasn't even responsible for this one—I just found myself like this. It's gotten completely out of control around here."

"I've noticed."

"It's all Identrope. All his plans are coming to a head. But something's wrong, something he didn't expect. There was some kind of an explosion—"

231

I nodded. "I was there when it happened."

"—that sent things all crazy. The explosion didn't just happen where you could see it and feel it. *It happened underneath reality.* Identrope's reality. This whole place—" Eastern gestured at the phony cavern and the amusement park beyond it. "This is some 'pink reality' out of Identrope's subconscious. Some wish-fulfillment dreamland, kid stuff. But it's already falling apart." She grabbed a piece of the nearest fake rock and broke it off. The substance crumbled in her fingers like loose sand. "Identrope's loading up toward his 'white reality'—when that happens, this place will get washed away in the flood. All the Madlands will."

"What else?" I touched her arm. "All that stuff you were digging into. Tell me."

"I got through." She smiled, the old Eastern showing behind Snow White. "He thought he could keep things from me. All his little secrets. But he couldn't. That's the problem with being just short of omniscient, omnipotent—you forget other people can do things, too." She brought her face close to mine. "Identrope thought that all of his data banks—the memory of this ultimate brain he's building—he thought all that was locked away tight, couldn't be penetrated. Because he'd been able to turn the wires leading in there into a simulation of a human nervous system, with the crystalline structure of the wires themselves acting as synapses under his control. But he forgot something. Metals aren't always crystalline. There's at least one that's liquid at normal handling temperatures."

"Mercury."

"That's right. It's a liquid, thus no crystalline structure. And thus no way for Identrope to bring it under synaptic control. I had complete access to the New Moon Corporation's laboratories—it was no problem for them to whip me up a set of thin capillary tubes filled with liquid mercury.

They're a bitch to work with, but I didn't need to use very long lengths of the stuff. Just enough to climb up into the web with, get close to Identrope's headquarters, and substitute the mercury capillary with one of the wires right at the back of his machines. The hardest part was drilling a hole through the fiberboard wall. Once I was hooked up, it was a cinch. Identrope has so much confidence in that metal-synapse defense, there's no security layers beyond it, not even a user password needed. I could read everything he had in there."

"What'd you find?"

"Get this. The New Moon Corporation is a front. For Identrope."

I laughed. "That figures."

"He'd been using it for some time now, to carry out his operations outside the Madlands. It's a blind front; none of the directors of the corporation, including that Harrison guy, knew they were actually working for Identrope all along. Then they all got ambitious, and started coming up with things on their own initiative. That's how they came up with that whole notion of assassinating Identrope. Harrison and the rest of the directors had been fed that line about the satellite out in the junkyard being some ancient communications device. That was a lie, too. But like good little entrepreneurial capitalists, they figured it was an opportunity too good to be missed, to put themselves way out in front of the Canal Ultime network in generating broadcast revenues. And they weren't going to sit around waiting for their marching orders to come filtering down from above. That's just not the kind of people they are. So they started their own plans into motion, and those just happened to include knocking off their secret employer, Identrope."

"Wait a minute. If the thing the New Moon technicians were working on out in the junkyard isn't a communications satellite . . . then what is it?" The bleak thought appeared in my head that the line I'd fed Rasty Mike and the Stone Units, that the satellite was a weapons system left over from the long-ago war, might actually be true. And the thing had been launched already, according to the news broadcast I'd seen.

"It's Identrope," said Eastern. "Or at least it's part of him. The satellite's not an ancient artifact at all. Identrope created it and had it planted out there. It's a control mechanism for the brain he's been building out of the web. The thing is analogous to the nonconscious sections of the human brain that regulate the electrochemical traffic of the nervous system. It's the last piece of Identrope's construct, the keystone of the whole white-reality project. It had to be kept distant from the rest of the network until Identrope had finished, and the web/brain was ready for it. A premature insertion of the satellite and its encoded programming would overload the network, burn it out to idiocy."

"And the web's ready now?"

Eastern shook her head. "I don't know. The satellite was launched ahead of schedule—it's heading for the web right now. I saw Identrope when he heard that the satellite had gone up. He's gone into a frenzy, trying to rush the last of the preparations into place. And that was before the explosion. Now there's no way of telling what condition Identrope and the web are in."

I shrugged. "Too bad for him if it isn't. And if it is—screw him. He can jerk himself off all he wants to, playing God in his own little pocket universe."

"You don't understand, Trayne. *The white reality has no limits.* If it happens—when it happens—it consumes all other reality. Identrope doesn't just achieve omniscience and omnipotence in the Madlands; he achieves omnipresence beyond it as well. The brain he's constructed from the web will achieve a flash-point critical mass. He won't be

234

God just here." Her voice lowered, tightening under this sure knowledge. "He'll be God everywhere."

That was it. Now I knew, what I'd known all along, in some hidden place of my heart and mind. Why I'd wanted to kill Identrope. Not the New Moon Corporation's money, or any small thing like that.

I'd run my own show for so long, even when I'd been working for the old Identrope. I couldn't change now.

Through the shabby walls of the cavern, a muffled voice boomed. My heart tripped when I thought it might have already happened, the grand conjunction between the segments of Identrope's new being.

"Listen!" Eastern grabbed my arm. "Come on—this way."

She led me out through the ride's backstage service door. We stepped out into the middle of the milling crowd, all of them craning their necks to look into the sky. The burning dirigible was directly overhead; the dancing light from the flames beat hot against the people's faces.

The voice shouted from P.A. speakers on top of tall metal poles. "The grand finale! It's showtime, folks!"

Fireworks went off beyond the dirigible, big burning chrysanthemums that turned the lifted, gape-mouthed faces to chemical reds and greens.

Against the crowd's cries of pleasure, Eastern shouted into my ear as she pointed. "There it is! That's the satellite!"

A speck of light showed in the distance. It bloomed into sprays of fire, an array of jets slowing it down for a majestic approach toward the web.

The crowd saw it and moaned happily as one, transfixed by the satellite's glory. It came on across the sky, like the final kiss of heaven.

235

35

THE crowd went wild.

The ecstasy of the masses—a surge of people from behind knocked me off my feet. By the time I managed to climb upright, elbowing and tugging at the dense pack around me, Eastern had been swept away from me by the human current. I caught a glimpse of her Snow White costume, one of the puff sleeves torn, as she roundhoused somebody in front of her. Then the crowd buffeted me in the opposite direction, and I lost sight of her.

I couldn't shout to her—the crowd's roaring and the thudding bombardment of the fireworks overhead filled the air tight. The appearance of the majestically approaching satellite, its size magnified by its continuous jets of flame and colored sparks, had driven the crowd to a new pitch of frenzy. They didn't know what was happening, what the significance of this new apparition was, but they could tell that a great moment was upon them. Identrope's broad-

236

casts had pumped them up for the Second Coming—maybe this was it, salvation written in skyrockets. Big sections of the crowd had started jumping up and down *en masse,* reaching up to the nearing satellite with their hands. A baby pinwheeled in the air, tossed by its enraptured mother.

The burning dirigible's flames were nearly swallowed up in the bursts of fireworks. The combined light brought the web dangling beneath into stark contrast, the interlinked strands black against the radiance. A network of diamond-outlined shadows overlaid the crowd's upturned faces and waving arms.

Another silhouette fell across me. I turned away from the satellite that all other eyes were fastened upon, and looked toward the perimeter of the amusement park. There, beyond the roller coaster and carousel, the bottom trailing edge of Identrope's web was fastened down, holding the burning dirigible and his headquarters underneath in place. Flares trailing down from the fireworks showed the forms of Identrope's faithful disciples who'd already been wired into his network.

One of the human shapes moved. I shoved away the arms in my face so I could see better. And saw that it was Snow White. Eastern, climbing up the web.

I fought my way through the crowd, counter to their jammed flow. A couple of mindless faces I had to put down with the slash of my forearm. I could see Eastern climbing higher into the web as I dived into the pack of bodies, driving the wedge of one shoulder between them.

The crowd thinned as I got toward the back of it. I shoved the last of the crowd aside, the feeble or the late-comers, and ran for the bottom of the web.

Back in the pseudo-L.A. I remembered, Identrope's web had been fastened to the ground with heavy-duty steel cables and huge masses of concrete. In this world's rearrangements, some kind of cheap carnival mentality had prevailed: the web was nailed down with nothing more than wooden circus-tent pegs driven into raw dirt. As I stumbled closer, a gust of wind hit the dirigible overhead; the web's lines tautened, and one of the pegs popped free, the others near it tugging loose.

I raised my hands and grabbed one of the web's horizontal strands. Above me, I could see the wind whipping the full skirt of Eastern's Snow White getup. "Eastern!" I climbed a couple of strands as I shouted. "What're you doing?"

The wind tore away my words, but I saw that she had heard me. She looked back down at me. "I'm going to him!" She grabbed the next strand and pulled herself up.

"What?" The web bucked as another pair of the wooden tent pegs snapped free from the ground. My foot slipped on the strand I stood on; I threw my arms around a horizontal and clung to it.

The whip-snap motion of the web had torn loose one of Identrope's wired disciples. The body ripped free of the neural wiring and feed tubes, and came tumbling down the web. One arm struck Eastern a glancing blow, knocking her back until she was able to clutch another strand. She looked dazed, breathless.

I started climbing again, working against the yawing back-and-forth drive of the web. As I got higher, closer to the middle of the web, the movement grew more extreme, the flexure unrestrained.

Another wave of fireworks went off, dazzling behind the flames. The dark rectangle of Identrope's headquarters building swayed beneath the dirigible's fire-rippled belly.

I'd managed to climb just beneath Eastern. I reached up and grabbed her white-stockinged ankle. The contact snapped her to attention; she kicked my hand away.

The web gave a deep lurch, the strands swaying like a

238

billowing sail. The burning dirigible seemed to leap closer to the bursts of fireworks. I looked down and saw that the last of the anchoring tent pegs had ripped loose. The bottom edge of the web flapped uncontrolled as the earth fell away.

More of Identrope's disciples tore free from their tubes and wires as the web's motion grew wilder. I clung tighter to the strands I'd gathered against my chest.

"Eastern!" I shouted past the fireworks' booming explosions. "Don't move! Just try to hang on!"

"Screw that—" She grabbed another strand and pulled herself up.

I kept up with her, climbing a few feet below. "What the hell are you trying to do?"

"Don't you see?" She looked down at me, reflected fire in the center of her eyes. "It's happening *now*—the satellite! The last piece! Look!" She took one hand away and pointed.

I looked, but heard it before I saw it. The hissing of its rocket panoply had swelled to a roar as it approached. The satellite's conjunction with the web was only a few meters away.

Another firework burst hit the web square on, just below the headquarters building. Multicolored sparks tore a gaping hole through the strands. Disciples with hair aflame plummeted past us.

I'd pressed my face against one of my upraised arms, but the glare of the explosion had still been enough to blind me for a few seconds. I could still hear Eastern's voice shouting down to me.

"I know what it's like! He showed me! The white reality—I can have it, with him!"

She'd made her choice. The only offer that counted more than the world. And greater than the world—her own soul.

"Now—"

239

A current like electricity, but singing up through my arms to my skull with the voices of angels, crackled in the strand I held. The web's interstices grew white with no heat; every loop glowed with the lashing of a submolecular life.

I looked over my shoulder, a luminous wind clawing my face. The satellite, the last component of Identrope's brain construct, had hit the web. The network strained with the impact, fire streaming through the open spaces. The interlaced neural fibers sizzled with the encoded program-stream fired through them.

A new wind, harder and fiercer than the one before, stormed around us, drawing the web out nearly horizontal from the burning dirigible. Eastern arched her back, arms locked straight from her grip on the strands, teeth clenched in ecstatic rictus. A light, slower and colder than the fireworks, swept across the web. I raised a hand against it, the radiance pulsing white through the bones.

Identrope came striding over the web.

Gravity and the storm bent around him. The only sign of the physical world's touch was his grey hair streaming mane-like in the wind, the tails of his preacher's black suit dancing. His grim, triumphant face had studied thunder, had eaten the darkness between each star's atoms.

He towered over me, the lance of his gaze pinning me to the strands. "You—" Syllable of wrath, basalt voice. "I did not expect to see you again. You have surprised me, Trayne. You won't again." He turned away, dismissing me with a raised hand. "Now there are no more surprises. There is only Me."

The strand under my feet snapped, the ends whipping against my legs as I fell partway through the web. The distant earth wheeled dizzying below me. I clutched the other strands tighter in my hands, fighting to pull myself up.

Wind stung my eyes, but I could see Identrope walking

over to where Eastern lay in the glowing net. He reached his hand down to her.

"I knew you would come." He took the hand she raised, and pulled her toward him. His bride. "What I showed you before was nothing, only the slightest brush of my fingertips. Now you will have everything. See all, and be all." He wrapped her in his embrace. "Worlds without end . . ."

Their burning became too bright for mortal eyes. My gaze was fire inside my skull as I watched, two figures becoming one inside a small sun's heart. I could just see the two faces, Eastern's raised to Identrope's, as they kissed. The white flame grew at that touch, transforming flesh to light.

Then a black spark. As though she had bitten his lip, and darkness had leaked out.

The coronal light reddened, hurtling down the spectrum. I could see Identrope pushing himself away from her, his face spasmed in pain. A convulsive thrust of his arms sent her falling back.

The web bucked, nearly throwing me, the strands cutting across my scarred palms. I lost sight of everything except stars spinning overhead.

In my hands, the electric singing of the web turned discordant, the spiraling notes of Identrope's cry. The light in the wires surged and jangled, the dark kiss corroding the thin chains.

The strand slipped from my grasp. I fell, arms flailing behind me for any hold—

And was caught. Eastern gathered me to her breast. One arm hugged me tight, her other hand gripping the black-burning web.

She brought her face close to mine, as though she would give me that kiss as well. But she whispered in my ear instead.

"He didn't know . . ." Her lips grazed the coiled skin.

"He wasn't there yet . . . not all the way." Wind battered against us, but I could hear each word. "But he knew everything then . . . when I kissed him. Became part of him. But then it was too late."

"Too late . . ." I spoke through clenched teeth, the earth tilting below us. "Too late for what?"

"He didn't know. Why I had come to him." Her voice became a wire piercing my skull. "He didn't know I had become infected . . ."

I turned my face against the storm to look at her, and saw that it was true. Under her skin, translucent soft glass, I saw the shapes of other things moving, becoming. She was deep in the processes of the *n*-formation disease.

Only one more word. "Why?"

"The only way." Eastern smiled, a thread of blood inscribed on her chin. "I let myself become infected . . . I did it on purpose. I took on the diseased bodies I found, until I was diseased. And then I could infect him. I became part of him . . . his heart, his brain." She closed her eyes. *"I killed him."*

I saw it was true. The web, the great thing Identrope had become, twisted about itself, the strands infused with rotting life, shapes unbridled. The connected wires tore apart, stitches in a corpse of air.

The wind tore me out of Eastern's loosening grasp. I had one glimpse of her dead face breaking open to a new beauty, radiance unbounding. Then I tumbled in night.

For a moment, I thought I rested facedown on a bed of stars. Then the sensing of gravity returned, and I felt earth and grass beneath me.

I lay on a rounded hillock, a rain of soft things filling my upturned hands.

Identrope's web, as it had come apart, and the secrets of his death had been whispered to me, must have been drift-

242

ing lower all that time. I could only have fallen a few yards to impact. My spine and shoulder blades ached, but I could move and sit up.

Morning light tipped the ridge of hills. In that red-tinged light, I looked around myself. Charred pieces of the dirigible's fabric were scattered around, like pages of a book that had finally been read to the end.

Another thing of cloth lay nearby, not burnt. The Snow White dress, empty now.

The soft things fell upon my brow as I looked up. The last pieces of the web separated from each other, each fragment drifting to earth.

I raised my hands and looked down into them. In my palms, and everywhere on the ground, were orchids of flesh, the petals infused with the transforming blood. The bright sheen of decay was upon them, and the stems were writhing snakes scaled with silver and black gems.

More things fell. The sky rained frogs, sick ones that huddled on the earth, and awaited their further change, every wet molecule shearing free of its bonds.

I picked one of the creatures up. It glared at me with red, all-knowing eyes, then convulsed and vomited up a pearl.

When the pieces of the frog had scurried away, the pearl remained in the hollow of my hand a little while longer.

Then it melted as well, a teardrop falling into the dark earth.

36

I walked back to the city. What was left of it.

A lot had already faded away. The bare-bones, plain-pipe-racks reality showed through the empty spaces. The bits that remained were muddled together, fragments of my old pseudo-L.A. and poor dead D's Joadoid world. Places that had enough of their own essence to remain a while longer, like crumbling rocks in a shrinking puddle.

I was sorry to see it all go. There was one consolation. I'd been worried that I'd been infected with n-formation, to the point of no return. But the disease had been part of this world—if the Madlands faded away, so would the disease. Maybe. I'd have to wait and see.

I went looking for one place in particular, and found it. That gave me a certain sad pleasure. I wanted at least one person to say good-bye to.

Paint flaked from the "Beautiful Girls" sign. I climbed the stairs to the ballroom, and found Nora sitting there.

"Hi." She smiled at me. She still had on the dime-a-dance dress, but she'd scrubbed her face clean of makeup and pulled her hair back into the ballet *chignon* I remembered from before. "I was hoping to see you again."

I nodded, taking a chair from the stack at the side of the room, and easing down to it. My fall from the burning sky had left me bruised and stiff. I leaned back. "Here I am."

"I remember things now." Nora looked out the dusty windows, then to me again. "The last time you came by, I didn't. Except that I knew you from somewhere else."

My turn to smile. "We go back a ways, don't we?"

"When it happened—all the fire and explosions and things—we could see it from here. Me and the other girls. And then they changed. They were all our old dance troupe, from when we did those broadcasts. From up there." She pointed to the ceiling, and the sky beyond. "That's when I remembered. Who you were. Who I was." She bit her lip. "And then they all went away. Just faded and were gone. Until I was the only one left here."

I didn't know if she'd understand, but I tried, anyway. "That's because Identrope's gone. He's dead. And now that he's gone, the Madlands are going, too. Just fading away . . ."

"Why?"

A shrug. "I don't know. Maybe the Madlands were Identrope; maybe he came from somewhere else, somewhere far away, and brought them with him. Maybe they were something he found here, and he became them. And we all played that happy game with him for a while. I just don't know."

Nora brought her level gaze to my eyes. "Am I going to fade away, too?"

"Maybe. Maybe not. You were getting realer and realer all the time. Maybe you're real enough now."

That same smile, sad as my own had been. "It doesn't matter. Does it?"

"I guess not." I shifted in the chair, and winced.

Silence entered the room and grew large, filling all the space to the walls. The crepe-paper streamers across the top of the bandstand had turned black, and the dust of distant funerals drifted over the windowsills.

I studied the knuckles of my hand. There was something I needed to say to Nora, but I didn't know what it was.

She looked at me pityingly. "You know what your problem is?"

"No. What is it?"

"All the time you were here, with me, and with the others . . . you never danced. You never learned. I suppose you were too busy. Everybody else danced, but you never did."

That was true. All the time I'd been a choreographer in a tuxedo, I might as well have been carved in stone. The old tapes I'd brought up from the archives had done all the demonstrations of steps for me.

The ballroom grew smaller around me, trapping me close to Nora's words.

She stood up and pulled me from the chair. "Come on. It's not too late."

The rehearsal studio's record player was behind the bar. She sorted through the black vinyl discs, found the one she wanted, and put it on the turntable.

The music started.

"Here." She took my hand, her shoulders in the curve of my arm. "Like this . . ."

I closed my eyes.

"See?" Nora pulled me around, a thing of wood and blood. "It's not that hard. Is it?"

"No." I shook my head. My feet knew no circular motion, and when they lifted from their iron tracks, stumbled against hers. "It's okay."

It didn't matter what the music was; we had evolved into some sort of easy waltz. I started to get the hang of it, enough to spin lazily to the center of the floor.

"That's it." Nora laid her head on my shoulder. "Just relax. You don't have to do anything at all."

Some other music came from outside. From the Madlands themselves, and any world they had ever held. A tidal motion, of dissolve and disappearance, until the rolling of that ocean's dark swell brought them onto the unadorned stone again.

I didn't know if Nora heard that music, too. For this moment at least, we were both in time to its constant beat.

We turned, and danced, in the afternoon's slow endless light.